Gilbert Abbott À Beckett, George Cruikshank

The comic Blackstone

Gilbert Abbott À Beckett, George Cruikshank

The comic Blackstone

ISBN/EAN: 9783743347380

Manufactured in Europe, USA, Canada, Australia, Japa

Cover: Foto ©Andreas Hilbeck / pixelio.de

Manufactured and distributed by brebook publishing software (www.brebook.com)

Gilbert Abbott À Beckett, George Cruikshank

The comic Blackstone

THE
COMIC BLACKSTONE.

BY

GILBERT ABBOTT à BECKETT.

WITH ILLUSTRATIONS BY GEORGE CRUIKSHANK.

NEW EDITION.

LONDON:

BRADBURY, AGNEW, & CO., 8, 9, & 10, BOUVERIE STREET.

1876.

LONDON :
BRADBURY, AGNEW, & CO., PRINTERS, WHITEFRIAR

TO THE

Commissioners of the Courts of Request,

WHO HAVE

SO OFTEN EXTRACTED MERRIMENT FROM A DRY SUBJECT

BY RENDERING

LAW A BURLESQUE AND JUSTICE A FARCE,

The Comic Blackstone

IS

WITH ALL DUE RESPECT, INSCRIBED BY THEIR OBEDIENT SERVANT,

GILBERT ABBOTT à BECKETT.

CONTENTS.

—•—

INTRODUCTION.

———————— — ——-

PART I.—OF THE RIGHTS OF PERSONS.

PART II.—OF REAL PROPERTY.

PART III.—OF PRIVATE WRONGS AND THEIR REMEDIES.

CONTENTS.

PART IV.—OF PUBLIC WRONGS AND THEIR REMEDIES.

THE COMIC BLACKSTONE.

INTRODUCTION.

Section I.—On the Study of the Law.

Every gentleman ought to know a little of law, says Coke, and perhaps, say we, the less the better. Servius Sulpicius, a patrician, called on Mutius Scævola, the Roman Pollock (not one of the firm of Castor and Pollux), for a legal opinion, when Mutius Scævola thoroughly flabbergasted Servius Sulpicius with a flood of technicalities, which the latter could not understand. Upon this Mutius Scævola bullied his client for his ignorance; when Sulpicius, in a fit of pique, went home and studied the law with such effect, that he wrote one-hundred-and-fourscore volumes of law books before he died; which task was, for what we know, the death of him. We should be sorry, on the strength of this little anecdote, to recommend our nobility to go home and write law books; but we advise them to peruse the Comic Blackstone, which would have done Servius Sulpicius a great deal of good to have studied.

The clergy and the Druidical priests were in former times great lawyers; and the word *clericus* has been corrupted into clerks, so that the seedy gentlemen who carry the wigs and gowns down to court for the barristers are descended from the Druids.

A contest sprung up between the nobles and clergy, the former supporting the common law, and the other the civil. Somebody having picked up a copy of the pandects of Justinian at a book-stall in Amalfi, introduced them into England, but King Stephen would not allow them to be studied. Roger Vacarius, however, set up an evening academy for adults, where he advertised to teach the pandects on moderate terms ; but the laity would not come to his school at any price. One · thing that contributed to save the common law from falling into disuse was the fixing of the Court of Common Pleas, which had formerly been moveable, following the person of the king, like Algar's booth or Richardson's show, with all the paraphernalia of a Court of Justice. It is probable that the Common Pleas had a van to carry the barristers' bench, the judge's easy chair, and the rostrum for the witnesses, from place to place ; but when it became fixed, it made it worth the while of respectable people to study the law, which was not the case when the legal profession was nothing but a strolling company.

To those who take up the study of the law for the mere fun of the thing, we say with Sir John Fortescue, " It will not," &c. &c., down to " other improvements."

SECTION II.—OF THE NATURE OF LAWS IN GENERAL.

THE term Law, in its general sense, signifies a rule of human action, whether animate or inanimate, rational or irrational ; and perhaps there is nothing more inhuman or irrational than an action at law. We talk of the law of motion, as when one man springs towards another and knocks him down ; or the law of gravitation, in obedience to which the person struck falls to the earth.

If we descend from animal to vegetable life, we shall find the latter acting in conformity with laws of its own. The ordinary cabbage, from its first entering an appearance on the bed to its being finally taken in execution and thrust into the pot for boiling, is governed by the common law of nature.

Man, as we are all aware, is a creature endowed with reason and free will : but when he goes to law as plaintiff, his reason seems to have deserted him : while, if he stands in the position of defendant, it is generally against his free will ; and thus, that " noblest of animals," Man, is in a very ignoble predicament.

Justinian has reduced the principles of law to three ;—1st, that we should live honestly ; 2ndly, that we should hurt nobody ; and 3rdly, that we should give every one his due. These principles have, however, been for some time obsolete in ordinary legal practice. It used to be considered that justice and human felicity were intimately connected, but the partnership seems to have been long ago dissolved ; though we cannot say at what particular period. That man should pursue his own true and substantial happiness, is said to be the foundation of ethics, or natural law ; but if any one plunges into artificial law with the view of "pursuing his own true and substantial happiness," he will find himself greatly mistaken.

It is said that no human laws are of any validity if they are contrary to the law of nature; but we do not mean to deny the validity of the Poor Law, and some others we could mention. The law of nature contributes to the general happiness of men ; but it is in the nature of law to contribute only to the happiness of the attorney.

Natural law is much easier of comprehension than human law ; for every man has within his own breast a *forum conscientiæ*, or court of conscience, telling him what is right and what is wrong. The judgments of that court of conscience are infallible, and its decrees are never silent ; for it is without an usher (which in this case means a husher) to preserve silence.

The law of nations is a peculiar kind of law, and it is generally settled by recourse to powder and shot, so that the law of nations is in the long run much the same thing as the cannon law.

But we now come to the municipal or civil law, which is the subject of the present chapter, though we have not yet said a word regarding it. Municipal law is defined to be " a rule of civil conduct prescribed by the supreme power in a state, commanding what is right, and prohibiting what is wrong." Such was the definition of Puffendorf, whose name is probably a corruption of *Puffing off*, for he puffs off the law most outrageously whenever he can find an opportunity of doing so.

It is called a " rule" to distinguish it from an agreement, for a rule must be complied with " willy nilly," according to Bacon, or " will ye nill ye," according to Coke.

It is a rule of " *civil conduct*," because the municipal law insists on civil conduct, particularly from omnibus cads and cabmen.

It is " *prescribed*," because one is bound to take it, and a very disagreeable pill it sometimes is to swallow. It is one of the beautiful provisions of the English law, that not knowing it forms no excuse for not obeying it. It is an ingenious fiction of British policy that every person in the kingdom purchases every Act of Parliament, and carefully reads it through; therefore, there can be no possible excuse for being ignorant of the laws that are made every session.

It is reported of Caligula that he caused the laws of Rome to be written in small characters, and stuck up so high that the citizens could not read them ; though, perhaps, the higher classes, who, it is presumed, could afford to purchase opera-glasses, were enabled to make themselves acquainted with the edicts.

Municipal law is a rule prescribed by the " *supreme power in the state*," and this brings us to the question of the origin of government. Some writers think that society, in its original state, chose the tallest man amongst them as king. If this had been the case, Carus Wilson might have disputed the English throne with Mr. Charles Freeman, the American giant. Perhaps the expression in the national anthem, " *Long* to reign over us," has given rise to this very extraordinary theory.

There are three forms of government—a democracy, where the mass takes such liberties in the lump, that there is no liberty left for allotment among private individuals—an aristocracy, which we need not particularly describe—or a monarchy, where one individual is absolute within a certain space, like the square-keeper of a square, who is fortunately the only specimen of pure despotism that this free country possesses.

Cicero thought a mixture of these three the best ; but Tacitus, who had better have been on this occasion tacitus indeed, and held his tongue, declared the idea to be a visionary whim ; for he seems to have imagined that the oil of aristocracy and the vinegar of democracy never could have coalesced. Tacitus, however, was out ; and, fortunately for us, the British Constitution presents the mixture in its complete form, and we trust will long continue what it is—"a real blessing to mothers," fathers, daughters, sons, and wives of Great Britain.

The House of Commons embodies the principle of goodness and purity, as a reference to the various election compromises and bribery cases will manifest. The House of Lords embraces the grand element of wisdom, as the reported speeches of various sagacious noblemen will at once prove ; while the Monarchy is the type of strength, the stability of the throne being provided for by her Majesty's upholsterers. Here, then, in the British Constitution is concentrated the milk of everything that is good, wise, and powerful. Woe to the revolutionary hand that shall attempt to skim it !

We now come to analyse a law. In the first place, it is declaratory ; in the second, it is directory ; in the third, it is remedial ; and in the fourth, it is vindicatory. The declaratory says so and so is wrong, and the directory immediately says it shall not be done ; but it sometimes contrives to say so in such very civil and mysterious terms as to leave people in doubt whether they may do a thing or may not, until they find all of a sudden they are put into possession of its true meaning, and punished for not having been able to under-stand it.

It is *remedial*, for it gives a remedy. Thus, if you are de-prived of your right, you have the remedy of a law-suit, which is a great luxury, no doubt, though rather an expensive one.

It is also *vindicatory*, for it attaches a penalty—and such is the majesty of law, that, whether right or wrong, he is sure to have to bear a portion of the penalty who presumes in any way to meddle with it.

Offences are either *mala in se* or *mala prohibita ;* but the *mala prohibita* differ very materially from the *mala in se*, of which many instances could be given. Piracy is decidedly a *malum in se*(a), but a *malum prohibitum* is that which is only made criminal by the law. For example, it was attempted to make baking on Sunday a *malum prohibitum*, so that a good dinner would in fact have been a *bonum prohibitum* if the anti-baking-on-Sunday party had succeeded.

The rules for interpreting English Law are extremely arbi-trary. Words are to be taken in their popular sense without regard to grammar, which is thought to have been always beneath the wisdom of Parliament. Grotius thought that the penalty on crime was a sort of tax on Sin, which might be defined without regard to Sin-tax. Puffendorf tells us, that the law forbidding a layman to lay hands on a priest (observe the pun, " a *lay*man to *lay* hands") applied also to those who would hurt a priest with a weapon, or in other words, " lay into him."

If words are still dubious after the lawyers are called in (and they have a knack of making matters more dubious than before), it is usual to refer to the context ; but this is, in many cases, only to get out of the frying-pan into the fire.

Next, as to the subject-matter. The words are always supposed (though it requires a tolerable latitude in the way of supposition) to have reference to the subject-matter. Thus a law of Edward III. forbids all ecclesiastical persons to purchase *provisions* at Rome, which would seem to interdict clergymen from buying anything to eat within the holy city. It seems, however, that this only has reference to the purchase of "bulls" from the Pope; though it is not unlawful to procure portions of "bulls," such as rump-steaks or sirloins of beef, from the papal butchers.

Next, as to the effect and consequence of words, if literally understood. "It has been held," says Puffendorf, "after a long debate," that when the words amount to utter nonsense, they are not to be in all cases strictly followed. Thus the Bolognian law, enacting that punishment should be inflicted on any one who drew blood in the streets, was at last held (after several medical men had been put to death) not to extend to surgeons who should bleed a man taken in the streets with a fainting fit. But, lastly, the reason and spirit of the law must be looked at (when there happen to be any). The following case, put by Cicero, is so nice, that we throw it into metre :—

A law there was, that in a water-trip
Those who should in a storm forsake a ship
   All property should in the vessel lose.
It happen'd in a tempest all on board,
Excepting one, who was by sickness floor'd,
   To leave the ship their utmost power did use.
The invalid, who could not get away,
Was with the wreck of course compell'd to stay,
   And with it he was into harbour wash'd.
The benefit of law he then did claim,
But when to sift the point the lawyers came,
   His claim with great propriety was quash'd.

The difficulty of saying what is the meaning of law led to the establishment of a perfectly distinct branch of jurisprudence, called equity. According to Grotius, equity "*non*

exacte definit, sed arbitrio boni viri permittit." Among other
boni viri, to whose *arbitrium* equity has left matters, was
the late Lord Eldon, who was so exceedingly modest as to
his judgments that he postponed them as long as he could,
and even when he gave them, such was his delicacy, that it
was often quite impossible to understand and abide by them.
It has, however, been said, that law without equity is better
than equity without law ; and, therefore, though in law there
is very often no equity, nevertheless there is no equity that
has not sufficient law to make its name of equity a pleasant
fiction.

SECTION III.—OF THE LAWS OF ENGLAND.

THE Civil Law may be divided into the *lex non scripta,*
the unwritten or common law, which was not originally in
black and white ; and the *lex scripta,* the written or statute
law, which was originally in black and white ; "though,"
says Coke, "yᵉ blacke in all our lawes did alwayse prepon-
derate."

By the unwritten law, we do not mean that any laws have
been communicated by word of mouth from one generation to
the other, for this would be reducing the common law to mere
talk. The western world being totally ignorant of letters—by
which it is to be understood that the alphabet was at that time
wholly unknown at the west end—our ancestors trusted to
tradition, and thus the laws became more familiar to them
than A B C ; and the earlier lawyers trusted to their recollection, which, no doubt, gave rise to the maxim, that liars—
of which lawyers is an evident corruption—should have long
memories. The Druids were certainly no disciples of Mr.
Carstairs, the celebrated writing master, of whom Lord Byron
is reported to have said, " I should have been a better writer
had I been guided by that man," and they probably despised
penmanship chiefly on account of their being wholly without

pens ; but Aulus Gellius has left this subject in the darkness that so naturally belongs to it.

Fortescue thinks our common law is as old as the primitive Britons ; and we are ourselves inclined to refer to the times of pure barbarism for the origin of our legal system.

Mr. Selden fancies we got a bit of it from the Romans, and that we picked some from the Picts ; so that, according to Selden, the English Law is a delicious jumble, and of this its confused state appears to give ample evidence. Bacon says, our laws, being mixed like our language, are so much the richer ; but Bacon always cuts it uncommonly fat when he gets on the subject of legal richness.

Antiquarians tell us that Alfred the Great compiled all the laws into one volume, which he called a dome or doom-book ; and, considering what people are doomed to by the law, Alfred could not have hit upon a happier title for his production. This book was lost in the reign of Edward the Fourth, or probably sold for waste-paper to the cheesemongers, which accounts for its having been looked upon as most decidedly " the cheese " from that day to the present.

In the beginning of the eleventh century, there were three different sorts of laws, the Mercian, the West Saxon, and the Danish ; out of which we are told, by Ranulphus Cestrensis, (who was, we suppose, " a gentleman, one *et cetera*,") that Edward the Confessor formed a digest of laws, which shows that the Confessor's digestion must have been first-rate ; and, indeed, he must have been something like Ramo Samee, the Indian juggler, who could swallow a stone and feel none the worse for it. Some say that Edward the Confessor's book was a mere crib from Alfred's, and Alfred has been called the *conditor* or builder of our law, while Edward the Confessor has been nick-named the *restitutor* or restorer. Being a confessor, we wonder he did not confess this fraud, if he had really been guilty of it ; but perhaps, on the *lucus a non lucendo* principle, Edward was called a confessor from his never confessing anything. Whoever may be entitled

to the authorship, these laws constitute the *jus commune,*
or *folk right,* as Edward the Elder rather facetiously
phrases it.

The goodness of a custom entirely depends on nobody being
able to say how it came to be a custom at all ; and the more
unaccountable it is in its origin, the better it is for legal purposes.   If this fine old principle were to be applied to the
ordinary business of every-day life, he would be the best
customer of whom the tradesman should say—" I can't think
how I ever came to trust or deal with him."

The unwritten law has three kinds of customs.   General
customs, which apply to the whole country, such as the
custom of going to bed at night, and getting up in the morning.   Particular customs, applying to particular places, such
as the custom of intimidating the boys at the Burlington
Arcade, by the presence of a man armed with a brazen-headed
tomahawk ; and certain particular laws that have obtained
the force of custom in some particular courts,—such as the
custom at the Court of Kingsgate-street, of making an order
on the defendant, and asking him how he will pay, without
hearing much of the evidence.

The judges decide what is a custom and what is not.   They,
in fact, make the law by saying what it means ; which, as it
scarcely ever means what it says, opens the door to much
variety.   " Variety is charming," according to the proverb ;
and the study of the law must, on this authority, be regarded
as one of the most fascinating of occupations.   " Law is the
perfection of reason," say the lawyers ; and so it is, when
you get it : but if a judge makes a decision that is manifestly
absurd or unjust, it is declared not to be law—for " what is
not reason," say the lawyers, " is not law :" a maxim which,
if acted upon, would have the effect of condensing the law
most materially, or perhaps exterminating it altogether.

The law is preserved in reports, of which there are many
thousand volumes ; so that any one in ignorance of the law
has only to purchase or borrow these—compare the different

decisions, and apply them all to his own case, when he will either be right, or have the happiness of correcting the law by a fresh decision telling him that he is wrong : which will, of course, be ample compensation for any little inconvenience he may have experienced.

The best of the old law treatises is Coke upon Littleton, by which obscurity has been rendered doubly obscure. Mr. Selden, whose acuteness missed the pun, might have said, that a bushel of Coke superadded to a Little Ton, was enough to put out the fire and extinguish the light ; but Mr. Selden has left it to us to make this observation. Coke upon Littleton is, no doubt, something on the model of Butter upon Bacon—the latter being a work that never was seen, though it is often alluded to. The former is said to be a mine of learning ; and, like all mining concerns, there is a good deal of mystery with not a little roguery mixed up in it.

Among particular customs may be instanced the customs of London, one of which is the custom of having a dish of sprats on Lord Mayor's day ; and another is the custom of making jokes, which the chief clerk always indulges in.

The civil law, perhaps, ought now to be noticed. It consists of the Institutes in four books, and the digests in Fifty, added to which are the Constitutions in twelve books ; and the Novels, or new constitutions, which like many novels of the present day, are not readable.

The Canon Law is made up of rare patchwork, in which various popes had a hand, and their contributions were appropriately enough called *extravagants*. In the reign of Henry the Eighth, it was enacted that there should be a review of the Canon Law, but like some of the reviews appointed to take place in Hyde Park, it was postponed, and nothing has been since done in it.

We need say no more of the Canon law, considering that it is subjected entirely to the common law, and does not in all cases bind the laity—but Spelman thinks that the term "son of a gun," is incidental to the canon law, for the law, was always sovereign, and the sovereign is said to be the father of the people.

We now come to the *lex scripta*, or written law—the oldest specimen of which is that glorious bit of old parchment known as *Magna Charta*—the sight of which sets many a British heart upon the beat at the Museum, where, on Easter Monday, the palladium of our liberties is an object of overwhelming interest.

Magna Charta is now chiefly useful as a subject for oratorical clap-traps. The scrawl is sadly indicative of the horrible state to which the discontented barons were reduced for want of " six lessons in the calligraphic art." John was made to sign as a *sine quâ non*—but the large spot of ink over the J. will be a blot upon his name as long as Magna Charta is in existence.

Statutes are of different kinds ; general or special, public or private. A public act regards the whole community— though there are exceptions—for, if Mr. So and So is advertised to appear as Othello at Covent Garden Theatre, it is a public act, and yet no one seems to care for it.

A special or private act regards only the party concerned ; as if there were to be an act to secure the profits of Waterloo Bridge, this would be an act in which no one but those who were paid for drawing it could feel any interest.

The mode of construing a statute gives fine scope for mystification ; and it has been said by the learned Barrington, who began his education for the office of a Botany Bay judge as an English pickpocket, that any one may drive a coach and horses through any Act of Parliament.

Penal statutes must be construed literally—thus if an act inflicts a punishment for stealing a shilling and *other* money, no one could be convicted under that statute for stealing a pound, because *other* money only would be mentioned.

When the common law differs from the statute law, the latter prevails—and a new statute supersedes an old one— which is just turning topside-turvy the principle which governs the common law, where the older the custom happens to be the better. The Wandering Jew and Methuselah are the two best authorities on questions of common law; but this is not germane to the subject.

If a statute that repeals another is itself repealed, the first statute is revived; another provision which is in the nature of law, though not in the law of nature. It is as if we should say that, if one man kills another, and he is afterwards killed, the first man revives—a position which none but a lawyer would insist upon.

Any statute derogating from the power of subsequent Parliaments does not bind, for Parliament acknowledges no superior upon earth—except, perhaps, Mr. Stockdale and his attorney Howard, who certainly showed themselves superior to Parliament by getting the upper hand of it. Cicero, in his letters to Atticus, had what is vulgarly termed a "shy" at the absurdity of "restraining clauses"—and he seems to think that if Parliament were fettered, it would be more like Newgate, for its acts would be little better than Nugatory. Cicero did not make this joke, but he laid the foundation of it; and as it is a maxim in law that *qui facit per alium facit per se*, we may give him the credit of it.

Lastly, an act of Parliament that is impossible to be performed is of no value—in which respect the acts that cannot be performed, resemble many of those which can be, and are carried into execution. It is, however, a rule admitting of many exceptions, for if Parliament were restrained from doing unreasonable acts, its proceedings would be necessarily greatly interfered with.

These are the materials of which the laws of England are composed—and they constitute a hash of the most savoury character.

Of equity we have already said something, and any one who is engaged in a Chancery suit will appreciate its blessings. Equity detects latent frauds, but there are exceptions to this rule, for equity would not assist the purchaser of a dining-table made of green materials, at a cheap mart for furniture. Nor would the Chancellor give his opinion as to whether any latent fraud had been practised. Equity will deliver a person from such dangers as are owing to misfortune or oversight; but if a man has the misfortune to fall into a cellar by an oversight of his own, he may wait a long time before equity will get him out of it.

Equity will give specific relief adapted to the circumstances of the case; but if a man has the tooth-ache, equity has no specific in the way of relief, except, perhaps, extraction—for Chancery will take the bread from the mouth, and may, therefore, as well extract the tooth from the jaw, for the latter without the former is superfluous. Such is the glorious nature of our constitution, that equity cannot touch the life though it may sweep away all the property.

A judge may not construe the law in criminal cases, except according to the letter—and sometimes it amounts to a dead letter.

We cannot conclude this account of the statute law, without observing that all eminent jurists say it ought to be consolidated; but this seems much less easy to do than to talk about. Several commissions have recently been appointed, and various reports have been issued, the last of which is the sixth of the Criminal Commissioners, who, however, are no less criminal than the others, for they have all made a horribly long job of it. We confess, that, figuratively speaking, the law requires boiling down, but we prefer trying to get at its essence by merely roasting it.

SECTION IV.—OF THE COUNTRIES SUBJECT TO THE LAWS OF ENGLAND.

SEVERAL of our law writers say, with their usual acuteness, " England is not Wales, neither is it Scotland nor Ireland ;" and, in fact, Spelman adds that " England is nothing but itself :" though, in our own day, we have seen that England has been anything but itself, so that the old learning on this head is quite out of date at present.

Wales continued a long time independent of England ; and Cæsar, who seized on almost everything, did not so soon seize upon that. The people lived, says Tacitus, in a pastoral state : having probably no other food but Welsh rabbits, until Edward the First introduced his heir to them as their prince ; and the people having shown the white feather, it is supposed that it was immediately taken from them and placed in the prince's hat—" where," says Fortescue, " it has continued ever since, as a badge of honour on one side, and servitude on the other." The finishing stroke to Welsh independence was given by the statute 27th Henry VIII., chapter 26, which may be said to have played Old Harry with their liberties. But while it gave Wales a frightful blow with one hand, it offered civil liberty with the other ; and Mr. Selden is of opinion that the expression a " topper for luck" originated with the circumstance alluded to. The only remnant of independence left to Wales has been taken away by the 1st of William IV., which puts an end to its independent law courts, which were, indeed, independent not of law alone but of justice. In those courts, law, instead of being paid for, as in England, through the attorneys, used to be purchased directly of the judge, who, instead of giving consideration to the facts, used to take a consideration from the parties, and decide accordingly

Scotland was an independent kingdom until the time of Anne, when the Union was carried out, and Scotland was declared to be a part of England ; but as nobody knew whether Berwick-upon-Tweed belonged to one country or the other, it is subject to neither or both. " And this," says Coke, " was making a regular Scotch mull of the business."

Ireland was, until lately, a distinct kingdom ; but since it has ceased to be distinct it has been a good deal confused, which is so far natural. Henry VIII. assumed the title of king, and afterwards recognised the title by the 35th of himself,* chapter 3, which is as though a pickpocket should steal a handkerchief and then pass a resolution in his own mind recognising his right to the stolen article.

At the time of the Conquest, the Irish were governed by the Brehon law ; but John, going over with a lot of legal sages, stuffed the Irish people with the said sage, which did not at all agree with their constitution. At length Edward the Third hit upon the old trick of abolishing the Brehon law, by saying that it never was law at all ; and hence the expression " Well I never ! did you ever ?"—an exclamation that Edward very probably used when pretending his utter ignorance that such a thing as the Brehon law had ever existed.

Laws passed in England do not bind Ireland, unless Ireland is named ; and when Ireland is named, it often seems to think itself only bound—to grumble. The union between Ireland and England was at length effected in 1800 ; and like man and wife, the two countries would go on very well together, but for the interference of certain pretended friends, who take pleasure in sowing dissension between them. Hibernia is at the present moment being urged to sue for a divorce, but the Agitator who has been working her up to ask for it has lately received a tweak of the nose,† which we

---

* 35 Henry VIII.

† The tweak alluded to in the text was the verdict of the jury on the man's trial.

are sorry Coke and other sages are not in existence to dilate upon.

Among the islands subjected to England is the Isle of Thanet, whose inhabitants devote themselves to the simple arts of peace, manufacturing Margate slippers, and polishing the shells of cockles, which they offer for sale to the strangers who visit their shores. The lesser islands of Dogs, and the Eel-pies, are also subjected to the laws of England ; but at the latter there is a sort of Lord Lieutenant, who keeps a tavern, and exercises a species of absolute monarchy, exacting tribute from the visitor, but extending hospitality in return for it. The thread of English law is carried through the well-known Needles to the Isle of Wight, and the ancient Isle of Isleworth, though locally subjected to three policemen, is bound by all the acts of the British Parliament.

The Isle of Man is a distinct territory, not subject to our laws ; and, indeed, if it were under the Queen, says Plowden, in his *Coruscationes Comicæ*, it would not be the Isle of Man, but the Isle of Woman. This Isle of Man continued for eight generations in the family of the Earls of Derby, until, in 1594, several daughters having been left by the deceased earl, the young ladies got up such a quarrel about the isle with the tempting name of Man, that the Queen settled the matter by seizing the island for her own use, and put a man in possession. At length the island became the property of the Athol family, but the title of king had long been disused, as well it might, for his Manly Majesty was a most absurd epithet to apply to any one. The contemptible little sovereignty was eventually purchased by George the First ; and the expression "I'm the Man for your money," probably originated from the circumstance alluded to.

There are several other islands, including Jersey, Guernsey, Alderney, (famous for its cows,) and Sark, remarkable for the ugliness of its name, which are not bound by British acts of Parliament, simply because nobody thinks it worth while to give them any laws at all until the last resort ; when, after

letting them go on in their own way till they have got themselves into a fix, there is an appeal to the Sovereign in Council. We do not know who is the present King of Sark, nor have
we any notion of the name of the Royal Family of Alderney.

Our colonial possessions are in some cases subject to the
English laws, but many have local legislatures, and a representative assembly has been recently given to New South Wales.
If the emancipated felons are to form part of the constituency,
it is probable that Newgate, and the various houses of correction, will send several members to the Sydney Parliament,
who, if they do not represent their own breeches-pockets, as
under the boroughmongering system used to be the case at
home, may nevertheless be supposed to represent the *élite*,
or rather the pick, of the pockets of other people.

'Let us now consider England, including part of the sea,
which is not subject to the common law, but to the Courts of
Admiralty ; for it is supposed that the judges of the Common
Law Courts, not being nautical men, would be unable to hold
the scales of justice steadily on the high seas, particularly
in the case of a storm or a hurricane. The Admiralty has
jurisdiction on the water, and the common law on dry ground ;
and very dry ground the common law is considered by those
students who have to go over it. The sea begins at low-
water mark, but the space between that and high-water mark
is subject alternately to the jurisdiction of the common law
or the Admiralty, according to whether the tide happens to
be high or low. For example, the coast of Battersea is subject alternately to Dr. Lushington, of the Admiralty, and to
Lord Denman, with the other common law judges. When
it is covered with water, the former is entitled to jurisdiction,
but when it is all mud and slush Lord Denman and his
learned colleagues may revel uncontrolled in it. It is, however, worthy of observation, that this jurisdiction is not often
claimed ; for when a client is at low-water mark, the lawyers
are seldom anxious to have anything to do with him.

England has two divisions, the one ecclesiastical, the other civil. The former is subdivided into provinces, sees, arch-deaconries, rural deaneries, and parishes. There are tow provinces, those of York and Canterbury, their province being to take care of themselves, and to bestow certain bishoprics, which are called seas or sees—probably from the amount that is annually swallowed in them. An archdeacon was originally called arch from a certain degree of clerical cunning ; and a rural dean is a sort of clergyman, we presume, with a strong taste for gardening.

A parish, of which there are about ten thousand in England, was, according to Camden—who, by the bye, did not build Camden Town—first formed by Honorius; but who Honorius was, Camden has not done us the favour to let us know. Sir Henry Hobart, who is as wide of the mark as Hobart Town is of Regent-street, thinks parishes were erected by the Council of Lateran, upon which Mr. Selden comes in and splits the difference, saying that, as both were wrong, perhaps it will be right to go as far as possible from either, by taking the middle of the term as the proper one. Some few places, such as marshes, were extra-parochial, until the clergy got them formed into parishes, and often took tithes from marshes, under the pretext of thoroughly draining them.

The civil division of England into counties, hundreds, and towns, began under Alfred, who made the discreetest man in the place the headborough ; an office answering to that of mayor, except that, instead of choosing the discreetest man, the other extreme has in modern times been usually resorted to.

A tithing is the same as a town or ville, and when incor-porated it always had a bishop ; but there are no records of there ever having been a Bishop of Pentonville : and if such a see existed, the look-out must have been somewhat of the dreariest.

A borough is a town that sends burgesses to Parliament ; but many fell into decay, and were called rotten boroughs in consequence   Besides these, there are small places called hamlets, such as the Hamlet of Hammersmith, where Shakspeare is supposed to have conceived the character of the Prince of Denmark.

Hundreds consisted of ten tithings, a tithing being composed of ten families; but "after the Revolution," says Bracton, "everything went to sixes and sevens, so that the tens and hundreds were lost sight of." Hundreds were, in some places, called wapentakes, probably from the inhabitants being accustomed to give and take a whapping.

The ancient distribution of hundreds being no longer applied to the land itself, has since been transferred to its produce; and hence we hear of a hundred of coals, a hundred of asparagus, and a hundred of walnuts.

Counties or shires are of ancient origin, and were governed by an Earl or Alderman; for, in very early times, all Aldermen were Earls, which does not say much for the Early aristocracy.

A county is also called a shire, and hence we have the word sheriff; whose proper duty it is to see to the execution of the law within the county, and also the execution of the criminals. If the old Saxon customs were now in force, the Sheriff, whoever he might be, would have to hang at the Old Bailey, not *in propriâ personâ*, but it would be his duty to hang capital offenders if there chanced to be any.

There are three counties palatine—namely, Chester, Durham, and Lancaster, which formerly had royal privileges. These have lost their fixity of tenure, for they have all been taken away; though at Lancaster the militia—consisting of an adjutant and four sergeants—is still allowed to exercise a sort of limited despotism.

We had almost forgotten to mention that the Isle of Ely though not a county palatine, is a royal franchise, where the bishop has it all his own way; thus realising the beautiful little allegory of the Bull in the China-shop.

So much for the countries subject to the laws of England.

CHAPTER I.

ON THE ABSOLUTE RIGHTS OF INDIVIDUALS.

MUNICIPAL law is a rule of civil conduct, and it is to be regretted that government clerks pay so very little regard to it. Its primary objects are rights and wrongs ; but it seems to have a greater regard for wrongs than for rights—often giving right to the wrong, and sometimes wronging the right in the most palpable manner.

Blackstone divides rights into the rights of persons and the rights of things ; but the division is not approved, for it has been held that there are no rights of things—but surely boots are things, and there is always a right boot, though the jurists insist that it is only the owner who has a personal right in it.

Rights are such as are due *from* a man and such as belong *to* him ; but some things that belong *to* one man are due *to* another, in which case it is hard to get at the right of it.

Persons are either natural or artificial ; but the law does not regard a man as necessarily artificial because, like an actor, he pads his calves ; but a corporation is an artificial person—and here it would seem that stuffing has really something to do with the distinction.

Absolute rights are such as belong to man in a state of nature, though absolute rights are often exercised by Eastern despots when in a state of ill-nature.

Human laws are principally intended to protect absolute rights ; but the laws often meddle with what seems absolutely right till there is nothing absolutely left of the original right, and absolute wrong is the consequence.

Natural liberty is the right inherent in all men at their birth ; but this natural liberty is soon at an end, for restraint begins in the cradle. Each member of society gives up a portion of his own individual liberty, in consideration of receiving the advantages of mutual commerce, says Coke, in his Institutes; but he does not go on to tell us the commercial advantages enjoyed by a newly-born baby.

This sort of modified power of action is called civil liberty, and anything interfering with that is considered to be taking a liberty of a most uncivil kind with the freedom of the subject. Thus, the statute of Edward the Fourth, prohibiting any but lords from wearing pikes on their shoes of more than two inches long, was considered to savour of oppression; but those who were in the habit of receiving from a lord more kicks than halfpence, would consider that the law in question savoured of benevolence.

Mr. Locke has well observed, that where there is no law there is no freedom; but Mr. Levy, the sheriff's officer—who understands the force of lock—has observed, tolerably well, that where there is a great deal of law there is often an infringement on liberty.

"Political liberty flourishes in its highest vigour," says Salkeld, "in these realms;" but Salkeld flourishes more about political liberty than political liberty flourishes about us; though, we confess, England has her share of it.

Every slave who sets his foot on British ground is said to be free, which gave rise to a bubble company for taking out earth to the Havannah in flower-pots from an English nursery-garden, for the slaves to stand upon and assert their freedom. Unfortunately, the speculators, and not the slaves, contrived to put their foot in it. Slavery is, however, now abolished by Act of Parliament; but it extends to blacks, and not to the white population, thus giving an opportunity to Coke—had he been alive to make the pun—that the boon has been bestowed with a *niggar*-dly hand by the legislature.

The history of the rise of our constitution is curious. It began with the great Charter, which the Barons wrested from John; but for the particulars of the wrestling match we refer to the sporting papers of the period. Henry the Third corroborated this statute, and other monarchs touched it up; which, considering the fuss that has been made about it, savours of the process of painting the lily, a proceeding that Shakspeare is justly indignant at.·

Charles the First edited a supplement, called the Petition of Right, and Charles the Second passed the *Habeas Corpus* Act, by which, among other blessings, a debtor could change his quarters to the Queen's Prison from Whitecross-street. Then came the Bill of Rights, drawn by the people, and accepted by William and Mary; which was followed by the Act of Settlement, relating to the Crown, which, it would appear from this, the sovereigns had previously had on tick, and it was therefore not settled for. The Reform Act, which followed, may be called the act of unsettlement, on account of the changes that have ever since been called for.

The rights of the person may be again divided into three; the right of security, by which a man has a right to be locked up in the station-house, if found drunk and incapable of taking care of himself; the right of personal liberty, by which a person may go wherever he pleases, if he has only the money necessary to pay the fare; and the right of private property, enabling every man to keep what he has got, when the Government has helped itself, through the medium of taxation, to all that it requires.

The right of personal security consists in the legal enjoyment of life, limbs, health, and reputation—from which it would seem that a man may draw his breath and stretch his legs without impediment. A man's limbs are understood to be those members which are useful to him in fight; and these, says Glanvil, include "ye armes with whych he may fyghte, and ye legges with whyche he may runne awaye, whvchsoever may beste suitte his whymme at ye moment."

In the eye of the law, the life and limbs of a man are of such value, that he may sacrifice the life and limbs of any one else in defending them. This, says Coke, is upon the good old English principle of tit for tat; but what is the origin of the word " tit," or what is the exact meaning of " tat," the old jurists have never told us.   There is no man so poor and indigent but that he may demand a supply sufficient for the necessaries of life,—though he may demand long enough before he will get them.   It is true, there are the Union Workhouses, where, if bread is asked for, stones will be given; and when a man has broken these, he may break his fast afterwards.

Next to personal security comes personal liberty, which consists in the power of moving from place to place,—a luxury often indulged in by debtors, occupants of furnished lodgings, and others, who prize liberty to such an extent, that the liberties they take are truly wonderful. *Magna Charta* says, that no freeman shall be imprisoned, except by his peers : and, if this be true, every policeman who walks a man off to the station-house, must be considered as a peer for temporary purposes.

The 16th of Charles the First gives to any one in prison the power of having his body brought before the Sovereign in council, that it may be determined if he is rightly in custody; but this glorious old privilege would give the Sovereign in council enough to do, if every gentleman who happened to have been " found drunk in the streets " should take advantage of it.

One of the great beauties of the *Habeas Corpus* Act is, that it prevents a Government from tyrannising, and yet as this would fetter the hands of Government, it may be suspended at the Government's will; and thus, says Fleta, " the subject is free, and yet not too free ; while Government is strong, yet not too strong," from which it appears this magnificent palladium of our liberties is neither one thing nor the other.

It now becomes a question, " What is imprisonment ?" Unlawfully detaining a man in any way, is imprisonment : and *semble* that if you take your neighbour by the button, and cause him to listen to a long story, you are guilty of imprisonment. An Omnibus driver, who loiters on the road, and thus detains his passengers, is also guilty of imprisonment.

Every Englishman has a right to live in England ; or at least, if he cannot live, he may have the glorious privilege of starving there. The Sovereign may not send a subject even to Scotland, Guernsey, or Sark, though George the Fourth sent Brummell to Coventry ; and our present Queen has been heard to tell Sir Robert Peel to go to Bath, when he has proposed measures contrary to the welfare and happiness of the people. The third right is the right of property, which the law peculiarly regards, and will not allow a man to be deprived of his property except by the law itself, " which often," says Fleta, " hath a happie knacke of stryppinge him."

It is a beautiful fiction of the English law that no man pays taxes without his own consent ; and, from this assertion, it would naturally be supposed that the tax-gatherers were the very idols of the people, who flocked round them, tendering specie and asking receipts for it. By legal imagery, the people are declared to tax themselves ; but Bracton, in a learned note, added " Hookey " to this assertion ; while Mr. Selden, by way of strengthening the comment, has subjoined " Walker," with his customary quaintness.

Besides the three great rights already touched on, there are a few auxiliary rights ; the first of which is the right of demanding justice—when you can afford to pay for it; and getting justice—when you are fortunate enough to obtain it.

The words of *Magna Charta* are these :—" *Nulli vendemus, nulli negabimus aut differemus, rectum vel justitiam ;*" meaning literally—" We will sell, deny, or delay, justice to no man." Who the " we " may be that make this promise it is hard to say, for nobody ever thinks of keeping it. As to justice never being sold, let any man look at the bill of costs he gets from his attorney. As to its being denied, let him seek justice in a Court of Requests ; and as to its being delayed, let him commence a suit in Chancery. Coke, who is the funniest fellow for a law writer that was ever known, says that any man " may have justice and right freely without sale, fully without denial, and speedily without delay,"— a burst of humour such as Old Coke very often favours us with.

The law cannot be altered, except by Parliament and the Court of Requests ; the latter having, in fact, greater power than the former ; for, while the one only alters the law, the other utterly demolishes it.   The sovereign may, it is true, erect new Courts, but they must proceed in the old way ; or he may turn a garret into a Court, as in the case of Vice-Chancellor Wigram, who was thrust—with the sword of Justice—into a three-pair back, where, to continue the figure, he had scarcely room to brandish the avenging weapon, with comfort to himself and satisfaction to the suitors.

The right of petitioning is another glorious privilege of Englishmen ; but they do not often get much by it.   Puffen-dorf, or somebody else, has said, " They who don't ask, don't want ; but those who do ask, shan't have ;" and *semble* that this is the sort of view which Parliament takes of any wishes, expressed or not expressed, which do not happen to coincide with the wishes of the legislature.

The last right at present deserving of mention is the right of having arms for one's defence ; and by the first of William and Mary, though it is the very last one would think of attending to, any man may walk about town with a gun, for the purpose of self-preservation.

Such are the rights and liberties of Englishmen, which are less understood than talked about, and less practically experienced than either.

CHAPTER II.

OF THE PARLIAMENT.

DEVOTING ourselves to our arduous task, we shall now treat of the relation men bear to one another in the way of government. The governors and the governed are relations in some sort: for the King, or Governor, is the father of his people, and one's father is therefore often called "the Governor." Of magistrates, some are supreme, and some subordinate; but the subordinate magistrates sometimes render themselves supremely ridiculous.

In tyrannical governments the supreme magistrate both makes and enforces the laws, acting in the double capacity of protector and punisher of the people, which is something like an actor combining the fathers, or benevolent old men, with the heavy business. When the magistrate makes laws, and enforces them also, he does as he pleases, but is not likely to please in what he does; and, therefore, in England the supreme power is divided into two branches—the one executive, consisting of the Sovereign alone; and the other legislative, to wit (as the lawyers say, though the wit is rather obscure)—*to wit*, the Parliament! Parliament is a word derived from *parler* to talk, and *mentir* to lie, and in this respect Parliament proves itself fully worthy of its origin. The antiquity of Parliaments is so great that no one can trace their beginning; and it is sometimes as difficult to say what is the end they are driving at. In England the Parliament used to be called *Wittena Gemote*, a meeting of wise or witty men; and probably the "three wise men of Gotham," who "went to sea in a bowl," were members of the *Wittena Gemote;* at least, if we may judge by the qualities of the collective wisdom which has succeeded the *Michel-Synoth*, or great council of the nation.

Glanvil, who wrote in the time of Henry the Second, in reporting a case in the Sheriff's court, from which it would appear that Red Lion Square was built very soon after the Invasion, alludes vaguely to a sort of meeting, which, it is said, was very likely to have been the Parliament; and as the body in question appears to have done no good, but rendered something quite obscure, the suggestion that it was the Parliament seems to be extremely feasible.

Antiquaries, who are "nothing if not at loggerheads" with one another, have disputed—first, as to who summoned the Parliaments; secondly, whether anybody summoned them at all; thirdly, if summoned, whether they came; fourthly, whether they came without summoning; fifthly, whether they came exactly when they were summoned; and, sixthly, if the same who were summoned, or sum-un else, actually came; none of which controversies do we think it expedient (just now) to go into. It is sufficient for our present purpose, that John, in the celebrated "bit of stiff," known as Magna Charta—that glorious bill drawn by the Barons, and accepted by himself—promised to summon the nobles personally, and the Commons by the sheriff and bailiffs; from which it would seem that the Commons were hunted up by the ancestors of the Slowmans, the Levys, the Thompsons, the Selbys, and the Davises.

Parliament can only be convened by the authority of the Sovereign, except on the death of either a king or a queen when if there be no Parliament in being, the last Parliament revives, which has caused Fleta to make the very indifferent joke, that "Whereas ye cattes have nine lives, ye rattes—meaninge ye Commones—have only two, and thatte seldome." If kings won't summon Parliament for three years, it seems that formerly peers might issue out writs; but if kings wouldn't summon peers, and peers wouldn't issue writs, the only way for the country to get over the stile, was for constituents to meet and elect members—a privilege that was taken away by the 16th Charles II.: so that in these days if sovereigns won't summon Parliament, there is really no help for it.

Wherever it is laid down in the law books that a thing can't be done, it may be assumed with tolerable certainty that the thing has been done ; and hence we find that though Parliament may not summon itself, it has summoned itself on several occasions, particularly in 1688, when the glorious revolution, by a piece of glorious irregularity, was fully accomplished. At the present time the happy idea of voting the royal income from year to year, renders it pretty certain that the Sovereign will summon the Parliament annually ; a practice which is " safe " to be adopted by every Sovereign. Parliament consists of the Lords and the King in one house, with the Commons by themselves in another, and the three together form a Corporation ; the Sovereign forming the head, the Lords the trunk, and the Commons the members. The King has the power of putting a negative on the measures of the Lords and Commons ; he can practise that prevention, which is familiarly said to be " better than cure;" and indeed the Nobility can check the people, while the Sovereign can check both ; an idea, no doubt, taken from the situation in the *Critic*, where the beef-eaters, the lovers, and the daughters are all unable to move, because of the hold they have over one another.

The Sovereign will be the subject of future chapters ; but we shall now take the liberty to anatomise the Lords, and will commence with a delicate dash at the Lords Spiritual.

The Lords Spiritual consist of two Archbishops and twenty-four Bishops, but the latter are, in one sense, almost as arch as the former. When Henry VIII. dissolved monasteries, there were also twenty-seven mitred abbots and two priors, the latter of whom enjoyed only a nominal priority; and the mitred abbots were probably so called, from meeting at the Mitre in Fleet-street—a tavern celebrated as the resort of Johnson—a copy of whose life in four volumes (two on each side) still adorns the chimney-piece.

The Lords Temporal consist of all the peers of the realm, some of whom sit by descent; and, indeed, the descent is in some cases terrific, from a very great man to a very little one. Some peers are as old as the creation; but, as such creations are frequently happening, there is no very great antiquity to boast of. The number of the peers is indefinite, and they may be made (as soap and candles are advertised to be sold) in large or small quantities.

The distinction of rank is said to be very desirable; because it preserves that scale of dignity, which proceeds from the peasant to the prince—rising like a pyramid from a broad foundation, and diminishing almost to a point—the Prince of Wales being the point in this case; or, as the lawyers would say, the case in point; and, it must be admitted, a very little one.

The Commons consist of all men of property who have not a seat in the Lords—and they all have a voice in the Commons, the members acting as voice conductors; but it is in most cases " *Vox et prœterea nihil!* "

These are the constituent parts of a Parliament; which, according to Coke, is so powerful that it can do anything or everything; and yet, with all this omnipotence, it frequently prefers doing nothing. Parliament has various privileges, one of which is the privilege of speech—and of this the members take advantage, by talking very much and very foolishly.

The privileges of the peers are numerous:—first, stands the right of killing the king's deer on the way to Parliament, but as there are no deer—in fact no game at all, but a few ducks on the ornamental water in St. James's Park, this sporting privilege is seldom taken advantage of. The peers may also be attended by the judges, but they are themselves far too good judges to subject themselves to such learned bores. A peer may vote by proxy, and enter a protest, the latter being a luxury, which a coughed-down peer is glad to take advantage of. All bills affecting the peers are to begin in the upper House, but what will be their end, or what end they have in view, is often a mystery.

The chief privilege of the Commons is to tax the people, which is declared to be nothing more than the people taxing themselves—a piece of logical *hocus pocus* which Sir Matthew Hale vainly endeavours to invest with that plainness which is said to be peculiar to the pike-staff. One of the great advantages connected with Parliament is, that it may be adjourned ; but a greater advantage still is, that it may be dissolved, and sent about its business altogether. When Parliament is dissolved by the Sovereign in person, *semble* that gravel is laid down all the way from the Palace to the House ; but this is not laid down by Coke, or indeed by any-body but Messrs Darke the dustmen. A Parliament may be extinguished by the royal will like a candle, or it may go out, by length of time, like a rush-light. A prorogation is a process something in the nature of snuffing, causing it to brighten up for an ensuing session.

CHAPTER III.

OF THE KING (OR QUEEN) AND HIS (OR HER) TITLE.

THE supreme or executive power is vested by our laws in a single person—though that single person very often happens to be a married one. Whether this person be masculine or feminine is of no consequence, and indeed Hale thought the sovereign ought always to be neuter.

In discussing the royal rights, we shall look at the sovereign under six distinct views, which is levelling royalty with the Cosmorama in Regent-street, where " six views " are constantly being exhibited. Our first view will be a glance at the title of the sovereign ; 2ndly we shall take a squint at his (or her) royal family ; 3rdly, we shall apply our quizzing-glass to his (or her) councils ; 4thly, we shall put on our spectacles to look into his (or her) duties ; 5thly, we shall indulge in a peep at his (or her) prerogative ; and, 6thly, we shall take out our gold-mounted opera-glass to look into his (or her) revenue.

First of the Title. It is of the highest importance to avoid those unseemly scrambles for the crown, which, while forming capital subjects for dramatic representation—*vide* Richard the Third—would be a great interruption to the business of every-day life, if they were at the present time liable to happen. The grand fundamental maxim, on the right of succession to the throne, must be taken to be this, that the crown is hereditary in all cases, except those in which it isn't.

In the infancy of a state, the chief magistrate is generally elective, and when Old England gets into her second childhood, but not till then, we may look for an elective monarchy in this country. At present we cannot form any conception of such a state of things. We cannot fancy Victoria canvassing the people, and having a central committee constantly sitting at the Crown and Anchor to promote her election. This may do very well in America, though it did not answer in ancient Rome, nor in modern Poland, in which last place, by the bye, it was natural to suppose that the candidate who got to the top of the Poll, should be placed at the head of the Poles—a pun which the learned Bracton might, with good reason, have boasted of.

2ndly. As to the particular mode of inheritance. The English crown descends in a line, but history tells us that this line is sometimes a very crooked one. Males are preferred to females, a constitutional maxim which may be traced to Lindley Murray, who declares in his grammar that "the masculine is worthier than the feminine." But the females don't all take an equal share, as in common inheritance, for had this been the case, the English crown would have dwindled, in the time of Mary and Elizabeth, to a couple of half-crowns, which would have much detracted from its dignity. The constitution is always very jealous of letting the crown get into the hands of an uncle—probably from the value of the jewels, for when jewels get into an uncle's hand it is difficult indeed to get them out again. It is a maxim that "the king never dies :" but this is a quibble, like that which asserts that "to-morrow never comes," for if kings never died, William the Conqueror would be now residing at Buckingham Palace, and granting occasional interviews to Sir R. Peel or the Duke of Wellington. The fact is, that when one king is cut off, another, like the head of a hydra, springs up to replace him, and the well-known burst of enthusiasm on the part of our present sovereign, who is said to have flourished her night-cap, exclaiming "Hurrah—hurrah—I'm Queen of England," was in conformity with the constitutional maxim alluded to.

We shall now proceed to trace the crown from Egbert, who found himself one fine morning a sort of seven in one, uniting in his own person all the kingdoms of the Heptarchy. In the course of 200 years we find the crown on the head of Edmund Ironsides, from whom it was claimed by Canute, who took a composition of 10s. in the pound, or in other words accepted half, but on the death of Ironsides, who deserved the second title of Leadenhead, clutched the whole of it. Edward the Confessor, who we have already seen never confessed anything, then got hold of the crown, which of right belonged to Edward, surnamed the Outlaw, who was probably keeping out of the way to avoid process. On the death of the Confessor, Harold the Second usurped the throne, from which he was pitched neck and crop by William the Norman, who pretended to have got a grant of it from the Confessor, and may probably have raked up some old cognovit given by Edward, which would after all account for his having the title of Confessor—a cognovit being, as the legal student will hereafter be told, a confession of a debt and a judgment. William the Conqueror having defeated Harold, at Hastings, left that delightful watering-place for London, and having tried on the crown it was found such a capital fit, that it was firmly fixed upon his head, and descended to his children.

It would be useless to trace the crown through its various vicissitudes—now being let out to fit the capacious head of the son of John of Gaunt, who "tried it on" successfully as Henry the Fourth, and now taken in to suit the delicate forehead of Elizabeth.

'The crown was at length laid aside for a time, in consequence of Charles the First being deprived of a head to wear it upon. James the Second subsequently ascended the throne, but soon "cut," and failing to "come again," he was declared, if we may be allowed a parliamentary parallel, to have accepted the Chiltern Hundreds. It is not at all improbable that the people acted with the utmost delicacy in reference to the absconding of James, and probably inserted in the papers of the day something like the following advertisement: —"If James the Second does not call at the Houses of Parliament on or before Saturday next, the crown, and other property which he has left behind him, will be immediately disposed of."

His Majesty continuing to play at hide-and-seek, a treaty was entered into with the Prince and Princess of Orange, which is called " the glorious revolution of 1688," which was effected without even so much as a row in the streets, or the police being called in to preserve order.

The remainder of the crown was settled on the heirs of the Princess Sophia, the Electress of Hanover; but what this remainder was, when some one else had got it all, we leave our arithmetically disposed readers to calculate.

After the death of Anne, George the First was honoured by that uneasiness in the head which is, according to Shakspeare, the natural consequence of wearing a crown, which has now descended—we hope without subjecting her to any head-ache at all—on our Most Gracious Majesty Queen Victoria.

The succession to the throne was formerly unconditional, but now it is limited to such of the heirs of the Princess Sophia as are Protestants; and some over-zealous persons have feared that her Majesty may imbibe Catholic notions by visiting Catholic nations—a fear which, we are bound to say, we do not participate. The Queen is, we know, devoted to the interests of the mass, but not to the mass performed in Catholic Churches.

Such is the constitutional doctrine of the descent of the crown, for which every good Englishman should be ready to draw his sword, or,—supposing him to be without a sword,—to brandish his walking-stick.

CHAPTER IV.

OF THE KING'S OR QUEEN'S ROYAL FAMILY.

THE Queen is either Queen Regent, Queen Consort, or Queen Dowager. The Queen Regent has all the powers of a king, and, in relation to her husband, is the highest possible illustration of the old adage that " the grey mare is the better horse." The Queen Consort is like other married women, but is separate and distinct from the king, though the Queen's Consort—*vide* Albert—is never desirous of quitting the side of the sovereign. Another privilege of a Queen Consort is that of paying no toll, and it would seem that Prince Albert might enjoy the luxury of bolting over Waterloo-bridge without satisfying the 'pike, and indulge in other freaks of a Rebeccaite complexion. The Queen Consort is also entitled to some money called Queen-gold, which is one mark out of every ten that any person will voluntarily give to the king, her husband. What may be the value of this revenue can be ascertained by calculating, 1st, What is a mark? and, 2dly, Who is fool enough in these days to make a voluntary offer of ten marks to the king? When the total of this is ascertained, ten per cent. of the amount will comprise the value of the Queen-gold alluded to.

In Domesday-book we find that out of rents due to the crown, there used to be reserved some money to buy wool for her Majesty's use, and oil for her Majesty's lamps, from which it would seem that the queens were famous for wool-gathering by candle-light. There are traces of this payment in the pipe-roll of Henry the First, from which it would appear that when the king was called upon to pay it, he used " to put that in his pipe and smoke it." Henry the Second seems to have understood how to collect this tax, for it is alluded to in the ancient dialogue of the Exchequer, written by Gervase of Tilbury ; but whether Gervase took his name from a Tilbury, or whether, being called Tilbury, his gig was nominated after him, we have no distinct evidence. Queen-gold afterwards fell into disuse, because there was no queen to look after it ; but Anne, the consort of James the First, tried it on, though it was, according to Spelman, *Nullum ire,* or " No go," and accordingly she abandoned her claim to it.

Another privilege of the Queen Consort is her right to a whale taken on the Strand, but there has been no whale in our days nearer to the Strand than Charing-Cross, where the skeleton of a whale was a few years back exhibited. There being no Queen Consort to claim the bone of the whale, the whale was not boned on behalf of royalty. The reason of this old claim is said to have been that the Queen Consort required whalebone for her wardrobe, and for that of her visitors, a reason which points of course to the English practice of ladies wearing stays—but Coke hints, that these visitors, if they wanted an entire whale, must have intended to make a very long stay with the Queen, or so much bone could not have been required.

In the present day the Queen is entitled to the Prince of Wales, but it is not likely there will be any bones about it, for no one would dispute her Majesty's prerogative with regard to the entire possession of the heir-apparent.

It is treason to compass or imagine the death of the Queen Consort ; but as we never yet saw a pair of compasses with which the death of a Queen Consort could be compassed, the statute—which is the 25th of Edward the Third—is never acted on. A Queen Dowager enjoys various privileges, among the most valuable of which is 100,000*l.* per annum. Any one marrying a Queen Dowager without special license from the King, is liable to forfeit his goods; but a Queen Dowager does not lose her title if she marries a private gentleman; for when Catherine, the widow of Henry the Fifth, married Owen ap Meredith ap Theodore—who was a mere man about town—she was not called Mrs. Ap Meredith ap Theodore—but she retained the name of Queen of England.

The Prince of Wales and the Princess Royal are peculiarly regarded by the laws, and so is the Prince of Wales's wife; but as Coke would say—" This is counting ye chickens before hatching them." The heir-apparent is Duke of Cornwall as soon as he is born, because there are certain revenues which it is thought advisable to clutch at the earliest moment possible.

The rest of the royal family may be considered in various lights; but as there is a probability that the royal couple, like the Bank of England, will be continually " adding to the rest," we shall postpone our remarks to a future period.

The only privilege enjoyed by the junior branches is, a seat at the side of the cloth of estate in the Parliament chamber; though we do not see how the cloth of estate can be more desirable than the horse-hair cushion of comfort. By the statute of Henry the Eighth, it was high treason to contract a marriage with the King's reputed children; but by the new act, the nuptial state may be entered into under certain restrictions; but if the conditions are not complied with, any one being present at the marriage incurs the penalties of a *præmunire*, which is " Important to the marrow-bones and cleavers," no less than to the friends of the happy—but treasonable couple !

CHAPTER V.

In order to assist the Sovereign, there are councils to advise him; and, though it is said there is wisdom in a multiplicity of councillors, there is more often folly in those by whom the monarch is guided.

First comes the Parliament, which we have already treated of; that is to say, given our readers a treat on that interesting subject.

Secondly come the Peers, who are by birth entitled to counsel and defend the king; but some of them get him into a scrape by their advice, and then leave him to get out of it as he can—which is the case when a ministry proposes something unpopular, and leaves the king alone in his glory, by resigning when the measure cannot be carried.

The advice of the peers being found, in olden times not worth having, the practice of asking it fell into disuse, until it was revived in 1640 by Charles the First, who must have lost his head, figuratively speaking, when he wanted the advice of the peers—as he did substantially lose his head after the said advice was given to him.

Any particular peer may demand an audience of the king; but some peers, who are not over-particular, demand audiences about nothing at all—as though Lord Brougham were to ask a personal interview with her Majesty to discuss his (Lord Brougham's) own individual merits.

Another portion of the king's council comprises the judges; but it does not seem that the sovereign has any power to ask their opinion about anything; and, considering that if he did ask opinions of all the fifteen upon one point he would scarcely find two alike, his inability to consult them is no great loss to him.

Then there is the Privy Council, the number of which is indefinite, consisting of persons chosen by the king; but it is conveniently managed that the opinion of most of them is never asked—which is a great protection to the country.

The qualifications of a privy councillor consist in his ability to take an oath; but no other qualification, either mental or otherwise, is requisite, as may be seen by the names of some of those who, at the present moment, belong to the privy council.

The duties of a privy councillor are generally "to keep and do all that a counsellor ought." Some of them fulfil this condition by keeping all they get, and doing anybody they can, with a zeal that is truly astonishing.

The Privy Council seems to have no original jurisdiction in anything but matters of lunacy or idiocy, which, it is said, properly belong to them. If any person claims an island, the Privy Council has jurisdiction; from which it seems that if the tenant of the Eel-pie Island were to be ejected for rent in arrear, it would be a matter for the Privy Council, instead of the broker.

By a late act, there has been created a tribunal, called "The Judicial Committee of the Privy Council," which adds another court of appeal to those already in existence, and thus supplies an opportunity for more law to those who in the inferior courts have not had enough of it.

The chief privilege of privy councillors is the security given them against attempts upon their lives, which renders it felony to "imagine" the death of any one of them. The reader will see the danger of allowing the imagination to wander to the possibility of a privy councillor popping from the hooks, or applying the foot with any degree of force to the bucket. This statute was made upon Sieur Guiscard attempting to stab Mr. Harley; but as this popular comedian is at present a member of the Drury-lane Company, it is evident that the Sieur Guiscard did not succeed in his murderous effort. The Privy Council may be dissolved at any time by the Sovereign, and in this respect it resembles a Seidlitz powder, which can be dissolved at a moment's notice.

The importance of the Privy Council has been getting, for many years, small by degrees and beautifully less. The only wonder is that, looking at some of the names, any importance at all is attached to it.

CHAPTER VI.

OF THE KING'S (OR QUEEN'S) DUTIES.

WE now come to the duties of the sovereign, which will form a very short chapter, though the prerogative, which comes next, will not be so briefly disposed of. The principal duty of the sovereign is to govern according to law, which is no such easy matter, when it is considered how frightfully uncertain the law is, and how difficult it must be to govern according to anything so horridly dubious. Bracton, who wrote in the time of Henry the Third—and a nice time he had of it—declares that the king is subject to nothing on earth; but Henry the Eighth was subject to the gout, and Queen Anne is thought to have been subject to chilblains. Fortescue, who was the Archbold of his day, and was always bringing out law books, tells us the important fact that "the king takes an oath at his coronation, and is bound to keep it;" but *semble*, say we, that if he did not choose to keep it he could not be had up at the Old Bailey for perjury. Fortescue deserves "a pinch for stale news," which was the schoolboy penalty, in our time, for very late intelligence.

To obviate all doubts and difficulties, a statute was passed in the reign of William the Third, which rendered matters more doubtful and more difficult. It was enacted that the "laws of England are the birthright of the people;" but there is such a thundering legacy duty, in the shape of costs, that few people like to administer and take possession of their precious birthright. The statute further goes on to say, that

" all kings and queens *ought* " to do so and so, and that " all officers and ministers *ought* to " do this, that, and the other; but, as Coke quaintly says in his dog French, " ought est sur son pied pour reang" (ought *is upon its feet*, the canine Norman or dog French for *stands,—pour reang* for nothing).

The duties of the sovereign are briefly set forth in the Coronation oath, which is arranged as a duet for the archbishop or bishop and the sovereign. There is, however, something evasive in the replies—for while the archbishop's question commences with the words " Will you promise and swear ?" the answer merely says, " I promise," and leaves the swearing part completely out of the question.

The coronation oath was formerly written in Norman French, but, having been looked upon as a farce, it has since been done into English, probably by a member of the Dramatic Authors' Society. The duties of the sovereign, then, are, 1st, To govern according to the law, which binds him to nothing ; 2nd, To execute judgment in mercy, which, as the sovereign can only be merciful at the suggestion of the Home Secretary, is not very practicable ; 3rd, To maintain the established religion, of which there are two, one for England, Ireland, and Wales; and another for Scotland. How the sovereign contrives to do both, is a problem we must leave to others to afford a solution of.

CHAPTER VII.

OF THE KING'S (OR QUEEN'S) PREROGATIVE.

IT is one of the beauties of our Constitution, that our natural liberties are only intrenched upon for the maintenance of our civil ; and thus, though it would be natural with many to take great liberties, civility is ensured by the wholesome restrictions that all are subject to. There cannot be a greater mark of freedom, than our being at liberty to discuss the prerogative, and with our usual freedom we take the liberty of doing so. Prerogative is a word derived from *præ* and *rogo*, which means to ask before; but this is a contradiction, for prerogative implies doing first and not asking even afterwards.

Prerogatives are either direct or incidental; for instance, it is a direct prerogative for a street-keeper to warn off the boys, but it is an incidental prerogative, to run after them with the cane when they decline going.

The direct prerogative concerns the royal dignity, which is kept up by assigning to the Sovereign certain qualities in bad Latin, and applying to him the term Imperial—which is also given to tips of hair on the chin, trunks belonging to travelling carriages, quart pots of full measure, and ginger-beer of a respectable quality.

This word imperial applied to the Sovereign means, that he is paramount in his own country, and is not regulated by any other laws than those which guided the bull in his celebrated tour (*de force*) in the china-shop. The Pope formerly claimed the power of controlling the King of England, and thus our allegory of the bull was liable to be rendered inapplicable by a Bull of his Holiness. "But," says Finch, "who shall command the King?" a question to which Finch is to this very day waiting for an answer. But if the Sovereign can do as he pleases, it naturally becomes a matter of anxiety what the people can do if the Sovereign don't please to do as he ought to do. In this dilemma we rush to Puffendorf for advice and consolation. We find in his law of N. and R. 1. 8, c. 10, that "A subject, so long as he is a subject, hath no way to *obliger* his prince to give him his due when he refuses it." *Semble* therefore, that in law the maxim does not hold good, that "Where there is a will there is a way;" and, indeed, many wills have been made away with; but this is a mere *obiter dictum* of our own, which we do not wish the reader to take particular notice of. In matters of private injury, it is usual for a subject to proceed against the Sovereign by what is called a petition of right, when " the Chancellor will administer justice " (*Hookey, Chap.* I.), " from the mere love of justice " (*Walker, passim*).

In cases of public oppression, the remedy is against the ministers, who may be punished for giving bad advice to the Sovereign. The advice, by a constitutional fiction, is never thought bad, because it is generally good for themselves; and thus the ministers somehow or other never get punished.

Throughout the whole of our Constitution there. runs a feeling like that of the uncles, the nephews, the nieces, and the beef-eaters in Sheridan's *Critic*. It is such a beautiful system of check and counter-check, that nobody can do this for fear of somebody else doing that; and therefore all are compelled to do t'other. The theory is, that neither Lords, Commons, nor King can do wrong; but the practice very often is for none of them to do right ; and there being no remedy, we are assured there can be no wrong, because it is a maxim that there is no wrong without a remedy. This is such consolation as it might be to a creditor, who could not get paid, to be told that he is not wronged, because he is not righted; and that, in fact, as there can be no debt without the money, so there being no money to be had, nothing can be owing to him.

Whether a sovereign may be sent to the right about is a subject too delicate for us to write about, and we can only refer to the popular song of *Over the Water to Charlie,* or hint at the mode in which James the Second, after playing his cards badly, was altogether cut by the people as the best way of dealing with him.

It seems that either House of Parliament may remonstrate with the Sovereign; but as one member was sent to the Tower for suggesting that the answer to the address contained " high words to fright the members out of their duty," this glorious privilege of remonstrance has been left in later times wholly unexercised.

It is a maxim that the King cannot be guilty of negligence

or *laches*, that, in fact, he can never be too late—a maxim that is very useful to him when going by a railway, for no *laches* can make him late for the train, which must be always ready for him. *Nullum tempus occurrit Regi* is the standing maxim, which means that the time never occurs to the King, or that he has no occasion to trouble himself as to what o'clock it is.

A third attribute of the King is his perpetuity; for it is a maxim that the King never dies, but, we presume, simply mizzles. Dying is considered too harsh a term to apply to majesty, and what is naturally death is civilly termed the demise of the Crown, or a repeal of the union between the Sovereign's body natural and body politic. This maxim seems to us to be a remnant of that gross feudal flattery which whispered to Canute that the king could never be capsized and swamped—which nevertheless the king might have been.

The royal authority is so great, that any other authority is a branch of it; the policeman's staff being a shoot from the same tree, and so in former times was the watchman's rattle.

The King may reject bills that are public, and refuse to pay those that are private: he may make treaties, coin money, and create peers; yet it is said he can do no wrong; "may ceo," says the old Norman jurist, "est un grosse Monsonge;" for, he adds in the quaint dog French of his time, "boko de Peers sont tray Movais." He may also pardon offences, which, considering the unpardonable lot he has to do with, must be a great luxury.

With regard to foreign nations, the acts of the King bind his own; and as America has no king, there is nobody to be bound; which accounts for its bonds, especially the Pennsylvanian bonds, being utterly valueless. The king sends and receives ambassadors, who, representing their masters, are not liable to any laws in this country. Thus, if the French ambassador were to pick a gentleman's pocket, the ambassador could not be punished; but the King of the French would be called upon to adopt the larceny, and either make restitution or fight it out. It seems also that if the representative of the Porte should dine out, and take too much sherry, though he should be found lying drunk in the streets, he could not be fined five shillings. This is the essence of the whole of the law, as found in the books, on ambassadors. It seems, however, that a legate can never be tied by the leg; but may hop off at any time. It did, however, once happen, that the ambassador of Peter the Czar was, in the reign of Anne, set upon by the Selbys of that rude era, and torn from his coach for a debt of fifty pounds, which so irritated Peter, that he sent a letter demanding the ears of the Sheriff to be forwarded by return of post to Moscow. If such a demand were made in these days, it could not be complied with, for the ears of the present Sheriff (Moon) are much too long to be transmitted through the post-office. Peter was, however, pacified by an illuminated copy of an Act of Parliament, passed expressly to prevent such things in future. The illumination of the act was, no doubt, intended to throw a light upon it.

The King may also grant letters of marque, enabling ships to seize the subjects and goods of a particular State; but, as we are not likely to get into that state, it may be said that of these letters of marque there is now no likelihood.

The King may also grant safe conduct, which is something like an order given by a tyrant in a melodrama, to see the juvenile tragedian safe without the lines, accompanied by an assertion, that when next the parties meet, they meet as deadly foes. Perhaps the safest conduct in the present peaceful times is never to put your name to an accommodation bill, and to avoid becoming a security to a loan society.

The Sovereign is generalissimo of the army, and has the power of manning forts; but at present there is only one fort to man, which is Tilbury Fort, where a man may be constantly seen manning it. There was formerly a tax for building castles; but these are now maintained by the owners, except

Jack Straw's, the Elephant, and a few others, where a sort of feudal revelry is kept up by those who choose to pay for it. To erect beacons is likewise a royal prerogative, but to knock the beacons down (*vide* the one in hand on the Goodwin Sands) is the prerogative of Neptune.

The King may also prohibit the exporting of arms, and he can also prevent the legs from leaving the country, by a *ne excat regno*. When royalty can hinder any one from going abroad, it is strange that Lord Brougham does not pray ou his own head the exercise of the prerogative.

The King is the fountain of justice, from which are supplied all the leaden reservoirs in Westminster Hall, and the Pumps at the inferior tribunals. The judges were formerly removable at the King's pleasure; but they were made fixtures by George the Third, and some of them manifest, at the present day, the most remarkable adhesiveness.

The Sovereign is supposed to be everywhere; and her present Majesty seems anxious to keep up the constitutional allegory, by running about here, there, and everywhere, when the weather will admit of it.

The King is also the fountain of honour, and lays it on— sometimes rather too thick—to those who are not quite worthy of receiving it. The King, as the head of commerce, may also establish marts and fairs; but it does not seem that the enormous Bedding Mart was established by royal interference, nor that Rag Fair owes its origin to the same high intervention. Weights and measures are also regulated by the Sovereign; but to very little effect, if we are to judge by the diminutive quantity of coals that go to a hundred, at some of the sheds in the metropolis.

With reference to currency and coining, over which the Sovereign has control, Coke lays it down, that money must be either gold or silver, from which it seems that Sir Edward had a soul above halfpence.

The Sovereign is also head of the church, and as such the royal assent is necessary to the validity of canons; but no assent could give validity to the cannon in St. James's Park, which is fit for nothing but old iron.

We have now gone through the whole of the royal prerogative, from which it appears royalty might do anything, if it could; but, as it can't, it is capable of nothing.

CHAPTER VIII.

OF THE KING'S (OR QUEEN'S) REVENUE.

THE Royal revenue is either ordinary or extraordinary; but what is ordinary for a sovereign, would be quite extraordinary for any other individual. It has subsisted time out of mind; and indeed the times must have been out of their mind, or mad, when they fixed the revenue at the enormous rate it was formerly fixed at.

The first item in the ordinary revenue consists of the temporalities of all bishoprics whenever a see becomes vacant; but these are now merely nominal: for there are always so many arms ready to thrust themselves into a pair of lawn sleeves the moment they are empty, that the Sovereign has no chance of making anything by a see continuing unoccupied. William Rufus had a knack of keeping the sees empty a long time, and not only pocketing the temporalities to a pretty tune, but refusing to give them up to the new bishop without a considerable sum, which he generally managed to get; for few prelates were long contented with enjoying only the capacious sleeves, and the pasteboard mitre.

Secondly, The King is entitled to what the law calls a corody, namely, to send one of his chaplains to be maintained by the bishop, until the bishop promotes him to a benefice. This plan of quartering hungry curates upon well-fed prelates has now fallen into disuse. It certainly partook more of the military than the civil law, and was founded on the old practice of billeting soldiers upon publicans.

Thirdly, The King is entitled to the tithes of places that

are extra-parochial ; but, since tithes have been commuted, this branch of the royal revenue might be deposited in the royal eye, without any detriment to the royal eyesight.

The fourth branch comprises the First Fruits, which are not, as some have supposed, the earliest crop of gooseberries in the parish, but the first year's profits of the living ; so that the parson would be compelled to live upon his wits during the first twelve months, or run into debt for that period to all the tradespeople.   These First Fruits, amounting annually to a great deal more than a plum, were originally gathered for the use of the Pope ; but Henry the Eighth, having thrown off the papal power, thought proper to bag the papal perquisites, and took possession of the First Fruits as a part of the royal revenue.

Queen Anne, however, to whom First Fruits, like unripe gooseberries, occasioned many a qualm, determined to give them up to augment the poorer livings, and the First Fruits have been preserved under the name of Queen Anne's Bounty.

The fifth branch consists of the rents and profits of the Crown Lands, including Regent-street and other sylvan retreats, which come under the jurisdiction of the Commissioners of Woods and Forests.   What there is woody about Regent-street, except the pavement, it is difficult to say ; and the connexion with a forest is still more dubious, except that it was a *branch* of the royal revenue.

Formerly the Sovereign had the right of pre-emption, or buying up provisions, to the preference of others, without the consent of the owner ; that is to say, he might have stopped the strawberry-women, as they walked into town, and bought every pottle of hautboys on his own terms; or he might have insisted on intercepting those waggon-loads of cabbages which pour into Covent-Garden Market, and have had them all put in at the very lowest figure for the use of the royal household. This privilege of pre-emption was, however, resigned at the Restoration, by Charles the Second, who agreed to take it out in beer, or, in other words, receive a duty of fifteen pence a barrel on all the heavy wet sold in the kingdom.

The seventh branch consisted of a charge for licences to sell wine; but as this was liable to evasion, by sloe-juice being sold instead, the revenue was abolished, and a compromise of 7000*l.* a year was taken by the Crown instead of it.

The eighth branch consists of fines for violation of the forest laws, which have for many years past amounted exactly to the same sum, which may be quoted in round numbers at 0*l.* 0*s.* 0*d.*

The ninth branch consists of the profits arising from proceedings in Courts of Justice; but as there is more plague than profit in all legal proceedings, the royal revenue may here be quoted at about the same as Pennsylvanian bonds, or shares in the bridge of Waterloo.

The tenth branch comprises whale and sturgeon, which belong of right to the king, when thrown ashore or caught near the coast; but the cunning fish seldom give royalty a chance of netting anything in this manner.

The king is, eleventhly, entitled to all legal wrecks; and "this," says Sir Peter Laurie, "is perhaps the reason why the King is called Rex, or Wrecks, in all legal documents." When the *Thunder* was wrecked by the reckless conduct of the crew of the *Lightning*, it does not appear that the sovereign claimed the former,

> As she lay,
> All the day,
> In the Bay of Lambeth-ho!

Twelfthly, the sovereign is entitled to all the gold mines in his dominions. As the Prince of Wales is a minor, perhaps he will be able to direct his royal parents to the mines alluded to.

Thirteenthly, the king is entitled to treasure-trove; that is to say, he may appropriate all the silver spoons, purses, banknotes, watches, pocket-handkerchiefs, and other valuables left

E

lying in the streets without any one to pick them up or own them. If a man throws his property into the sea or on to the earth, he is supposed to have abandoned it, and the sovereign may claim it; so that if a gentleman, coming from a dinner-party, throws a handful of halfpence amongst a crowd, it seems that the sovereign might beat off the mob and pick up the copper.

Fourteenthly may be classed waifs, or property thrown down by a thief in the act of flight; so that if a pickpocket takes a handkerchief, and the king should happen to witness the act, he may cut after the thief in the hope of picking up a waif, by the article being thrown down, or dropped by the delinquent.

Fifteenthly are estrays, or animals found wandering about without an owner; and, considering how many donkies are in this erratic state, it is a wonder that this branch of the royal revenue is not more productive. It would, however, be converting the Court of Buckingham Palace into a Green-Yard, if this source of income were to be looked after by the sovereign; and hence it is that cabmen can leave their horses on the rank, without fear of the animals being treated as estrays, and walked off to the palace for the benefit of royalty.

The sixteenth branch consists of confiscated goods, including deodands, or things forfeited on account of their having caused death by accident. If a wheel runs over a man and kills him, the wheel belongs to the king; and if an ox tosses up an individual so high that he never comes down again, (alive,) the king may enjoy the horns as a part of his revenue.

The seventeenth branch arises from escheats, or lands for which there are no heirs; but these lands are so scarce that there are no grounds for the supposition that the royal revenue derives any advantage from them.

The eighteenth branch of the king's revenue consists in the custody of idiots, or the right of appropriating the lands of a *purus idiota*, or right down fool—a class so numerous, that it was thought the property of the barons would gradually get into the hands of the sovereign ; and, therefore, on petition, the estate of a *non compos* may be committed to the care of some one, for the benefit of the heir, for "the lords were naturally fearful," says Fleta, or Fleeter, who is not quite so slow a coach as some of the jurists—"the lords were naturally fearful that the Crown should make idiots of them all, and bone their property."

It seems then, that out of eighteen sources of income, there is really nothing worth speaking of, to be got ; and consequently, it is usual for the House of Commons to vote a Supply first, and then think about the Ways and Means of raising it.

We now come to the extraordinary branches of the revenue, and shall begin with the land-tax, which is a substitute for hydages, scutages, talliages, and other outlandish pretexts for getting hold of money.

In ancient times every knight was bound to attend the king in battle for forty days in a year ; but as it would be very inconvenient for a civic knight to give his personal assistance in the wars, the matter came to be compromised for a sum of money called a scutage—and afterwards a hydage, probably in allusion to the hyding—or hiding—from which the compromise preserved the parties paying it.

Afterwards came the practice of subsidies, which consisted of money taken from the Commons, under the guise of their having granted it. These subsidies have now subsided into a land-tax.

Next comes the malt-tax, which is thought to be a proper penalty on the very uncourtly practice of biting the initials into pewter pots ; and the customs form a part of the revenue including butlerage, or the right of taking two tons of wine from every ship—a process which, considering the quantity of vessels that carry no wine at all, savours so much of getting blood out of a stone, that we are not surprised at the practice being abandoned.

The excise we need hardly allude to, for every one knows, by personal experience, the nature of it—there being scarcely a single article of consumption, that is not partly consumed by the excise duty.

The post office, the stamps, and the duty on hackney carriages, are also branches of the revenue—so that the badge on the omnibus conductor's breast is like so much money taken from his very heart—a remark that will also apply to the cab-driver.

The Assessed-taxes come next, and embrace the duty on windows; which constitute a terrible look-out for those who have to pay it. These taxes also comprise the impost on horses and dogs—which are said by Buffon to be the natural companions of man; but it is hard that man should have to pay so dearly for their company.

The tax on hair-powder used to fall heavily on the briefless barristers, but they have rushed recklessly into horsehair, and run their heads into a species of composition wig, which combines the lightness of wire with the durability of cat-gut. Armorial bearings are also liable to a duty; and it is therefore not safe to seal a letter with anything but the top of a thimble, lest, by adopting a more elegant contrivance, the tax-gatherer should pounce down upon you for what he may call a crest; though it is in fact nothing but a chance device on a second-hand wafer-stamp. There is also a duty on pensions, perhaps to make up for the absence of duty on the part of those to whom the pensions are payable.

The first purpose to which the revenue is devoted is the interest of the national debt, which commenced in 1693, just five years after the glorious revolution of 1688, and was probably one of the glorious results of it. The national debt has increased several millions, in spite of the efforts of certain commissioners for reducing it. These gentlemen now and then announce the fact of their having rubbed off a few pounds at one end, while, somehow or other, a few thousands have been rubbed on at the other.

If, till the debt is paid off, the commission is to be continued, it may be fairly pronounced immortal. The only method of getting rid of it would be for the sovereign to file a petition at the Insolvent Court in the name of the nation, and solemnly take the benefit of the act, in the presence of all the fundholders.

The whole of the revenues already described were given up by George III. to the public, in lieu of an allowance which was called the civil list—from the extreme civility on the side both of the king and the people. Some complaints have been occasionally made of the large amount of this civil list; but when all things are considered—the state-coach, the drawing-rooms, the levees, the palace dinners, and last, but not least, the royal progresses, we do not see how her Majesty can " do it respectably" for less money than is paid to her.

It will have been seen, from our view of the royal prerogative and revenue, that the sovereignty is tolerably well hedged in with restrictions, and has, after all, very few opportunities of rendering itself obnoxious.

The army is at its beck and call, but the Commons must vote the money for supporting it; and an army without pay would be little better than a steam-engine without steam, or the beadle of Burlington Arcade without his brass-bound bludgeon. It is true the sovereign has the run of the treasury, but there is seldom any money in hand, for it is always spent first and raised afterwards. It is not now as it was in the days of the Johns and Richards, who, directly they usurped the throne, used to jump into a cab and rush to the Horse-Guards, " to secure," as Hume tells us, " the crown and treasure." These days of royal roguery are gone, and we may now venerate the crown and respect the sovereign, without feeling called upon to address to Englishmen those emphatic words, " Take care of your pockets."

CHAPTER IX.

OF SUBORDINATE MAGISTRATES.

We have hitherto considered only the Chief Magistrate, but we now come down to the subordinates; and when we say that we shall begin with the Sheriff, the drop from the throne to the shrieval office-stool appears indeed terrible.

First, of the Sheriffs. The Sheriff is an officer of very great antiquity, his name being derived from two Saxon words, which we don't print, because if we did, we could not read them ourselves, and we think the reader would find himself in the same predicament. In Latin he is called Vice-Comes, or Deputy of the Earl, though literally it means Viscount; but Viscount Moon, or Viscount Rogers, would sound so absurd that the term Vice-Comes is no longer applied to a sheriff. The Earls formerly did the duties themselves; but, finding that there was now and then a man to be hanged, the Earls turned the matter over to the sheriffs, who afterwards relinquished the task to Jack Ketch, the Sheriffs only reserving the right to introduce their friends to illustrious criminals.

The Judges now choose the Sheriffs; but in the time of Henry VI. the king, having tried to make a sheriff, was told he could not, by Sir John Prisot and Sir John Fortescue, who delivered, probably in a duet like the following, the opinion of all the judges :—

Sir John Prisot.
Oh, no. You must not mention it.

Sir John Fortescue.
Your Majesty has err'd.

Sir John Prisot.
A sheriff you can never make.

Sir John Fortescue.
You can't, upon my word.

Both together.
From book to book we 've search'd all day,
  And have perused a set
Of old reports—but cannot find
  A King-made sheriff yet.

Notwithstanding this judicial distich, the King occasionally amused himself by making a sheriff, and even to the present time what are called pocket-sheriffs are now and then manufactured by the hands of Royalty. The Sheriff, like the sun flower, lasts only a year, though he partakes occasionally of the holly-hock, which may be cut down one year and spring up the next, for a sheriff that has blossomed once may again flower into shrievalty.

The Sheriff is like a telescope, a pencil-case, or a trombone, including two or three official divisions in one, and requires drawing out before he can be fully appreciated; for he is a judge, a keeper of the peace, and a bailiff.

His judicial capacity is often a good deal like judicial *in*-capacity. It was formerly limited to forty shillings, which was about as much as it was worth; but it has since been extended to twenty pounds, by virtue of a writ of trial.

As the keeper of the king's peace, the Sheriff is, for the time being, the first man in the county; that is to say, he is expected to be the first to rush on at a row, when there is a probability that the only advantage in being the first man in the county will be the privilege of being the first to get his head broken. He is bound to pursue and take all traitors; so that if either Sheriff should happen to see a traitor standing at the corner of Threadneedle-street, he would be bound, as Sheriff, to bolt after him. He may also summon the *posse comitatus*, or, in other words, call upon the tag-rag to assist him in capturing or pursuing a felon. The Sheriff, however, cannot try criminal offences; " For," says the facetious Fortescue, " it would be too much of a good thing that the Sheriff should try a man first, and hang him after-wards; for, of course, having to hang him, he has a direct interest in finding him guilty."

The Sheriff is also bound to execute all writs; and for this purpose he has officers called bailiffs, who frequently undergo martyrdom at the spout of the pump, and pass through other ordeals in their endeavours to catch that particular bird which their writ indicates. "The Under-sheriff," says Dalton, "is derived from the old Saxon word Under, signifying beneath, and Shriff or Shreff, which means the Sheriff."

After the Under-sheriff and the Bailiff, comes the Gaoler, " an officer," says Coke, " who is the have ye to the bailiff's catch ye; for he keeps fast or has in custody the bird that the bailiff has caught; and as there is no catch ye no have ye, so the gaoler, who doth have the gaol bird, would be useless without the bailiff who doth catch him."

We now come to the Coroner, whose office is very ancient; and indeed the Lord Chief Justice of the Queen's Bench is *ex officio* the chief coroner in the kingdom, so that it really *semble* that Lord Denman might insist on sitting upon any-body whenever he happened to feel an inquisitorial fit come over him. The Coroner is elected by the freeholders; and formerly none but a discreet Knight could be chosen. In these days, however, a discreet Knight is not often to be found, and the office of Coroner is consequently given to mere Esquires, in whom discretion is not looked for. If any person dies suddenly, the Coroner must sit on the body, where the death happens; but, if a man is drowned by falling into the sea, it does not appear that the Coroner is bound to dive after the body and sit upon it. Another branch of his office is to sit upon wrecks, which can only be done when the top of the mast is sufficiently out of the water to enable the Coroner to sit in safety. He is also to inquire about treasure-trove, which gives him jurisdiction over mudlarks, who seek for coals at low water, and bone-grubbers, who rummage in dust-holes.

We now come to Justices of the Peace, who are a very miscellaneous set, beginning with no less a person than the Sovereign, and finishing with the Solons who adorn the various benches of Magistrates. The duty of a Justice of the Peace is to suppress riots and affrays, and to hear and determine felonies; but if a justice sees an affray, he is often too much afraid to rush in and put an end to it.

After the Justice comes the Constable, a genus of which there are two species, the High and the Petty. The Petty Constable is as old as Alfred, but how old Alfred might have been we are unable to say with certainty. The Constable is armed with very great powers; and there is one at the Burlington Arcade who is armed with an instrument of slaughter, but, happily for the nation, he never uses it. Nevertheless, when the constable has nothing better to do, he may be seen breathing on the brass nob, and rubbing it up with his pocket handkerchief.

The Surveyors of the Highways form the next branch of subordinate magistrates; and their duty formerly was to call the inhabitants of the parish together, and order them to bring materials for repairing the roads. If this were now the case, the Dukes of Cambridge and Devonshire would be obliged to contribute a few blocks of wood to pave Piccadilly. To avoid this sort of inconvenience, a paving rate has been imposed; though there is no doubt that any inhabitant might claim the provisions of the statute of Henry the Eighth, and insist on mending his own ways, instead of paying a rate for doing so.

Lastly, we will consider the Overseers of the Poor, who sometimes literally over-see or over-look the cases of distress requiring assistance. The poor law of Elizabeth has been superseded by a much poorer law of William the Fourth, the one great principle of which is to afford the luxury of divorce to persons in needy circumstances. It also discountenances relief to the able-bodied, a point which is effected by disabling, as far as possible, anybody who comes into the workhouse. The Poor Law is administered by three Commissioners, who spend their time in diluting gruel and writing reports—trying experiments how little will suffice to prevent a repeal of the union between the soul and the body.

CHAPTER X.

OF THE PEOPLE, WHETHER ALIENS, DENIZENS, OR NATIVES.

HAVING treated of the Sovereign, we now come down to the small change, or in other words, we turn from her Most Gracious Majesty the Queen, to his Most Miscellaneous Majesty the People.

The people are divided into aliens and natural born, though the latter are not necessarily born naturals. Natural born subjects are such as are born within the ligeance, or allegiance of the Sovereign ; but aliens are such as are born out of it.

Allegiance is the tie which binds the subject to the Sovereign, and the form is derived from the Goths ; who, under the feudal system, held their possessions under some lord, to whom they were vassals. The only remains of this system are to be met with at the Gothic Cottages in the Regent's Park, the tenants of which swear fealty every quarter to the lord or his house-agent. Formerly there was mutual trust between the tenant of the soil and the owner, but this trust has been much broken in upon, by the modern practice of "shooting the moon," which hath destroyed that sylvan state of simple confidence which formerly existed.

The vassal was formerly expected to defend the lord against his enemies ; so that if the landlord of a house got into a street row, his vassals or lodgers were expected to take part in it. This was called *fidelitas*, or fealty, the tenant taking an oath to protect the lord of the soil ; but this is now commuted into an undertaking to pay the taxes, including a police rate,

which secures the lord and the vassal also from violence.
The oath of allegiance to the Sovereign is still taken by attorneys and barristers, on being admitted to practise ; but in
consequence of their number, it has been arranged as a solo
and chorus for the officer of the Court, and an unlimited
number of voices, which chime in together, expressing their
horror of the Pope, without knowing who the old gentleman
is ; and declaring that it is not lawful to murder foreign
princes in the public street, as if any one in these days ever
thought of assassinating continental royalty in Regent-street,
or any of the leading thoroughfares.

It seems, however, that all subjects owe allegiance to the
Sovereign, whether they have taken the oath or not ; and it
is very probable that the ideas of most people would be
much the same on the slaughter of foreign princes, without
going through the ceremony of swearing the awful affidavit
alluded to.

Every person born within the English dominions owes
allegiance to the Sovereign from the moment of birth, being
at once under the protection or particular patronage of royalty.
The immense quantity of allegiance payable from persons
of large families may therefore be conceived ; and it must be
held as a constitutional doctrine, that twins cause a double
accession of loyalty. Local allegiance is something of the
nature of portable gas, for it is movable, and only lighted up
in the bosoms of aliens during their residence in this country,
after which it may be turned off, or otherwise extinguished.

It seems that allegiance is as much due to the usurper as
to the rightful Sovereign, and must be paid to whomsoever is
on the throne for the time being. If, therefore, a lunatic
should get into the throne-room in the Palace, and, sitting on
the throne, proclaim himself king, it would seem that the
royal housemaid would owe temporary allegiance to the
madman, until a policeman should regularly dethrone him,
and walk the usurper off to the nearest—that is to say, a much
more humble—station.

Allegiance is due to the person, and not to the dignity alone ; for, in the time of Edward the Third, the Spencers were banished for refusing allegiance to the person of the King, and offering it to his crown, which was something like the notion of bowing to Gesler's hat, which, through Sheridan Knowles's " William Tell," every one is acquainted with. The sad tale of these Spencers led to the introduction of spencers with no tail at all, several centuries afterwards.

Natural born subjects have rights that nothing but their own misbehaviour can forfeit ; such as the right of buying lands, if they have got the money to pay for them.

This glorious privilege may be enjoyed by the meanest subject, under the circumstances last alluded to.

An alien may purchase lands ; but if he does, the Sovereign is entitled to them.   Nevertheless, an alien may hire a house to live in, though the King of the Belgians, when he first came to London as an alien, occupied only lodgings, being those on the second floor of Hagger's oil and pickle shop in Oxford-street.   The Prince, who is now the Lord of the Belgians and their soil, was then the vassal of Hagger, to whom he did weekly homage to the tune of thirty shillings.

An alien may trade freely ; so that Verey dispenses dinners in strict conformity with the provisions of our glorious Constitution.

Children born out of England, whose father or grandfather, by the father's side, is in allegiance to the English Sovereign, are natural born subjects ; and, therefore, the summer visitors to Boulogne are in no danger of producing a crop of young aliens—a result which would deprive the Sovereign of many subjects, and not only the *Sovereign*, but the *Emerald*, the *Princess Maude*, the *Ondine*, and the *Queen of the Belgians*, of a great number of passengers.

The children of aliens, when born in England, are considered as natural born, and Pagliano's Hotel contributes annually a large stock of subjects to the British monarchy.

A denizen is an alien, who, by the Royal prerogative, is

made a natural; being, in fact, an animal something like a
mule, which, being between the horse and the ass, generally
partakes mostly of the latter.   The denizen is indeed almost,
not quite, a natural.

Naturalisation can only be achieved by Act of Parliament;
but even when naturalised, neither an alien nor a denizen can
be a member of Parliament—a dignity that naturals only are
thought worthy of.

There have been one or two attempts to introduce an Act
for the general naturalisation of all foreigners; but the nearest
approach to it is the statute naturalising certain persons who
have served two years in the army or navy, and some who
have been three years fishing for whales; which really ex-
hibits such a strong turn for natural history, that naturalisation is the smallest compliment which can be paid to it.

So much for " the People," who have always got a number
of " People's Friends," ready to serve them in all sorts of
ways; but serving them out is the most usual course that is
taken.

CHAPTER XI.

OF THE CLERGY.

THE people are divided into the clergy and the laity, the
former of whom will be the subject of this chapter; and a
very lively chapter may be expected in consequence.

The clergy have several privileges, some of which were
taken from them at the Reformation, in consequence of their
having become impudent from the great liberties allowed to
them.   Many of the personal exemptions still continue.   For
instance, no one can be compelled to sit upon a jury, after he
has taken orders; though *semble* that the persons at the free-
list office in the theatres, notwithstanding their having taken
orders, are liable to serve as jurymen.   A clergyman cannot

be chosen to any temporal office, such as bailiff or constable ; so that a curate cannot be a bailiff at a lock-up house, nor could a rector act as a policeman in a street riot. A clergy- · man is also privileged from arrest, in going to and returning from the performance of duty, or, as the Norman Jurist ex- presses it, " il ne faut pas commettre un tel faux pas de nabber il parsone, et lui porter hors de la pulpite jusqu'à maison de fermer au cle." (One must not commit such a false step, as to nab the parson, and carry him out of the pulpit to the lock-up house.) Formerly, a clergyman had what is called the benefit of clergy in cases of felony ; a privilege which, if a layman had asked for, he would have been told, that the authorities would " see him hanged first." The last remnant of benefit of clergy was the benefit allowed every May-day to the sweeps, who were vulgarly called the clergy ; but this has been almost swept away by the Ramoneur—a very up- right invention, which, disdaining to force itself into holes and corners, leaves the soot to ignite in the crevices of the chimneys.

The clergymen have, however, several disabilities ; for instance, they cannot sit in Parliament, but " that's not much," as Othello (one of Nature's clergymen) very properly observed, for there are many occasions, such as a financial discussion, when exclusion from the House of Commons must be regarded as a privilege, rather than a disability. Formerly a clergyman was not allowed to trade, but was restricted to the cure of souls. It does not seem, however, that even in the days of doubtful orthography—for our ancestors never could spell—a parson might have occupied himself in the drying of fish, which is certainly in one sense undertaking the cure of soles ; for we do not find that Shakspeare's beau- tiful line in Hamlet, " Excellent well, you 're a fishmonger," was ever applied to any reverend contemporary of the Swan of Avon.

· It having been determined that a contract with any com pany, of which any spiritual persons were partners or members, was void—and this having been decided to be the law—another law was passed in the reign of her present Majesty to decide that it was not, or, if it was, it never ought to be. It might be a hint worthy of adoption by the repudiating States of America; for as there are, no doubt, spiritual persons among them, they may as well shuffle out of their liabilities, by reference to the fine old principles of English law, and thus give a sacred character to one of the sublimest swindles ever attempted in any age or country. By the new act, parsons may trade in joint-stock companies, their evanescence giving them, no doubt, a sort of ethereal character. The 'clergy may also trade in books, or in anything connected with keeping a school, which admits of their adding to their income by selling ink and various other scholastic commodities.

We shall now consider the various ranks and degrees of the clergy, commencing with an archbishop, who is the greatest gun in the Church, according to all the canons. Archbishops were formerly elected by all the people; but' the tumultuous scenes that arose were a great scandal; and indeed we cannot fancy his Grace of Canterbury placarding the town with posters, calling upon the public to " vote for Howley," or defacing the walls of the episcopal palace with the words, " Howley for Canterbury."

Archbishoprics afterwards came to be conferred by the sovereigns till Gregory VII. exhibited a bull, declaring that princes should not meddle in the manufacture of prelates. Henry VIII., however, put an end to the Pope's pretensions, by giving the power of electing an archbishop or a bishop to the bishops themselves; that is to say, when his Majesty has made his own choice, he gives the prelates the power of conforming to it; or, in other words, rams a bishop down their throats, thus forcing them to swallow him.

An archbishop is a sort of inspector of all the bishops in his province; but he does not call them out like an inspector would so many policemen, to examine their mitres, and see that their lawn sleeves are properly starched, before going on duty in their respective dioceses.   An archbishop may call out the bishops, just as a militia colonel may call out the militia ; and it is his duty to look after the spiritualities of a vacant see, while the Crown takes care of the temporalities, which are the only remunerating part of the business.   If a bishop does not fill up a vacant living in his diocese within six months, the archbishop may ; but the bishop has generally too much archness to give a chance to his superior.

The archbishop also takes the first presentation to a living which may occur in a bishop's diocese, so that a bishop's mouth waters a good deal before he is suffered to quaff the sweets of patronage.   The Archbishop of Canterbury has also the privilege of putting the crown on the heads of the Kings and Queens of England ; but this seems to be more a hatter's business, and we, therefore, do not enter into it.

Bishops have authority over the manners of the people ; and we wonder, therefore, that the Bishop of London does not favour us with a book on etiquette.

Several alterations have been made, and others contemplated, by the Ecclesiastical Commissioners appointed by Act of Parliament in the reign of William IV., to unite certain sees, by cutting through the barrier or isthmus that divided them.

We now come to deans and chapters, which would form a chapter of themselves, only there is no occasion for it.   A dean and chapter are a sort of council to advise the bishop, who, however, seldom asks their advice ; or, if he asks it, scarcely ever takes it.   A dean formerly superintended ten canons, but this must have been in the days when the Church was disposed to be militant.   The bishop is the superior of the dean and chapter, with the power of visiting them and " correcting their excesses ;" which surely cannot mean administering soda-water after they have been rather convivial ?

An archdeacon comes next to a bishop, and visits the clergy, leaving his card formally with some, and dropping in to tea, in a friendly manner, no doubt, with others.

Rural deans, in these anti-rural days, are nearly out of use. They had nothing to do but pry into the domestic affairs of the parochial clergy. They were called rural, very likely, from their love of country occupations, such as fishing for preferment, and making hay during sunshine.

We now come to the parson, a name derived from the word *persona*—a person; because the parson is a person; that is to say, he is in the parish decidedly " somebody." He is sometimes called the rector or ruler, but why, we cannot tell; for there is no rule to account for it.

Formerly, the monasteries appropriated to themselves the valuable part of a living, and contracted with some curate to do the work; the monasteries acting then, much as the " sweaters " do now, making a very good profit upon a task which they gave a beggarly sum to another party to execute. Henry VIII., however, determined to sweat the monastic sweaters; for, at the dissolution of monasteries, he swept away the institutions, and pocketed the good things that belonged to them. The Crown having afterwards granted these things out to laymen, gave rise to what are called lay-appropriations, hands having been laid upon them by those who were most inappropriately possessed of them.

These appropriators used to get the duty done very cheap by a vicar; and there being much competition among the clergy, vicar's work was done on such very low terms, that there was an alarming sacrifice of the interests of the parish-ioners. This led to an Act being passed to protect vicars, by providing for their being better paid, and some of the smaller tithes were settled on the vicar; who, on the principle of " little fishes being sweet," no doubt eagerly clutched at them.

The duties incumbent on a parson are first to act as the incumbent, by living in the place where he has his living. By a recent Act, a parson absenting himself from his parson-age for upwards of three months in a year, forfeits a third of the value of his benefice, and so in proportion; so that if he stays away a whole year, he will have more to pay than to receive, and thus realise the homely picture of the man who is said to have won a shilling and lost eighteenpence.

There is only one way of becoming a parson or vicar, but five at least of ceasing to continue so :—1st. By dying, or going quite out, like an exhausted rushlight. 2nd. By taking another and a better benefice, or, following the allegory of the light, being removed from a japan to a plated candlestick. 3rd. By being made a bishop, or undergoing a sort of conversion from simple tallow to superior sperm. 4th. By resignation, or, still pursuing the simile of the light, suddenly going out, nobody knows why. And 5th. By deprivation, that is to say, being deprived of one's benefice altogether, and expelled from the clerical profession, which is like a gas lamp completely cut off from the company's main.

A curate is the lowest grade in the church, for he is a sort of journeyman parson, and several of them meet at a house of call in St. Paul's Church Yard, ready to job a pulpit by the day, and being in fact "clergymen taken in to bait" by the landlord of the house alluded to.

From the clergy we come next to the churchwardens, who keep the church, and represent the parish. They also keep the accounts: and, in some cases, like that of Alderman Gibbs, these accounts are so literally kept, that it is hard to get hold of them. The churchwarden may keep order in the church ; and if a boy giggles, it is the duty of the churchwarden to frown, or even to kick the juvenile's shins, if he should be near enough.

Parish clerks and sextons are also particularly regarded by the common law, which must be very common to regard such exceedingly common people. The parish clerk was formerly often in holy orders, but any one may be a parish clerk, excepting, by-the-by, Macbeth, who was utterly disqualified for the post, inasmuch as he could not say "Amen," according to the authority of Shakspeare.

THE Civil State includes every one of the laity who does not belong to the military or maritime state. But there are some of the military, such as the sentinels on duty at the Park, who are in a very civil state, when asked a civil question.

The Civil State consists of the nobility and commonalty, the former of which resembles, in some respects, "ginger beer from the fountain," the Sovereign being the fountain from which alone it is possible to draw nobility.

The Sovereign may invent any titles he pleases; but those now in use are Dukes, Marquesses, Earls, Viscounts, and Barons.

A Duke is derived from the Latin word *dux*, a military leader; and perhaps the practice of soldiers wearing dux or ducks in the present day, has something to do with it. In the time of Elizabeth, the order of Dukes became extinct; but it was galvanised fifty years afterwards. A Marquess is the next degree of nobility, and is so called from the Teutonic word *marche*, a limit, because the Marquesses originally watched the limits of the kingdom; but whether they acted as a sort of coast-guard, or as a police on the frontiers, or as beadles to beat the bounds of the kingdom, we are wholly at a loss to make up our minds about. An Earl is a title so early, that it is impossible to trace its origin. It is supposed that after the Norman conquest, William made Earls of those who were the earliest to do him homage. The Saxons had their Ealdormen, which got corrupted into Earldermen, or, greater corruption still, into Aldermen. An Earl was at one

time called a Count, from an old Norman pun of the Conqueror, who said " he could *Count* upon his *early* friends ;"
but, as the pun died off, the title was discontinued, leaving
nothing to keep it in remembrance but the word County.

The Sovereign, in writs, always styles an earl his " trusty
and well-beloved *cousin*," a reason as old as Henry the Fourth,
who had really cousined, or cozened, all the Earls, and was
related to every one of them.

The next degree is that of Viscount, or vice-comes; which,
though we have turned on the gas of research from the main
of history, we are unable to throw a light upon.

The last, and most general degree of nobility, is that of
Baron, which was formerly so numerous, that the King summoned only the greater ones to the council of the nation, and
the others gradually became extinct, except the barony of
Nathan, the holder of which, though not enjoying a seat in
'the peers, occupies a seat in or near the (Kennington)
Commons.

Peerages were formerly annexed to lands ; and even now
there are some piers—such as those of Westminster-bridge—
which only exist by the hold they have upon the soil ; but
this sort of tenure has now become very uncertain.

Peers are now created by writ or by patent ; so that, when
a sheriff's officer serves a person with a writ, he is said to be
made *a-ppear* (*a peer*) by the writ being served on him. But
every one who is summoned by a writ is not ennobled, and
it is now usual to make peers by the batch.

Let us now examine the privileges of nobility, the first of
which is the right of being tried by one's peers, the last case
being that of Westminster-bridge, which, when tried by its
piers, was sentenced to have its head entirely removed, and
was so far disgraced as to be brought down to a lower level.

A peer or peeress cannot be arrested in civil cases. Peers
always give a verdict upon their honour ; and there is something, therefore, very aristocratic in the term, " 'Pon honour !'
which is, probably, the reason why dandy footmen and shop-

boys, "out for the day," generally make use of it. A peer cannot be deprived of his nobility, except by death or by attainder; though, in the reign of Edward the Fourth, George Neville, Duke of Bedford, was reduced to such a seedy state, that he was degraded on account of his poverty. It is probable that he attended Parliament in a cotton-velvet robe, and a squirrel cape instead of real ermine; while, instead of the ducal coronet—irredeemably pledged, and the ticket out of date—he sported a sort of theatrical property, made of tinfoil and mother-of-pearl, cutting, in every respect, such a very shabby figure that the peers, amid loud cries of "Turn him out," got unceremoniously rid of him. The Act of Parliament by which it was accomplished was termed an "Act for Cutting the Tin Kettle from the tail of George Neville, Duke of Bedford." It is said, that if a Baron wastes his estate, the King may degrade him; but some Barons are in the habit of degrading themselves, by wasting their estates, without any interference of the Sovereign.

The first dignity beneath that of a Peer was a *vidames*, a title so old, that antiquarians quarrel greatly as to what a *vidames* was; though they agree pretty well in believing that such a thing as a *vidames* never existed. The first personal dignity after the nobility is consequently now settled to be that of a Knight of the Garter, instituted by Edward the Third to preserve tidiness in the stockings of the aristocracy; a point that has been beautifully kept in view by Shakspeare, who makes Hamlet wear his stockings about his heels, until he visits England, where it is supposed he has been invested with the Garter, and he consequently always appears in the last act with his silk hose properly adjusted.

Next comes a Knight Banneret, or a knight made by the Sovereign in person on the field of battle; so that, if a civil war should break out in London, her Majesty might rush to Lincoln's Inn-fields and manufacture knights bannerets. After these come the Baronets, an order instituted by James the First to raise money to meet a bill for the reduction of Ulster.

Next follow the Knights of the Bath, instituted by Henry the Fourth, and so called from the ceremony of taking a bath the night before their creation. This fact about the bath is given on the authority of a case in Shower.

William the Fourth instituted a Guelphic order, and a few knights were installed; but the instalments not being regularly kept up, the order expired.

Knights are called in Latin *equites;* and, indeed, all nations call their knights by some name connected with a horse, excepting the Scotch order of the Thistle, which seems to show that the Scotch knights are akin to another and a much more homely quadruped.

St. Patrick is the name of an Irish order; but St. Patrick's day, particularly in the morning, is more associated with the idea of dis-order than order; at least, it is generally considered so.

The lowest order of knighthood is that of the Knights Bachelors, the first of whom was Alfred's son, Athelstan, who must have been a single young man; and his wretched fate proves that he was ultimately " taken in and done for."

" These," says Coke, " are all the names of dignity;" but Sir Edward confounds together Esquires and Gentlemen, leaving the subject confoundedly obscure, according to the usual custom of the quaint old jurist. It has been said, that any one who wore coat armour was an Esquire; in which case the supernumeraries at Drury-lane, clothed as they are in block-tin dish-covers, must be considered Esquires while engaged in the performance of Richard the Third, but no longer. Camden, who was himself a herald, and blew the trumpet vigorously for any one who paid him, makes four degrees of Esquires. First, the eldest sons of knights, and their eldest sons, in successional crops, like broad beans or radishes. Second, the eldest sons of younger sons of peers, and their eldest sons in like succession; so that Baron Nathan's youngest son's eldest boy's firstborn male infant would be an Esquire, supposing the Barony of Nathan to be acknowledged as a branch of the tree of English aristocracy. Third, Esquires created, like Baker's mangles, by patent. Fourth, Esquires who are so called from holding a place of trust under the Crown; but it is not decided whether the waiter at the Crown and Anchor comes under this head, as holding a place of trust under the Crown, the words " and Anchor " being rejected as surplusage.

As for Gentlemen, says Sir Thomas Smith, he who can live idly, and bear the port and charge of a gentleman—that is to say, can pay what is charged for port, and sit idly over it—shall be taken for a Gentleman. A Yeoman is one who hath land that brings him in forty shillings a year; but *semble* that a crossing, the sweeping of which produces forty shillings a year, does not constitute the sweeper a Yeoman.

The rest of the community are tradesmen, artificers, and labourers, who must all be styled, in legal proceedings, by their estate or mystery; but the estates of most of them would be a mystery indeed to any one attempting to describe them.

Such is the Civil State, which we have stated as civilly as circumstances will admit of.

CHAPTER XIII.

OF THE MILITARY AND MARITIME STATES.

THE Military State includes the whole of the soldiery from the Commander-in-Chief down to the raw recruit, or the private who has the honour of being stationed at the post of Storey's-gate, who is alluded to by the poet, in the fine line—

" The post of honour is a private station."

In a free country, it is said that the soldier is an object of 'ealousy, chiefly, we suppose, on account of the impression

made by a red coat upon the fair sex.   As to any other kind
of jealousy the soldier creates, we are certainly not aware of
it, unless it be the natural jealousy felt by a police-man at
the superiority of the steel bayonet over the wooden staff, and
the cartridge-box over the lantern.   A soldier does not put off
the citizen when he becomes a soldier; and consequently
many of our gallant army whose wives are washerwomen,
carry out the clothes in time of peace, and others lend a
hand in the mangling—which, according to the old jurists, is
not out of character with their slaughtering propensities.
The laws of this country do not recognise a standing army;
so that even, when on service, the soldiers are said to go to
the *seat* of war—thus showing that a *standing* army is never
contemplated.

All historians agree in declaring that Alfred invented the
Militia, when every man in the kingdom was a soldier; and,
considering what sort of soldiers the militia usually are, we
should say that every man, woman, or child might have been.
In those days, the Dukes led the soldiers, and had such
power, that Duke Harold, although the wrongful heir, was
strong enough to push from off the throne one Edgar Atheling, the rightful heir—an event, which if the Saxons had
had a taste for melo-drama, would have made a fine subject
for a piece, introducing " a grand combat of two "—including all the popular business of Harold cutting at Edgar
Atheling's toes, while Edgar Atheling jumped up exclaiming,
" No, you don't! " with a wink at the prime minister.
Then, of course, would have come the grand last movement
of clashing of swords together across the stage, till both
disappear at the wing, when Harold would have returned
alone, with both swords, in token of victory, and taken his
seat on the throne—in which position he might have been
" closed in " by the scene-shifters.

We have already, in a former chapter, spoken of the
necessity a Knight was under to go for a soldier in case of
war, but in peace the country was protected by a statute of

Henry the Second, making it obligatory on every man to keep a certain quantity of arms; but it does not appear there was any law insisting on his knowing the use of them. These persons were, however, now and then called out, arms and all; and it is presumed this was done, as Camden hints, "to ennjoye a joyke at ye expennsse of ye people."

It is not, perhaps, generally known, that the whole of the dreadful row between Charles the First and the people, arose out of a dispute about the militia—the King pulling at them one way and the Parliament the other. The militia all the while was in those days just what it is in these—very indif-ferent.

After the restoration of Charles the Second, the King's right to do what he liked with the militia was recognised; and there is still a remnant of them who rent a coal-shed at Lancaster, which is called the *dépôt*, and from which three corpulent sergeants—for they are all officers and no men— would emerge in case of an invasion. During the election riots, the Lancaster militia put itself under the protection of the two policemen in the town; but, in the glorious language of the Constitution, "the militia are, after all, our great defence against foreign aggression." "After all" means of course, when every thing else had been tried; and then, we say, Let England throw herself into the arms of the three sergeants at the coal-shed at Lancaster.

Besides the Militia, there is also the Yeomanry, who are more often called into service, and have several times dis-tinguished themselves by keeping back the boys at proces-sions and on other public occasions. We had almost for-gotten to mention the Volunteers, who formerly had the command of all the parochial engines, pumps, and fire-lad-ders. That these troops would have stood fire manfully there can be no doubt, for their valour under an incessant pelting of water, was frequently put to the test during showers to which they were so often exposed, that it was once in contemplation to add an umbrella to the regulation bayonet. The Lumber Troop must not be forgotten, whose last recorded exploit was an encounter with the landlord of the public-house where the troop has its quarters.

Martial Law is a sort of law in which the military authorities do as they like with their own, and hang soldiers wholesale for the sake of preserving discipline. This can only be done in time of war; and it is now quite settled, that if a lieutenant hang a private for the mere fun of the thing in time of peace, it would be murder, for it is against *Magna Charta;* so that it is fortunate for the heads of her Majesty's Foot that *Magna Charta* was hit upon.

There is an annual Mutiny Act which provides for the government of the army; and, according to this, any soldier shamefully deserting a post—such as walking away from the lamp-post at Storey's-gate—or sleeping on the said post (he must be a deuced clever fellow to manage that)—or giving advice to a rebel (unless perhaps he advised a rebel to be off about his business)—or making signs to the enemy (though surely he might shake his fist at the foe)—would be liable to any punishment, from death downwards to a drill, or from the strong-room upwards to the scaffold.

There are, however, privileges belonging to the soldier, such as the right of making a will when on actual service, by merely saying how he wishes to dispose of his property; so that, in the field of battle, if a soldier sees a cannon-ball coming towards his head, he has only to say, " I give and bequeath all I have to so and so;" and if any of his comrades should have heard what he said, and live to repeat it and remember exactly what it was, there is no doubt that the will would be a very good will in its way, and certainly quite strong enough to convey as much property as would probably be left by

" The soldier who lives on his pay,
And spends half-a-crown out of sixpence a day."

The Maritime State is the next topic we have to touch

upon; and when we think of the glory of the Navy, the valour of the British tar, the hearts of oak, and all the rest of it, our timbers naturally begin to shiver, and we involuntarily go through a sort of mental Naval hornpipe as a tribute to the maritime prowess of Britannia, who has ruled the waves, the whole waves, and nothing but the waves, from time immemorial.

The mode of manning the Navy is, in time of war, to resort to the liberty of the press, or, in other words, to seize hold of any one who comes in the way, and make " a heart of oak " of him, whether his heart may be disposed to sympathise with wainscoating or not, and to turn him at once into a British tar, by pitching him on board a vessel. Some doubt has been thrown on the legality of impressment, but Sir Michael Forster, who is a regular special pleader, makes out that it must be a law, because it is mentioned in other laws, though there is no law in existence to which the other laws refer; and consequently, as A is to B, so is B to C, which makes it as clear as A B C that A may B (e) pressed to go to C whenever there is any occasion for his services. Thus the power of impressment resides somewhere; but where that somewhere is, nobody knows; and, as we are fortunately at peace, nobody thinks it worth while to inquire. It has recently been enacted that no seaman shall serve more than three years against his will, unless he is made to serve longer, and then he must; so this boon to impressed seamen helps them out of their difficulty much in the same way as the Irishman lengthened his ladder, by cutting a bit from the top and joining it on at the bottom.

The privileges of soldiers and seamen are great; for, if the soldier loses his arms in battle, there is Chelsea Hospital to lend him a hand; and a sailor who is deprived of both his legs by a cannon-ball, has nothing to do but quietly to walk into Greenwich.

HAVING commented on the people in their public relations, we now come to private relations, including Master and Servant, Husband and Wife,—which, by-the-by, is a relation something like that of master and servant, for the wife is often a slave to the husband,—Parent and Child, and Guardian and Ward—the latter being a sort of relationship which is seen upon the stage, where a choleric old man with a stick is always thwarting the affections of a young lady in white muslin.

We shall begin with Master and Servant—showing how such relationship is created and destroyed. There is now no such thing as pure and proper slavery in England ; so that a servant of all-work who says, " Hang that door-bell,—I am a perfect slave to it," has recourse to a fiction.

England is so repugnant to slavery, that directly a negro sets his foot on English ground he is free ; but if he has lost both his legs, he cannot of course put his foot on British soil, and would remain a slave to circumstances. A menial servant is so called from the word *mœnia*, which signifies walls, and arises probably from the practice of brushing down cobwebs from the *mœnia*, or walls, with a Turk's-head, or hair-broom. The old doctrine of a month's wages or a month's warning is always acted on in London, except when a servant refuses to obey his master's orders, when it seems the master may give the servant kicks—and kick him out—instead of halfpence.

Another species of servants are called Apprentices, from the word *apprendre*, to learn ; and thus a barber's apprentice learns to shave on the faces of poor people, who, in consideration of their paying nothing, allow themselves to be practised on by beginners who have never handled the razor.

Next come the Labourers, whose wages were formerly settled by justices of the peace at session, or the sheriff; but now the master settles the wages, or, if he does not settle, he is a very shabby fellow for failing in doing so.

Stewards, Porters, and Bailiffs come next; but no one would think of having a bailiff as his servant, unless there were an execution in the house, and the bailiff were thrust into livery to save appearances.

A master may correct his apprentice for negligence; and if a grocer's apprentice neglects to sand the sugar, the master may give him the cane for neglecting his business.

A master may maintain or assist his servant in an action at law; and if one's footman happens to be a rightful heir in disguise, the master may lend him the money to go to law against the wrongful heir, for the purpose of recovering the property.

A master may assault a man for assaulting his servant, on the principle, probably, that in a row, as in everything else, the more the merrier.

" If any person do hire my servant," says F. N. B. 167, 168—but whether F. N. B. is a policeman or what, it is impossible to say, for we only find him alluded to in the books as F. N. B. 167, 168—"if any person do hire my servant," says he, " I may have an action for damages against both the new master and the servant, or either of them." This glorious old privilege is rather obsolete, for we do not find the courts much occupied in trying actions between ladies and gentlemen and their late menials.

The master is amenable, to a certain extent, for the act of his servant; and, therefore, if a servant commit a trespass by order of his master—such as if a gentleman riding by a field were to order his groom to jump over into it and pull up a turnip—the master, though he did not eat the whole of the turnip, or any of it, would be liable for the trespass. If an innkeeper's servant rob a guest, the innkeeper is liable, on the principle of like master like man; for the law very reasonably thinks that, if the servant is a thief, the master very likely may be.

If I usually pay my tradesman ready money, I am not liable if he trusts my servant; but if I do not usually pay him any money at all, then I am liable to pay the money—when he can get it out of me. This is on the authority of Noy's Maxims—and a maxim is always supposed to contain the maximum of wisdom.

By an old statute, called "An Act for the better and more careful use of the Frying-pan," it is provided that any servant who sets the house on fire by carelessness shall forfeit 100l., or go to the workhouse, where the servant would forfeit so many pounds of flesh by the spareness of the diet; but this act, savouring too much of the spirit of Shylock, is now seldom acted on. A master is liable if anything is thrown from the window of a house; but it has been decided that if a house should be on fire, and a servant should throw himself on the indulgence of the public, by jumping amongst the crowd and should hurt any one, the master would not be liable, for this would not be wilful damage.

If a pea-shooter be discharged from the garret, and the pea enter the eye of a passenger, the *pater-familias*, or master of the house, is, in the eye of the law, answerable for the pea in the eye of the stranger; for it is a common-law right, inherent in every one, to protect his own pupil.

Such are the leading features of the law of master and servant. The modern tiger has not been regarded by the ancient Constitution; but we find in *Petersdorff's Abridgment a quaint allusion to the legs of footmen, some of whom, he says, appear to be regularly calved out for the prominent situations they occupy.

* Vide MS. marginal note, in pencil, in the author's own copy of this able work.

WE now come to treat of Husband and Wife, and shall inquire, first, how marriages may be made, which will be interesting to lovers ; secondly, how marriages may be dissolved, which will be interesting to unhappy couples ; and lastly, what are the legal effects of marriage, which will be interesting to those who have extravagant wives, for whose debts the husbands are liable.

To make a marriage three things are required ;—first, that the parties *will* marry; secondly that they *can;* and thirdly, that they *do;* though to us it seems that if they *do*, it matters little whether they *will*, and that if they *will*, it is of little consequence whether they *can ;* for if they *do*, they *do ;* and if they *will*, they *must;* because where there is a *will* there is a *way*, and therefore they *can* if they *choose ;* and if they *don't*, it is because they *won't*, which brings us to the conclusion, that if they *do*, it is absurd to speculate upon whether they *will* or *can* marry.

It has been laid down very clearly in all the books, that in general all persons are able to marry, unless they are unable, and the fine old constitutional maxim, that " a man may not marry his grandmother," ought to be written in letters of gold over every domestic hearth in the British dominions. There are some legal disabilities to a marriage, such as the slight impediment of being married already ; and one or two other obstacles, which are too well known to require dwelling on.

If a father's heart should happen to be particularly flinty, a child under age has no remedy, but a stony guardian may be macadamised by the Court of Chancery ; that is to say, a marriage to which he objects may be ordered to take place, in spite of him. Another incapacity is want of reason in either of the parties ; but if want of reason really prevented a marriage from taking place, there would be an end to half the matches that are entered into.

A considerable deal of the sentiment attaching to a love affair has been smashed by the 6th and 7th of William IV., c. 85, explained by the 1st of Victoria, c. 22,—for one Act is always unintelligible until another Act is passed to say what is the former's meaning. This statute enables a pair of ardent lovers to rush to the office of the superintendant registrar, instead of to Gretna Green ; and there is no doubt that if Romeo could have availed himself of the wholesome section in the Act alluded to, Juliet need not have paid a premature visit to the " tomb of all the Capulets."

Marriages could formerly only be dissolved by death or divorce ; but the New Poor Law puts an end to the union between man and wife directly they enter into a parochial Union. Divorce, except in the instance just alluded to, is a luxury confined only to those who can afford to pay for it ; and a husband is compelled to allow money—called ali-money —to the wife he seeks to be divorced from. Marriages, it is said, are made in Heaven, but unless the office of the registrar be a little paradise, we don't see how a marriage made before that functionary can come under the category alluded to.

A husband and wife are one in law—though there is often anything but unity in other matters. A man cannot enter into a legal agreement with his wife, but they often enter into disagreements which are thoroughly mutual. If the wife be in debt before marriage, the husband, in making love to the lady, has been actually courting the cognovits she may have entered into ; and if the wife is under an obligation for which she might be legally attached, the husband finds himself the victim of an unfortunate attachment. A wife cannot be sued without the husband, unless he is dead in law ; and law is really enough to be the death of any one. A husband or a wife cannot be witness for or against one another, though a wife sometimes gives evidence of the bad taste of the husband in selecting her.

A wife cannot execute a deed; which is, perhaps, the reason why Shakspeare, who was a first-rate lawyer, made Macbeth do the deed, which Lady Macbeth would have done so much better, had not a deed done by a woman been void to all intents and purposes.

By the old law, a husband might give his wife moderate correction; but it is declared in black and white that he may not beat her black and blue, though the civil law allowed any man on whom a woman had bestowed her hand, to bestow his fists upon her at his own discretion. The common people, who are much attached to the common law, still exert the privilege of beating their wives; and a woman in the lower ranks of life, if she falls in love with a man, is liable, after marriage, to be a good deal struck by him.

Such are the chief legal effects of marriage, from which it is evident, says Brown, that the law regards the fair sex with peculiar favour; but Smith maintains that such politeness on the part of the law, is like amiability from a hyæna—an animal that smiles benignantly on those whom it means mischief to.

CHAPTER XVI.

OF PARENT AND CHILD.

WE now come to the tender subject of parent and child, which Shakspeare has so tenderly touched upon in many of his tragedies. Macduff calls his children " chickens," probably because he " broods" over the loss of them; and Werner, in Lord Byron's beautiful play of that name, exclaims to Gabor " Are you a father?" a question which, as the.

Hungarian was a single man, he could not have answered in the affirmative without rendering himself amenable to the very stringent provisions of the 45th of Elizabeth.

Children are of two sorts—boys and girls : though the lawyers still further divide them into legitimate and illegitimate.

The duties of a parent are maintenance and education ; or, as Coke would have expressed it, grub and grammar. That the father has a right to maintain his child is as old as Montesquieu—we mean, of course, the rule, not the child or the parent is as old as Montesquieu—whose exact age, by the bye, we have no means of knowing.

Fortunately, the law of nature chimes in with the law of the land ; for, though there is a game, called " None of my child," in which it is customary to knock an infant about from one side of the room to the other, still there is that natural στοργη in the parental breast that fathers and mothers are for the most part willing to provide for their offspring.

The civil law will not allow a parent to disinherit his child without a reason ; of which reasons there are fourteen, though there is one reason, namely, having nothing to leave, which causes a great many heirs to be amputated, or cut off, even without the ceremony of performing the operation, with a shilling. Our own law is more civil to parents than the civil law, for in this country children are left to Fate and the Quarter Sessions, which will compel a father, mother, grandfather, or grandmother, to provide for a child, if of sufficient ability. If a parent runs away, that is to say, doth spring off from his offspring, the churchwardens and overseers may seize his goods and chattels, and dispose of them for the maintenance of his family ; so that, if a man lodging in a garret leaves nothing behind him, *that* must be seized for the benefit of the deserted children. By the late Poor Law Act, a husband is liable to maintain the children of his wife, whether legitimate or illegitimate ; and we would therefore advise all " persons about to marry," that though it is imprudent to count one's chickens before they are hatched, still it is desirable that chickens already hatched, and not counted on, should be rigidly guarded against.

It being the policy of our laws to promote industry, no father is bound to contribute to a child's support more than twenty shillings a month, which keeps the child continually sharp set, and is likely to promote the active growth of the infantine appetite.

Our law does not prevent a father from disinheriting his child; a circumstance which has been invaluable to our dramatists, who have been able to draw a series of delightful stage old men, who have a strong hold on the filial obedience of the walking ladies and gentlemen, who dare not rush into each other's arms, for fear of the old gentleman in a court coat and large shoe-buckles being unfavourable to the youth in ducks, or the maiden in muslin. Heirs are especial favourites of our courts of justice—much as the lamb is the especial favourite of the wolf—for an heir with mint sauce, that is to say, with lots of money, is a dainty dish indeed to tempt the legal appetite.

A parent may protect his child; and thus, if one boy batters another boy, the parent of the second boy may batter the first boy, and the battery is justifiable, for such battery is in the eye of the law only the working of parental affection; though it is rather awkward for parental affection to take a pugilistic turn in its extraordinary zeal to show itself.

The last duty of a parent is to educate a child, or to initiate him into the mysteries of Mavor at an early period. Learning is said to be better than houses and land—probably because it opens a wide field for the imagination—that Cubitt of the mind—to build upon.

The old Romans, says Hale, used to be able to kill their children; but he adds that " the practysse off cuttinge offe one's own hair was thougghte barber-ous." This atrocious pun reminds us of the cruelty of a certain dramatist of modern times, who used to write pieces and take his own children to see them, thereby submitting his own offspring to the most painful ordeal, for they were compelled to sit out the whole performance, and were savagely pinched if they fell asleep, while they were, at the same time, expected to laugh and look cheerful at every attempt at a joke which their unnatural father had ventured to perpetrate. In conformity with the maxim that *" paterna potestas in pietate debet non in atrocitate consistere,"* it is believed that a child in such a dreadful position as that which we have alluded to, might claim to be released by his next friend, for the time being, the box-keeper.

A parent may correct his child with a rod or a cane—a practice originally introduced to encourage the growers of birch, and to protect the importers of bamboo, as well as to promote the healthy tingling of the juvenile veins; and a schoolmaster, who is *in loco parentis,* is also empowered to do the like by an old Act of Parliament, known as the statute of Wapping.

Children owe their parents support; but this is a mutual obligation, for they must support each other—though we sometimes hear them declaring each other wholly unsupportable.

Illegitimate children are such as are born before wedlock; being, like Richard the Third, " sent before their time into this breathing world :" and though there is a fine maxim, to the effect of its being "better late than never," it is, in some cases, better to be late than too early. They are said to be *nullius filii,* or nobody's children : but so many people are now the children of mere nobodies, that all the old prejudices on this point against innocent parties are becoming quite obsolete, as they ought to be.

There is now no distinction between the two kinds we have named, except that one cannot inherit, and the other can ; but some of those who can can't, and some of those who can't are enabled to do what is far better—namely, to give instead of taking.

CHAPTER XVII

OF GUARDIAN AND WARD.

A GUARDIAN is a sort of temporary parent to a minor,—a kind of tarpaulin thrown over the orphan to shield him from the storms of life during his infancy—or, if we may use an humbler illustration, a guardian is a kind of umbrella, put up by the law over the ward, to keep off the pelting of the pitiless storm till the years of discretion are arrived at. There are various kinds of guardians, such as guardians by nature, and guardians for nurture, who are of course the parents of the child ; for if an estate be left to an infant, the father is guardian, and must account for the profits ; but as the father can control the child's arithmetical studies, it is easy for the latter to be brought up in blessed ignorance of accounts, and thus the parent may easily mystify the child when the profits of the estate are to be accounted for. The mother is the guardian for nurture ; that is to say, she is expected to nurse the infant, and the law being very fond of children requires the mother to look to the infantine wardrobe. It also invests her with absolute power over the milk and water, and the bread and butter, making her a competent authority—from which there is no appeal—on all points of nursery practice.

Next comes the guardian in *socage*—so called, perhaps, from the quaint notion that guardianship generally extends to those who wear socs—or socks—which is further borne out by the fact that guardianship in socage ceases when the child is fourteen years old—which is about the age when socks are relinquished in favour of stockings. These guardians in socage are such as cannot inherit an estate to which a child is entitled, for Coke says that to commit the custody of an infant to him who is next in succession, is " *quasi agnum committere lupo*," to hand over the lamb to the wolf, and thus says Fortescue, in one of those rascally puns for which the old jurists were infamous. " the law, wishing the child to escape from the *lupo* has left a *loop-hole* to enable him to do so." Selden has cleared this pun of a good deal of its ambiguity by changing the word *lupo* into *loop-ho*, but Chitty and all the later writers are utterly silent regarding it

By the 12th of Charles II. confirmed by 1st Victoria, any father may appoint, by will, a guardian to his child till the latter is twenty-one ; but it is twenty to one whether such a guardian—called a testamentary guardian—will be able to exercise proper control over the infant.

Guardians in chivalry have been abolished, and so have the guardians of the night, who on the *lucus a non lucendo* principle, were called watchmen, from the fact of their never watching.

The Lord Chancellor is the general guardian of all infants, and especially of idiots and lunatics, for as Chancery drives people mad, it is only right that Chancery should take care of those who are afflicted with insanity, and who may be called the natural offspring of equity.

Having disposed of the guardians, let us come to the wards, or, as Coke would say, " having got rid of the wolf, let us discuss the lamb in an amicable spirit." A male at twelve years of age may take the oath of allegiance ; but this does not apply to all males, for the Hounslow mail * can take nothing but two insides and the letters. At fourteen a boy may marry if he can find any one fool enough to have him and at twenty-one he may dispose of his property, so

* The learning on the subject of the Hounslow Mail is fast becoming obsolete a regular mail-cart having been recently substituted for the cab that previously carried it.

that he may throw himself away seven years sooner than he can throw away his money. By the law of England a girl may be given in marriage at seven, but surely this must mean the hour of the day at which she may be married, and not the age at which the ceremony may be performed. Formerly, children might make their wills at fourteen, but as they could not be expected to have a will of their own, it has been enacted that no will made by a person under twenty-one shall be valid. Among the Greeks and Romans, women were never of age, and if they had their way in this country a good many of them never would be. This law must have been the civil law, for its consideration towards the fair sex on a matter of so much delicacy as a question of age betokens extreme civility. When this wore away, the Roman law was so civil as to regard them as infants till they were five-and-twenty—which was meeting the ladies half-way by treating them as little innocents for the first quarter of a century of their precious existences.

Infants have various privileges, such as the common law privilege of jumping over the posts at the corners of the streets, and playing at hop-scotch or rounders in retired neighbourhoods. Another infantine privilege is the juvenile amusement of going to law, which a child may do by his guardian or his *prochein amy*, or next friend—though, by the bye, he must be a pretty friend who would help another into a law-suit. A child may certainly be hanged at fourteen, and certainly may not be hanged at seven, but the intermediate period is one of doubt whether the infant culprit is hangable. Hale gives two instances of juvenile executions in which two infant prodigies were the principal characters. One was a girl of thirteen, who was burned for killing her mistress; and the other a boy still younger, who, after murdering one of his companions by a severe hiding, proceeded to hide himself, and was declared in legal language, *doli capax*—up to snuff—or, to follow the Norman jurists, *en haut du tabac*, and hanged accordingly. It is a fine maxim of the English law, that an infant shall not lose by *laches*, or, in other words, that the stern old doctrine of *no askee no havee* does not apply to a child who is entitled to something which he neglects asking for.

An infant cannot bind himself, but he may be " stitched in a neat wrapper "—that is to say, a Tweedish wrapper—at his own cost, if he thinks proper to go and pay ready money for it. An infant cannot convey away his own estate, but he may run through his own property as fast as he likes, for if he has a field he may run across it—in at one end and out at the other—whenever he feels disposed for it. An infant trustee may convey an estate that he holds in trust for another person, though he may not be a party in a conveyance on his own account, yet he may, nevertheless, join a party in a public conveyance, such as an omnibus. An infant may present a clerk to the Bishop, but if the Bishop don't like the clerk, he may turn upon his heel ; but still the presentation does not fall by lapse into the laps of the Bishop. An infant may bind himself for necessaries, such as food and physic ; thus, if he gives a draft to pay for a pill, or contracts with a butcher to supply what is requisite and meet, he will be clearly liable.

In weighing the disabilities and privileges of infants, we come to the conclusion, that, to every six of one, there will be about half-a-dozen of the other.

CHAPTER XVIII.

OF CORPORATIONS.

IN addition to natural persons, the law, in honourable emulation of Madame Tussaud, of wax-work notoriety, has constituted certain artificial persons. These are called bodies politic, bodies corporate, or corporations, and they stick together like wax, in which respect they bear a still closer resemblance to the artificial persons in Madame Tussaud's collection.

Corporations are either aggregate or sole. When aggregate they consist of many, such as the mayor and common councilmen of a city—and precious common councilmen some of them are; the head and fellows of a college—nice fellows some of *them* are also; and the dean and chapter of a cathedral church, which endures, of course, until the end of the chapter. Corporations sole consist of one person and his successors, such as a king, or a bishop, or a parson. This is the origin of the doctrine that the king never dies; for it is always, as the boys say, "One down and another come on," so that in fact the throne, like the curds and whey house at Hyde Park Corner, is never vacant. "The parson," says Coke, "*quatenus* parson shall never die," and the same may be said of the street-keeper, who, *quatenus* street-keeper, enjoys official immortality. The glorious old constitutional watchword of "Never say die," probably has its origin in the circumstance hinted at.

Another division of corporations is into ecclesiastical and lay; the former being spiritual, such as bishops and parsons in the present day, and formerly monks, abbots, or priors; but it is doubtful whether the priors were prior to the monks. Lay corporations are such as the society of antiquaries, for the study of antiquities; and of course the members are expected to be well up in all the old jokes, which are better known as the "ryghte merrie mysteries of Miller." There are also eleemosynary corporations, such as hospitals, where legs are amputated *gratis*, from those poor persons who would otherwise be thrown upon their own hands for surgical attendance.

Having described the various kinds of corporations, we shall now ask:—first, how they are made; secondly, what they can do; thirdly, how they are visited; and fourthly, how they may be dissolved or got rid of.

A corporation is made by the sovereign, who uses the words "*Creamus, erigimus, fundamus, incorporamus,*" and the sovereign is guilty of the grossest tautology in doing so. A corporation must have a name, and Romeo, therefore, when he asks " What's in a name ?" betrays a frightful ignorance of the beautiful passage in *Gilb. Hist. C. P.* 182, where it is prettily laid down that the name is the knot by which a corporation is combined, and without the knot it is not a corporation at all—" a point," says Coke, " that is by the mass a knotty one."

We come, secondly, to the rights and powers of a corporation ; the first of which is the right of perpetual succession ; for as every man has a right to live till he dies, so every corporation has a right to exist till its existence ceases. This indeed is said to be the very end for which corporations were established ; that is to say, their very endlessness is the end they are designed to answer. Thirdly, they may sue, or be sued ; quod or be quodded ; grant or receive, give or take, borrow or lend ; and, in fact, do as they please with their own just like other people. A corporation may have a common seal, by which it is bound ; for though the members may pass their words, it matters not what they say till the corporation sealing-wax renders it incumbent on them to stick to it. A corporation may make by-laws ; but these by-laws, by the by, may have the go-by given to them if they are contrary to the law of the land—a rule which is as old as the twelve tables of Rome ; but we forget the date of those dozen specimens of classic mahogany. We have, however, done wisely in taking a leaf out of the tables alluded to.

A corporation has some disabilities, and is incapable for instance of being committed to prison, for there can be no catchee where there is actually no havee. A corporation is prevented from purchasing lands without a licence from the sovereign, by certain acts called the statutes of *Mortmain,* which means a dead hand, probably from the fact that these corporations were dead hands at making a bargain.

Our next inquiry is " How may these corporations be visited ? " a question that would seem to need a reference to the book of *étiquette,* for when we talk of a corporation being visited, we allude, of course, to its liability to be called upon. The sovereign is the visitor of the archbishop ; and we presume that the bell at Lambeth palace, with the brass plate beneath it, inscribed with the word " Visitors," is for the exclusive use of royalty. Lay corporations are said to have no visitors, and the lord mayor of London sometimes appears to value this exemption, for if he is a stingy person he never asks any one to dine with him.

An eleemosynary corporation may be visited by the founder and his heirs, so that any genuine guy may leave his card as a visitor at Guy's Hospital.

We will consider, lastly, how corporations may be dissolved, for even the goodly pearl is capable of dissolution in the gem-destroying vinegar. A corporation may be dissolved by civil death, but no uncivil death—such as murder—can put an end to it. It may be extinguished by act of parliament, or, in other words, by the law, which is as it were dissolving a corporation in hot water ; by surrender, which is a sort of suicidal exit, when the corporation asks itself the question, " to be or not to be ? " and prefers the latter ; or, thirdly, by forfeiture of its charter through negligence or abuse, which formed a pretext in the reigns of Charles and James the Second for seizing the charter of the city of London. This led to an act being passed after the Revolution, enacting that the franchises of London shall never more be forfeited for any cause whatsoever, and thus the lord mayor and corporation have a *carte blanche* for any amount of foolery, a privilege that they one and all, in turn, take unlimited advantage of.

In the foregoing chapters we have given an account of the rights of persons, which are equally the privilege of the peer and the pot-boy, the gallant soldier, the sailor, the tinker, the tailor, the ploughboy, the apothecary, and the thief. May the pride of the first never disdain the humble merit of the second ; and may the valour of the third and fourth, added to the industry of the fifth and sixth, ameliorate the condition of the seventh ; while oh ! may the healing art of the eighth restore, in a moral sense, the degraded ninth to that position, which in accordance with the rights of persons, any person has a right to occupy.

PROLOGUE to PART II.

———◆———

THE Second Part of BLACKSTONE touches on Real Property—though, by-the-bye, any property that is not real, can scarcely be called property at all—and this division of the subject is said to comprise the rights of things, which, as everybody likes to know the rights of things, will be a very popular topic with the multitude.

PART II.

CHAPTER I.

THE law of England distributes things into two kinds—real and personal ; though we should personally be really sorry to leave our things to be distributed by the law, for if we did, we should not expect to see much more of them. Things real are such as are fixed and immoveable, which cannot be carried out of their place, such as a ministry that will not resign, and looks upon itself as the real thing, or just the thing, to carry on the Government. Lands are called things real, because they cannot be moved ; but goods are called personal, because they can be moved, as landlords sometimes find out when they discover that the moon has been cruelly shot by an unprincipled tenant. In treating of things real, we shall consider—First, their sorts ; but, by-the-bye, those individuals who have nothing that is real, must be terribly out of sorts : Secondly, the tenures by which things real may be holden—we have seen a man at a fair hold a real red-hot poker in his hand, but by what tenure we never could find out : Thirdly, the estates which may be had in them : and Fourthly, the title to them, or how they may be got, and how they may be lost, the latter being a point that the law is very fond of arriving at. Things real consist in lands, tenements, and hereditaments. Land means anything substantial, but it don't mean a substantial dinner—tenement means anything that can be holden, though it don't mean a woman's tongue, which the owner can hold sometimes—and an hereditament means anything that can be inherited.

Hereditaments are of two kinds—corporeal and incorporeal; the first of which will be treated of in the present chapter. Corporeal hereditaments can only be such as affect the senses, though it is not necessary they should be calculated to drive people mad; nor was the Cock Lane Ghost, who frightened a few individuals out of their wits, a corporeal hereditament. They may all be comprised under the name of Land, which signifies any ground or soil whatever; so that a flower-pot with mould in it is the lowest species of real property, though when it is on the outside of an attic window, it assumes a somewhat higher position. Land also includes castles, except, perhaps, castles in the air. Water is also Land in the eye of the law, because the law takes a dry view of everything, and looks not at the water, but at the ground beneath it.

Land also comprises everything above and everything beneath it; so that the owner of the soil may carry a building to any height he pleases, even as far as the very clouds themselves, which would, perhaps, be the height of absurdity. He may also go downwards, to the very centre of the earth; but if he went beyond that point, the landlord at the immediate antipodes would have an action of trespass. Land, therefore, does not mean the mere face of the earth, but the very "bowels of the land," which Richmond, when he seemed bent on showing his dominion over the soil, expressed his intention of marching into. If a man grants only water, he grants nothing but a right of fishing, which may be called possession with a hook, and can scarcely be said to descend in a right line to one's posterity. By the title of water nothing passes, except a right of fishing—though, by-the-bye, water itself often passes by the title of milk—but by the name of land anything terrestrial will pass, except, perhaps, fullers' earth, which is the only instance that we are aware of, in which the earth itself cannot be regarded as real property

CHAPTER II.

It seems that Coke, in his pleasant squib on Littleton— for surely he who throws a light on another may do so by aiming a squib at him—has described an incorporeal hereditament as a right issuing out of a thing corporate, whether real or personal; such as a rent issuing from land, which is not the same as money got by raising the wind, though rent is sometimes paid by resorting to the latter process.

There are ten sorts of incorporeal hereditaments; so that, as we have already said, they must be out of sorts indeed who have not the enjoyment of any one of them.

The 1st is an Advowson, or the right of presentation to a church; which would indeed be an unsatisfactory kind of introduction if it applied only to the church, instead of the good things connected with it. Advowsons are of three kinds: 1st. Presentative, where the patron presents his clerk to the bishop, who is expected to institute the said clerk, or rather to "let him regularly in." 2ndly. Collative, where the patron and bishop are one; in which case Coke insists, in a lengthy chapter of eighty-six pages, that "the bishop cannot present to himself unless he were one beside himself, in which case he would be stark-staring mad, and therefore *non compos*, and *reang de bishoppe de too.*" 3dly. Donative, when the King, or any subject, by his license, has founded a church, which the patron is allowed to give without presentation. "And this," says Spelman, "is an illustration of the patron's *willy* being superior to the bishop's *nilly;* the latter going for *nil* in opposition to the *will* of the former."

Tithes form the 2nd species of incorporeal hereditaments,

though a recent jurist says that tithes ought rather to be the tenth, because they are the tenth part of the profit yearly arising from lands.

Tithes are not payable on animals *feræ naturæ*, or, in other words, wild beasts; so that the proprietors of the Zoological Gardens are not bound to settle on the rector one in ten of all the tigers, bears, lions, or cassowaries, that may be added within the year to the live stock alluded to.

Tithes are due to the parson, who is entitled to the tenth of almost everything; and there is a case in the books, where a parson claimed the Xth of a hogshead of XX, which he held must be equivalent to half, because X is the half of XX.

There are three ways of being exempted from the payment of tithes; namely, composition, custom, or commutation, to which some unprincipled persons have occasionally added a fourth, by bolting and leaving the tithes unpaid, to the extreme disgust and decided *damnum* of the parson.

A composition is where a parson makes hay while the sun shines, by getting a good round sum in his own lifetime in discharge of the tithes which would have been payable not only to himself but his successors—a practice which savoured so much of covin towards future incumbents, that a law was passed in the 13th of Elizabeth, to prevent parsons and vicars from making away with the property of their churches for more than three lives *or* twenty-one years,—a statute which consequently fixes seven years as the average duration of human existence.

Secondly, is a discharge by custom, which is sometimes only a partial discharge, as where the parson is accustomed to take the twelfth cock of hay instead of the tenth, in consideration of the hay being made for him,—unless, indeed, the parson be such a jolly old cock that he can make his own hay, in which case the *modus decimandi* would not operate. Sometimes also the parson accepts two fowls instead of a tenth of all the eggs,—which is, in fact, counting his chickens after they are hatched,—and the reduction is made in consideration of the labour employed in sitting on the eggs; from the risk and anxiety of which the parson thus saves himself.

Thirdly, Commutation, which provides that the parson shall take his tithes in money, instead of rushing into poultry yards, and carrying off one goose out of ten, or going personally into the hay-field and cocking a cock or two into a cart for his own use; "a plan by which, it is true," says Fortescue, "he made cock-sure of his tithes, though at a sacrifice of his dignity."

The 3rd incorporeal hereditament is the Right of Common, which is of four sorts, namely, pasture, piscary, turbary, and estovers. Common of pasture is the privilege of turning out ducks and jackasses, or other animals, to indulge in the luxury of a meal of buttercups among a lot of boys flying kites, pitching stones, or playing cricket in all directions. Common of piscary is the right of fishing, which presents a curious contradiction to the science of mathematics; for in fishing it requires only one line to make an angle, while in mathematics two lines are required before an angle can be formed. Common of turbary is a right of digging turf, but unless it is for a lark, this right must be regarded as rather *infra dig.* Common of estovers is the privilege of cutting wood from another's estate, though Williams, J., has declared that any one cutting another person's wood deserves to be made to cut his own stick with remarkable rapidity.

The 4th kind is that of Ways, or the right of going over another person's ground, which is, in fact, the right of getting into the way of other people.

Offices form the 5th kind, such as the office of beadle; though the stout and worthy beadle of the British Museum is himself anything but *in*corporeal.

Dignities constitute the 6th, and franchises the 7th sort of incorporeal hereditaments. The former speak for themselves; but a franchise is a branch of the royal prerogative existing in a subject; such as the right of killing bucks, does, and roes, in a royal forest. Whether the does and roes alluded to are the celebrated John and Richard, of legal celebrity, we are not aware, and none of the jurists have helped to solve the problem.

The 8th, 9th, and 10th descriptions of incorporeal hereditaments are corodies, or the right of sustenance, which may be had at any respectable workhouse ; annuities, which must be well understood by those who enjoy them, but are not worth the trouble of describing to those who don't ; and rents, including rent-service, rent-charge, and a few others. Rent-service has fealty attached to it, as where a policeman is put into an empty house to let it—which, by-the-bye, he never thinks of attempting. A rent-charge is a rent-payment charged upon land, with the power of distress—a power which the law loveth to exercise, for distress is the very essence of law in general. Rack-rent is rent of the full value of the tenement according to some, but in the opinion of others it is thought that rack-rent means a rent so high that the tenant is on the rack how to succeed in getting it together.

CHAPTER III.

OF TENURES, OR THE MANNER IN WHICH REAL PROPERTY MAY BE HELD.

ALL real property is held—and it is generally pretty tightly held by those who possess it. This tenacity of property is such that the thing holden is called a tenement, the holder a tenant, and the mode of holding a tenure. There is another mode of holding, called holding hard, which is frequently used in conveyancing—by the cad of the omnibus.

Tenements are of two kinds—frank tenement, or free holding, and villenage, of which there are different degrees, including pure villenage and villein socage. A pure villain is such a very low sort of villain that he must do whatever his landlord commands; but socage villains, or villain socmen, are not such villanous villains, inasmuch as there is a limit to their villany, the services required of them being certain and definite.

The most honourable species of tenure was knight-service, which was to attend the King in his wars; but sovereigns in these days, instead of fighting boldly, invariably fight shy, so that knight-service, or attendance on the King in his wars, is now merely nominal. There is also a tenure by grand serjeanty, by which the tenant bound himself to do some special service, such as acting as champion at the coronation; but as all improper characters are scrupulously kept out by the police, the valour of coming forward in a suit of armour, and offering to fight anybody who disputes the title to the crown, is rather questionable. The champion, however, pockets the gold cup and a few other valuable coronation "properties," so that he can afford to throw down a large theatrical gauntlet, which by-the-bye is invariably "smugged" by some subordinate as a perquisite.

Knight-service eventually was found so inconvenient that the knights gave money instead of going to battle, and thus paid themselves off, rather than run the risk of being paid off by the enemy.

By the 12th of Charles II. all military tenures were destroyed at one blow, for knights being of no service had long since converted knight-service into a farce of the broadest character.

Socage subsequently became the most general kind of tenure; so that the tenants, to use the quaint notion of Glanvil, "rushed precipitately from boots and spurs to simple socks—or socs; which is, no doubt, the origin of the word soc-age."

Free socage has several kinds, the chief of which are petit-serjeanty, or little service, such as giving the King annually an arrow, or a lance—but it does not seem that lancing the King's gums once a year would amount to petit-serjeanty;

tenure in burgage, where the tenant lives in a borough—so that the Southwark people afford a specimen of this class ; and gavelkind, where all the sons take alike, so that when a father gives his boys a thrashing all round, he in fact only illustrates the good old principle of gavelkind.

We now come to villenage, from which copyhold tenures are derived, so that any copyholder is a villain in the eye of the law ; and it is perhaps on this principle that the printer's boy who carries to and fro or holds the copy, is termed a devil, to show the alarming state of villenage he has fallen into.

A copyhold must always exist in a manor, which must have a court attached to it, with a jury consisting of two tenants at least, or the manor is lost ; so that if manners do not always make the man, it requires two men to make the manor.

A part of the ground of a manor was called folk-land, or land for the folks who lived upon it, who were downright slaves to the owner ; and as they were called villains, it is probable that Folkstone was, at one time, a very villanous neighbourhood. When the Normans came over to this country they did not proceed to kick out the villains, but allowed them to remain on the land, until at last the villains got a better title to the land by custom than the lords themselves by conquest ; for the stewards of the manors merely looking on and taking notes, the villains referring to the copy on the rolls of the court, declared themselves copyholders to all intents and purposes. The essentials of a copyhold are—1st, that the lands should be part of a manor, and consequently of right belonging to somebody else ; 2ndly, that they have been demised by copy of court-roll immemorially ; for if any one can remember the transaction it is bad, because the thing will not bear thinking of.

There is a fine payable on the death of the tenant or alienation of the lands, and this fine is now in most cases limited by law ; because, says Glanvil, " when the landlords could lay on as large a *fine* as they liked, they made a very *fine* thing of it." The italics are Glanvil's own, so that the joke must be given to him, though later writers, including four of the Chittys, have made a severe struggle to obtain the merit of it. Ancient demesne is a sort of privileged villenage, the villains who enjoy it having the privilege of paying no taxes, and of holding a court of their own to try their own rights to their own—and, perhaps, other people's —property. The villains, however, can only alienate their land by surrender, instead of passing it by the usual conveyance ; but a recent writer has thought it necessary to state in a note, that though the villains may not pass their land by the usual conveyance, there is no law to prevent them from going past their own houses in a rail-road carriage or omnibus.

In addition to the lay tenures there used to be the spiritual tenure of *frankalmoign*, by which religious corporations held lands on condition of singing masses for the soul of the donor. These masses amassing too much in the hands of the church, and weak-minded persons, attracted by the notion of having psalms sung for them, having been let in to a very pretty tune, the statute of *Quia emptores* was passed in the 18th of Edward I., to prohibit all such donations for the future. Many of the parochial clergy still hold their lands by this tenure, which accounts for a congregation being occasionally startled by a demand of their prayers for some one who would never be thought of either by parson or people, but for the necessity of observing the conditions by which the Church retains possession of the deceased's property.

CHAPTER IV.

BEFORE we go any further we mean to consider an estate—but we shall be very brief, though an estate is just the sort of thing we should like to dwell upon.

A freehold estate of inheritance is either a fee-simple or a fee-tail, and estates are probably called fees, because the lawyers generally contrived to pay themselves pretty well out of them.

The true meaning of the word fee is the same as feud—a feud signifying a row, because fees, which arise from law proceedings, are the result of a squabble.

A fee-simple is an estate that a man may leave to whom he pleases; and it is, perhaps, called fee-simple because it is sometimes very simply or foolishly disposed of. " Hence the tenant," says Bracton, " makes good his own title to be called a simpleton."

It used to be thought that a fee or freehold might remain in abeyance—that is to say, without an owner—but modern lawyers cannot tolerate the idea of a fee with nobody to take it, and the doctrine is therefore exploded.

We must now consider a limited fee, which we must take care not to confound with a half-guinea motion, which is a very limited fee indeed, but is not an estate of inheritance, because one's heirs are not likely to see much of it. These limited fees are divided into fees base or qualified, and fees conditional.

Base fees are fees with a qualification subjoined; though, by-the-bye, a barrister who takes a base fee, or, in other words, receives less than is marked on his brief, has seldom any qualification at all, either as £n advocate or a gentleman.

It is a base or qualified fee, if an estate were granted to A and his heirs, beadles of the Burlington Arcade; for if any of the heirs of A should cease to be beadles of that Arcade, the grant is entirely defeated.

A conditional fee is perhaps the lowest of all fees in its ordinary sense; for when a barrister agrees to receive a fee conditionally on winning his cause, it is a conditional fee that he bargains for. A person seised in such a fee, or caught at such a trick, would deserve to suffer in tail by a general endorsement, without limitation or restriction of any kind. An estate held by a conditional fee is when it is granted to B and his heirs male; so that if he has only daughters, they cannot have the estate.

When an estate is granted to a man and his heirs, he has what is called a fee-tail, from the French word *tailler*, to cut, because his heirs must eventually cut him out, or because he may in some cases cut off his own tail, by cutting away the rights of those who come after him.

Tail-general is where an estate is given to a man and all his heirs whoever they may be, which is a sort of tag-rag and bob-tail; but where the gift is restrained to certain heirs, the estate is tied up—like the head of a Chinese Mandarin—in a special tail.

Among the incidents of a tenancy in tail, are—first, the right of the tenant in tail to commit waste by felling timber, breaking windows, and other similar acts of mischief, which, if tenant in tail were a troublesome young scamp, he would most probably like to be guilty of. The Marquis, who rode his horse into the drawing-room of a furnished house he had taken for the season, was guilty of waste, because he was not seised in tail, though his horse might have been.

Estates tail could not at one time be aliened at all, but it is now quite settled that a man may cut off his own tail under a recent statute which abolished fines and recoveries; for, although the law always delighted in fines, it never favoured recoveries—for an estate in the hands of the law is generally considered to be past recovery.

CHAPTER V.

OF FREEHOLDS NOT OF INHERITANCE.

A FREEHOLD not of inheritance is an estate, held for one's own life, or for the life of somebody else; so that, a cat having nine lives, it would seem that a grant to a cat and his heirs would be almost as good as an estate in tail, for it would extend to so many lives as to make it nearly equal to a freehold.

A tenant for life has the right to enjoy the land in whatever way he pleases; so that he may roll about in the asparagus beds, play at leapfrog over the gooseberry bushes, or indulge in any other species of enjoyment which he thinks the land is capable of affording him. He must not, however, be guilty of waste on the premises, such as felling timber; but he is not prohibited from domestic waste, such as neglecting to eat his crusts, or buttering both sides of his bread "as some folke," says Spelman, "dydde formerlie."

If a tenant for life sows the land, and dies before harvest, the executors are entitled to the crop; and it seems that if a tenant for life has planted mustard and cress, but dies before it comes up, his personal representatives may enjoy the salad.

These profits are called emblements, and the doctrine of emblements applies not only to corn, but to roots—though not to fruit trees; so that the heir would have the apples, but the executors would have the parsley, and, perhaps, the rhubarb. Fruit-trees are not included, because they are not planted annually for immediate profit; but if a gooseberry bush, recently put in, bears fruit the first year, and the tenant for life dies, it would be difficult to say whether the gooseberries would vest in the heir or the executor. The better opinion seems to be, that it would be better for the executor to relinquish the new gooseberries than to go to law with the heir, which might play old Gooseberry with both of them.

There are one or two other kinds of life estates, which it is not necessary to go into. Among them is tenancy by the curtesy of England. Any gentleman endeavouring to keep up his tenancy by curtesy alone—without being able to pay the rent—would very soon be curtsied out by his landlady, or bowed or kicked out by his landlord. There is also tenancy in dower, where a widow gets one-third of her husband's estate. But a recent act has made it so easy to bar the dower, that the widows are generally done out of their thirds; and instead of the corn, the fruit, or even the vegetables, there is nothing left but the weeds, with which the unfortunate widows can console themselves.

CHAPTER VI.

OF ESTATES LESS THAN FREEHOLD.

ESTATES less than freehold are of three sorts : 1st, for years ; 2d, at will ; and 3d, by sufferance.

An estate for years is where a man takes premises on a lease, which may be for half a year, or even a quarter ; but still it is a lease for years, because the law does not take notice of anything less than a year—for the law has nothing to do with halves—never doing anything by halves—and will not recognise quarters ; "for the law," says Jones, "giveth quarter to nobody."

The law of England has a peculiar division of time ; and though the old wags have said in the books, that "legal time shoudde bye ryghte be sixe-eighte time—for thatte sixe and eighte pence be ye lawyer's fee"—still the old wags have thrown no light upon the subject.

A year, says Cocker, consists of 365 days, except in leap

year, when there are 366, but the 21st of Henry the Third merges the added day in the day before ; so that, on the 28th of February, to-day is, in fact, to-morrow, while the day after is, by act of Parliament, yesterday, for all legal purposes. A month is either lunar or calendar; but a month in law is lunar, unless otherwise expressed,—for there is a natural affinity between law and lunacy. A day includes all the twenty-four hours, for the law makes no distinction between day and night, but loveth the darkness of the latter better perhaps than the light of the former.

We are, however, losing sight of an estate for years, which is often called a term, because it must have an end or *terminus ;* but it might as well be called a railroad, as far as that goes, because every railroad must have a *terminus.*

Estates for years must also have a certain beginning and a certain end ; but so must almost everything, except a jack-towel, which has neither one nor the other.

It is a settled principle of law, that an estate is a freehold if it is for one's own life, or for anybody else's ; the latter being called, in the sort of Cockney French of the jurists, who probably picked it up at Boulogne during the long vacation, an estate *pur auter vie.* But an estate for 1000 years is only a chattel, and less than a freehold, which we can hardly understand, unless the *auter vie* should be such another *vie* as that of Methusaleh or Widdicomb ; but even then the estate for 1000 years would have a small majority in its favour.

A freehold must commence immediately and not *in futuro,* because there must be seisin ; but a lessee for years need not be seised, though his goods may be seized, and probably would be seized if he neglected to pay the rent of his premises.

A tenant for a certain number of years is not entitled to emblements, because if he is fool enough to plant peas in February, and he is compelled to march out of possession in March, he must leave the peas and take the consequences.

In the same way, if he has sown wheat in June, and is compelled to quit at Midsummer, he cannot reap the wheat, nor reap the benefit to be derived from it.

An estate at will is where the lessor may kick out the lessee at pleasure; as where A lets to B, and A changes his mind directly B has moved in his goods, and A orders B to be off, and B, being merely tenant at will, is compelled to mizzle. It is evident that lessor gets the best of it in an estate at will; and, as to *lessee*, "it is clear," says Salkeld, "the *less he* has to do with such an estate the better.

An estate at sufferance is where a man is not actually kicked out, but is clearly kick-out-able; as if he has taken a lease for a year, and the year has expired, and he either won't or don't go—he is a tenant at sufferance. When, however, tenant at sufferance becomes insufferable, the landlord must enter and oust him, or he will be guilty of *laches*, or neglect. But if tenant locks himself in, the landlord can avoid *laches*—or *latches*—by forcing the bolts, after a regular process of ejectment.

By recent statutes an insufferable tenant at sufferance must pay double rent if he refuses to go after regular notice, but if he has been in the habit of paying no rent at all, the penalty will not be a very heavy one.

CHAPTER VII.

OF ESTATES UPON CONDITION.

HERE we come to Estates upon Condition—which are sometimes estates that are sadly out of condition, and must be considered as estates that a man may call his own if he can, but if not he mustn't.

An estate on a condition implied by law, is where a man has a grant of the office of beadle—the implied condition attached to which is that he do act as beadle, or he might be ousted by the grantor and his heirs for ever. Thus the Beadle of Golden Square runs after imaginary boys at least twice a day, in order to fulfil the condition on which his office is held ; for if he did not make some show of this sort, the cane would become a mere badge of indolence, rendered more conspicuous by authority. This would come under the head of non-user, for which any public office would be forfeited ; and a beadle, having nothing to do, often walks an applewoman off to the station-house, lest, by non-user, he may be considered useless, and lose his appointment.

On the principle of either non-user or mis-user, all forfeitures of estates proceed ; as, if a man had taken a house for a few years, and he has the impudence to call it his own freehold and sell it, he incurs a forfeiture of his lease— "which is," says Coke, "the *leased* punishment that can be given him." Felons used to forfeit their estates, but as they often got better estates in New South Wales, it did not signify. The law was therefore altered, and the descendants of felons may now take—whatever they can get, from their worthy ancestors.

An estate on a condition expressed will be understood at once, by reading the words, and taking them to mean what they say—which in a legal definition is very unusual.

Some conditions are void :—1st. If they are impossible ; as, if an estate be given to Lord Brougham, on condition that he keeps himself out of mischief. This would be clearly an impossible condition, and Brougham would have the estate. Here the law is at variance with its general principle ; for while it requires impossibilities in many cases, it doth in this instance set its face against them. 2ndly. A condition is void if it is against the law ; as, if an estate be granted to B, on condition that he do stick a bill on the gate of Buckingham Palace—this condition would be void, and B need not stick the bill, but he would take the freehold.

Some estates on condition are held in pledge ; as, where a man borrows £200, and grants an estate of £20 a year till it is paid, after which the estate is at an end—and this is called a Welsh mortgage. Why it should be called Welsh is a puzzler, for it has nothing Welsh about it, any more than a Welsh wig or a Welsh rabbit. Next comes a mortgage—*mort-gage*, or dead pledge—called dead, because the estate is dead to the mortgagor if he does not look alive and pay off his mortgage in good time. A mortgagor has, however, the equity of redemption, which is the privilege of taking his estate out of pawn, by paying up the principal and interest at any time within twenty years after the mortgagee has taken possession ; so that mortgagee is kept for twenty years in a precious state of uncertainty as to whether he shall say "Mine own is not mine own," which is extremely possible.

The other estates on condition are estates by statute merchant, statute staple, and elegit. The two former are intended to benefit commerce ; but as they are nearly obsolete, we leave it to commerce to make what it can of them. An estate by elegit is where a plaintiff occupies and enjoys half the defendant's lands and tenements ; as, if defendant has a two-stall stable, and plaintiff turns a horse into one of the stalls ; or if the former has a lot of chickens, and the latter takes by *elegit* every alternate egg that may be laid in the poultry yard. This troublesome sort of estate may be ended by the payment of the debt that gives rise to it. These estates are chattels and no freehold, so they go to the executor instead of to the heir, though, by a little alteration in the spelling, these estates may be said to go to the *heir* or *air*, for property of all kinds will vanish *in tenues auras*, when the lawyers once get a hand in it.

CHAPTER VIII.

ESTATES may either be in possession or expectancy—much in the same way as a bird may be either in the hand or in the bush ; and the doctrine that one of the former is better than two of the latter, may also apply to some estates, particularly when the bush happens to be that very thorny one —the Court of Chancery.

Estates in possession may be very soon disposed of—too soon, indeed, by some who are forced to sell their property. We shall knock them all down in one lot, by saying that estates in possession are estates that one actually possesses ; though estates in expectancy are the subject of some of the very nicest law—the law being, by-the-bye, very nice for the lawyers, though anything but nice for the clients who pay for it.

An estate in remainder is where a man, having the fee-simple, grants a lease of twenty years to A, and after that to B ; as, if a person should treat A to the first drink of a pot of porter, which is afterwards to go to B. Here A is seised of the whole pot during the term of his drink, but afterwards B comes in as the remainder-man. In the first case there is only one estate, though there are two interests ; and in the second case, there is only one pot of porter, though two drinks, and consequently, two distinct interests are carved out of it. So there may be an estate to A, remainder to B, remainder to C ; which is like the well-known measure vulgarly known as three-outs to a quartern of gin, where A is in possession of the whole quartern, till B, who is a sort of tenant in expectancy, has a term (that is to say a glassful) carved or rather poured out of it, with the residue of the quartern to C, who takes whatever may be left, as the remainder-man.

It is a maxim of law that an estate in remainder must be preceded by an estate in possession, which is tantamount to saying that something must be taken before anything can be left; but there is often nothing left when the law begins to take, and thus the remainder-man finds nothing remaining. It is another rule of law that a remainder commences at the same time as the estate that precedes it; so that the remainder-man gets his estate, in the eye of the law, before he gets it at all—but he does not get it in his own eye, or if he does, it is just as much as he may put in his eye and see none the worse for it.

Remainders are either vested or contingent; a vested remainder being one that will certainly be had if the party entitled to it lives long enough, and a contingent remainder being one that a man who is entitled to it will get, if nothing occurs to prevent his having it. To revert to the allegory of the liquor: it is a vested remainder that falls to B, if A may only drink half, because B must have some of it; but it is a contingent remainder when B is to have a drop, supposing that A happens to leave any. A contingent remainder may be dubious on many grounds: 1st. as to person; as, when A has a pint of porter, with remainder over to the first comer, then the moment somebody comes the remainder vests in him, though till then it hath been contingent. This is the same as an estate being left to A, with remainder to B's eldest son; then, if B has no son, the remainder is never vested.

A remainder may also be contingent, where the person is certain, but the event on which it is to take effect is dubious; as where land, or a pint of beer, is given to A, and in case B survives, or drops in after the first draught, then with remainder to B. Here the person is certain; but there the event is dubious, for B may not survive—that is to say, not

come till all the porter is drunk up—and then there is of
course no remainder. There can be no remainder on any
estate less than a freehold, or, to come back again for the
sake of familiarity to the beer, there can be no gift over, or
contingency, on less than a pint; for the estate or drop of
porter would be too insignificant. Contingent remainders
may be defeated—as by surrender; and to pursue the simile
of the beer, the remainder may be destroyed either by being
spilt, or by the remainder-man executing a surrender, and
saying he don't want any.

We now come to an estate in reversion, which Sir Edward
Coke describes as a return of the land to the original
grantor; as when the lord of the soil lets his back-attic for
one week, he has the reversion at the end of the week—if
the tenant will go out quietly. It may be proper to observe that, when a greater and a less estate meet in the same
person, the less is merged in the greater; as where the back-
attic lodger takes the entire floor, he is tenant of the whole
floor, and not of the mere attic: so if tenant of the first
floor marries the lessee of the whole house, it is a tenancy
of the entire house, and the first-floor merges in the rest of
the building. It is now settled that one term of years may
merge in another; and it is also settled—which looks very
like a settler—that 1000 years may merge into one—if the
one is the reversion; which is something on the same
principle as six-and-twenty in an omnibus, or any other
tremendous crammer that might be cited.

CHAPTER IX.

OF the four ways of holding an estate described in the title of this chapter, the first is decidedly the best, because the holder of an estate in severalty has it all to himself; like the Member of Parliament who got up to address the House, which made every one run out of it.

An estate in joint tenancy is where two or more persons have one and the same interest, by the same conveyance, at the same time, and held by the same possession. First, they must have one interest; though, if they quarrel, they will probably have had a division, which the wisdom of the law does not guard against. It must come to them by one conveyance; but whether that "one conveyance" shall be the Parcels' Delivery Company, or the railroad, does not appear to signify. Joint tenants must have one and the same title: but *semble*, that a nobleman would not refuse an estate in joint tenancy with the Lord Mayor, whose title cannot be one and the same with that of the peer, who would nevertheless "take," as the legal phrase characteristically expresses it. There must also be unity of time to constitute a joint tenancy; but it does not appear that a mere difference in their watches would defeat the estate, nor would one of them being in London, and the other at Bath, where there is a variation of some minutes in the clocks, prevent them from having an estate in joint tenancy. If this rule as to time were very stringent, the property in the parish of St. Clement's would be placed, by the irregular conduct of its very eccentric *horloge*, in constant jeopardy. The joint tenants must have one and the same possession;

or, as the law term has it, they must be all seised at once —for the law is so very fond of " seizing," that it applies the term to the acquisition of property, and it is certainly a word that expresses pretty accurately the law's own mode of acquisition.

Out of joint tenancy arises the doctrine of survivorship, by which the longest liver is entitled to the whole estate ; but if they both die at the same moment—by shipwreck, for instance—we should like to know which of their two heirs would take the property. It is probable, that if the ocean swallowed up the joint tenants, the estate itself would be gulped down by the tempestuous sea of Chancery. It is an important question, how a joint tenancy may be severed or destroyed, for joint tenants may wish to part, and one may make the other very uncomfortable. For instance, suppose two people are joint tenants in a house, and they both want to live in it. As it belongs equally to both, neither could prevent the other ; and if both wanted to occupy the best room, or both insisted on putting up their feet on the bars of the same fire-place, endless litigation would be the consequence.

The law, foreseeing this sort of thing, provides that there may be a writ of partition, and the jointure may be dissolved ; " for Chancery," saith Coke, " can dissolve, that is to say, it can swallow and digest, melt or otherwise make away, with anything."

Estates in coparcenary are such as descend to two or more persons ; as, where a man's next heirs are females, the estate goes to them all, an arrangement the law delights in, because it is probable that handing an estate over to the ladies is almost equivalent to making it immediately the subject of litigation. Coparceners have not the benefit of survivorship, which is, perhaps, a rule made out of consideration to the fair sex, who could not enjoy an estate, if living to grow old were one of the conditions of getting it.

Tenants in common are such as have different interests

in the same estate, as in the celebrated case of the oyster, where the clients came in for the shells, and the lawyer took the fish. Here they were all tenants in common of the native, but the oyster was a sort of separate interest carved out of the shells, which the clients held as long as they found it convenient.

It may be as well, before concluding this chapter, to remark that the illustration of the oyster is not taken from the well-known rule in Shelley's case ; but to seize the fish, and give the shell, is the rule in almost every case where it can possibly be acted on.

CHAPTER X.

OF THE TITLE TO REAL PROPERTY IN GENERAL.

TITLE is defined by Sir Edward Coke to be *titulus*, a definition in which the Latin dictionary curiously coincides with the very astute old jurist. A title is the means by which a man hath the just possession of his property, and there must be several requisites to form a title to land, which differs in this respect from a title to nobility, which is often conferred on those who have none of the natural requisites of nobility.

The lowest degree of title is naked possession, which is such a title as a man has who is bathing in the Serpentine ; but his naked possession may be put an end to by his being ordered out of the water when the term for bathing has expired.

The next step is the right of possession, which arises when a man has booked a place in the boxes of a theatre, but is kept out by some one who has the wrongful possession. Here the rightful possessor is disseised until the intruder, who has the actual possession, is seized and turned out by the box-keeper. The right of possession may however be lost by negligence, as when the actual possessor is allowed to sit without being disturbed by him who has the right of possession until after the end of the first act, beyond which period no places can be kept, although they may have been taken. There may, however, be a right of property without even a right of possession, which is equivalent to the law saying, "Such a thing ought to be yours, but nevertheless you shall not have it." This occurs when a disseisor—the genteel legal name for a man who takes what don't belong to him—happens to die; then the son of the disseisor has a right to the possession, and the owner has a right to the property—if he can get hold of it. This is called a mere right, which is in many cases a mere humbug. A complete title to lands therefore requires a right of possession joined with a right of property; but the crafty Fleta, perceiving that people did not always get their property even when they had this *jus duplicatum* or double right—the two affirmatives sometimes resulting in a practical negative—the knowing Fleta laid it down that possession was also necessary in order to constitute a good legal title. It follows, then, the law gives you a title to what is your own :—1st, if you have a right to it; and 2nd, if you have actually got hold of it, when if you can manage to keep it, you will have the full privilege of doing so. Such are the incidents of a title to real property in general, which means that the law generally surrounds all property with the little difficulties alluded to.

CHAPTER XI.

OF TITLE BY DESCENT.

Long has it been one of those beautiful maxims in which our law is luxuriantly rich, that "what one man loses another gains;" but, supposing a man to lose his senses, which he often does when he goes to law, we should be glad to know who gains them. At all events, it seems quite agreed that law is a matter of gain and loss, whereof the latter decidedly preponderates. The methods of acquiring on the one hand, and losing on the other, are reduced by Coke to two, namely, descent and purchase ; though, if we had been asked to say the two methods by which property may be legally lost, we should have at once defined them to be Common Law and Equity.

Descent is the title by which the estate of the ancestor is cast upon the heir; but if the estate of the ancestor consists of Wallsend coals, it may be very inconvenient for the heir to have them cast by descent upon him.

Descent depends upon consanguinity, which is either lineal or collateral, the former being the sort of relationship that exists between old Jones and young Jones, supposing young Jones to be the son of old Jones ; and all the little Joneses would be lineal descendants through as many generations as there happened to be of them. Collateral consanguinity is the sort of relationship existing between a couple of gooseberries, growing on different branches of the same root; as, if Smith (the root) has two sons (the branches) each of whom has a son (a gooseberry), there is a clear collateral consanguinity existing between the young Smiths, that is to say, the early gooseberries. Several alterations have been made in the law of descent, which did not come into operation until the 1st of January, 1834; and Mr. Stewart has discovered, with his usual acuteness, that persons who died before 1834, will not be expected to comply with the law that came into operation after that date, an indulgence which those who died previous to 1834 will no doubt fully appreciate.

By the old law, an estate could never ascend, or go up, but always descended ; and indeed even now the law rather delights in knocking property down, for an estate goes down to the son, before it goes up to the father, who only takes it if the owner has no son to come in for it. But by the same law, paternal ancestors take before maternal ancestors, or, in other words, the law never falls back upon the mother until the father is quite exhausted. A second rule is, that the law casts the estate on the male issue before the female, which we can only account for by presuming that the law, in its gallantry towards the ladies, is unwilling to cast upon them anything they may not be strong enough to sustain the burden of. A third rule is, that males shall inherit alone, and women altogether—the latter being a cunning device of the law to get property into its own hands; for by giving an estate to a lot of women, a quarrel amongst them is insured, and the estate getting into Chancery, the law has its pickings out of it. A fourth rule is, that the lineal descendants *ad infinitum* shall stand exactly in the same position as the ancestor would have done, had he been living; so that all the posterity of Baron Nathan will be expected to dance hornpipes among new-laid eggs, because that was frequently the position in which their ancestor placed himself. A fifth rule is, that if lineal descendants fail, collaterals shall take; or, to revert to the simile of the gooseberry bush, if the root has no branches the estate shall go to the gooseberries; "but this,' says Bracton, "is sending the estate to old Gooseberry;" a remark that could only have been made for the sake of the joke, for there is certainly very little legal learning comprised in it. A sixth rule is, that the brother shall shut out the uncle—a proceeding, by-the-bye, that appears to be very un-nephew-like. Thus, if John Stiles has a brother, the uncle is shut out until there is a failure of brothers; whereupon if there should be a glut of uncles, the oldest uncle—like the oldest hand at a game of whist—is allowed to count the family honours. The seventh and last rule is, that male stocks in collateral inheritances shall be preferred to female; so that if land descends from John Stiles, who marries Lucy Baker, the Stileses shall for ever shut out the Bakers, who, like the old woman and her pig, will not be able to pass over the Stiles, as long as one of them remains in existence.

In former editions it has been customary to give elaborate

directions for searching for the heir of John Stiles, and it has been usual to add a table of consanguinity, through the various ramifications of which that illustrious person—like a needle in a bottle of hay—may be looked for.

We shall not, however, take the reader through the awful labyrinth, pouncing at one moment upon Stiles's paternal grandfather's mother, now plunging down after his maternal grandmother, then suddenly emerging from the blood of the Bakers, to wade through the collateral consanguinity of the Whites, the Thorpes, and the Willises. No : if Stiles's heir is an object of interest to any particularly curious reader, let him exercise his own ingenuity in searching for Stiles's heir amid the amusing puzzle of bits of riband, squares, hexagons, octagons, demi-hexagons, demi-octagons, hands, lines and numbers, which in the *Table of Descents* given in the ordinary editions of Blackstone surround the name of

---

John Stiles,

THE PURCHASER.

CHAPTER XII.

OF TITLE BY PURCHASE; AND FIRST, BY ESCHEAT.

A PURCHASE in its vulgar sense is giving money for a thing and getting it ; but as the law contemplates the possibility of giving money for what one never gets, as well as getting what one never pays for, the word purchase in its legal signification is very large, for the law calls every man a purchaser who has got hold of property almost anyhow. The word purchase is derived from *perquisitio,* and there are five methods of purchasing, the first being escheat, to which, probably on account of its final syllable (cheat), the law gives the preference. Escheat is a sort of interruption to the course of descent, by which the original lord gets his estate back into his own hands, by an escheat or cheat—the former being merely the long and the latter the short of it. The law of escheat is founded on the supposition that the blood of the last tenant is extinct and gone, so that, as Coke says, "yᵉ tenant failing in bloodde yᵉ lordde walketh in and bones yᵉ propertie." There are three modes by which escheats may arise: 1st. Where the tenant dies without relations, not even a brother or an uncle, then "yᵉ lordde," says Coke, "doth supplie relations by coming in and cozening yᵉ tenant out of his possessions." A monster cannot take by the law of the land, though giants—who are monsters—have taken prodigiously at Greenwich Fair, and it does not seem that their caravans became escheated.

Illegitimate children are incapable of being heirs, the law calling them *nullius filii* (the children of nobody), which is in fact having a game of None-of-my-child, at the expense of the very ill-used individuals alluded to.

Aliens cannot be heirs; so that if Lord Lyndhurst's doctrine were the right one, no Irishman could inherit English property. The *dictum* has, however, been much doubted, and the noble Lord himself has contradicted it. An alien cannot even purchase land, until he is made a denizen, or translated from a foreigner into a British subject, when he may take whatever he can get hold of. Our dramatists afford specimens of the art of denization by translating French into English, though the subjects of their denization do not always take to the extent that might be desired.

Another cause of escheat was attainder, by which the property of all the felons in Newgate or elsewhere would escheat to the lord; so that the lord of the soil actually had an interest in all his grantees getting hanged as speedily as possible.

By a recent act all men who are hanged after the 1st of January, 1834, shall enjoy the privilege of leaving their property to their heirs, unless murder or petty treason have been the crimes they suffer for. This enjoyment is however a luxury that few—for want of property to leave—have been able to take advantage of.

Before concluding this chapter it is necessary to observe, that there is no escheat in the case of a corporation, and therefore the Lord Mayor and Aldermen of London may all go and be hanged, without the doctrine of escheat coming into operation. In such a case as this the donor would have the lands again by reversion, if the donor could be found, which perhaps might be the case if he were advertised for, something in the following fashion :—

"The corporation of London having been dissolved (by hanging, or, as the case may be), any gentleman who gave any lands is requested to apply at the Mansion House, London, when he will hear of something to his advantage."

In this case the little Greshams would claim the site of the Royal Exchange, and the heirs of Waithman would demand the strip of granite set up like an isolated ninepin at the top of Farringdon-street, in memory of their illustrious ancestor.

So much for escheats : but it never has been decided whether, if a dust contractor should be convicted of high treason in the middle of his contract, the rubbish would escheat to the owner of the soil, or whether the law would come down with the dust to the heir of the contractor.

CHAPTER XIII.

OF TITLE BY OCCUPANCY.

SINCE we began writing the present elaborate work, we have made it a rule never to sit down to a fresh chapter without reading through the whole of the Statutes at Large, to see what the law originally *was ;* and we then turn to the recent acts, to see what the law *is* on the subject we are about to treat of.

Title by occupancy appears to have been a sort of title that a man acquires to a place in the pit of a theatre, which he takes by the mere act of jumping into it. We had arrived at this conclusion when we lighted on the 29th Car. II., c. 3; and we gradually kept reading up to the 14th of Geo. II., when, having got as far as chapter 20, we discovered that the title of common occupancy is utterly extinct and abolished. We therefore considered it useless to put the match to that mine of learning with which we were ready to explode, and batter away the barriers to legal knowledge, for, as title by occupancy was semismashed by the 29th Car. II., and received the finishing blow from the 14th of Geo. II., it is not quite consistent with the plan of this work to say anything more upon the subject.

In accordance, however, with the quaint practice of the old law-writers, we feel justified in beginning to talk about something else when we find there is nothing to be said about the matter which nominally forms the subject of our chapter. We therefore rush precipitately from title by occupancy to the consideration of islands rising in the middle of seas and rivers. These belong to the king, if they start up suddenly, like ghosts through stage traps; but if they collect together by slow and imperceptible degrees, like the building of the Nelson column, they go to the owner of the land adjoining. Land left dry in the middle of the sea sometimes belongs to the first occupant—the Goodwin Sands to wit—but when the tide comes up, the occupant is glad to release his claim by means of a regular conveyance.

It is a maxim, that whatever hath no owner is vested by law in the sovereign; but this is hardly correct, for an infant left deserted, without an owner, on the step of a door, with a flannel waistcoat on, is vested in the flannel, without being vested in the sovereign.

CHAPTER XIV.

TITLE by Prescription has been held by some to be the title which a chemist has to charge for medicine, because he has generally the prescription to show for it. Prescription, however, is a title of which no one can remember the origin—a doctrine which was very agreeable to those pretenders to the English throne who found it convenient not to remember that any one else had a better claim to it, and they carried their shortness of memory so far, as very frequently to forget themselves.

The inconvenience of having title by prescription dependent on such a very vague business as a matter of memory, induced the legislature to pass the 2nd and 3rd Will. IV., c. 71, which materially shortens the time of prescription. A right of common cannot be defeated by showing the commencement of it, after thirty years ; so that a donkey, who has enjoyed the luxury of a rollic on the village green during the period alluded to, cannot afterwards be ousted by a reference to the period at which he was first invested with the Order of the Thistle. After sixty years—and it has been quaintly said by all the judges sitting in Banco, that donkeys never die—the animal's right becomes absolute, unless he has, from time to time, had the consent of the owners. Forty years will give a right of way ; so that if a man can contrive to commit a trespass uninterruptedly for forty years without interference, he may, at the end of that time, turn round and snap his fingers at the heir or the tenant, whether in tail or not in tail, and all who may come after him.

The use of light is indefeasible, if used for twenty years,

K

provided the window tax is punctually paid; and therefore, if I knock out a window in order to pry into my neighbour's premises, my neighbour is justified in running up a brick wall slap before it, unless he tacitly submits to my impertinence for twenty years, after which I might batter down his brick wall, if he attempted to build one.

It now becomes a question what may be prescribed for; and, though the jurists have laid it down that incorporeal things, such as rights of way or common, only can be prescribed for, the chemists have laid it down that corporeal matters, such as the gout, a cold, or even chilblains, may be the subjects of a prescription. A prescription, before the recent act, could only be claimed by him that had the fee, and he who has the fee—being the physician—generally prescribes, so that the 2nd and 3rd Will. IV. made very little difference in this respect. The lord of a manor cannot tax strangers by a prescription; probably because the dose would be rather too strong for them.

There are one or two other incidents attending a title by prescription, which it is not necessary to name; for property is too well looked after, in these days, to admit of its being claimed by others in consequence of those to whom it of right belongs forgetting to look after it. Prescription is, in fact, letting in number two, through the original owner neglecting to look after number one; but this is a piece of *laches* that very rarely happens.

CHAPTER XV.

OF TITLE BY FORFEITURE.

EVERY one is aware that amid the numerous games played by the law is the game of forfeits, of which it seems there are eight varieties; and if variety is charming in the singular number, the law of forfeiture, with no less than eight varieties, ought to be a most fascinating topic.

Property may be forfeited by crimes and misdemeanors: such as treason and felony, drawing a weapon on a judge, or striking any one in a court of justice. It seems, therefore, that whenever the court is over-crowded, and people on the back benches begin to push each other about for the purpose of getting a place, and come to blows—however mild—they are all liable to forfeit all their property, if they happen to have any. Drawing a weapon on a judge is happily obsolete; but we have seen a disappointed suitor shake his umbrella at a puisne behind the puisne's back, while attending a summons at chambers, which is in some sort drawing a weapon on a judge, though the "books" are silent on the subject. Lands may be forfeited by alienation, or conveying them to another contrary to law, such as alienation in mortmain, or dead hand, the term being applied chiefly to lands given to monks, who, as may have been already observed, were dead hands at a bargain. The motto of a corporation being "Never say die," the lands could not be transferred to a corporation without a license. The clergy, however, soon set to work, and concocted the beautiful system of fines and recoveries, which was one of the most delicious bits of legal cobwebbery that was ever spun by monkish mummery. Several of our early legal blue-bottles were taken by these webs; and old Coke delighted to tangle himself and others in the curious yarn, but the Turk's head of Law Reform has brushed away the whole of it.

Property may be forfeited by lapse, which signifies a slip; and "thus," says Selden, "the proverb of 'Many a slip 'twixt the cup and the lip,' is verified." How Selden makes out any connection between the property and the cup, or the tenant and the lip, we don't exactly see; but we should be sorry to disturb the authority of any of those quaint dogmata that the old jurists so often revelled in.

Another mode of forfeiture is simony, or presenting any one to a benefice for money; a sort of thing that is done every day by certain loop-holes which the law, notwithstand-

ing its pious horror of such transactions, leaves to be taken
advantage of.   There have been some curious decisions as to
whether it is simony to bargain for a parson's living, when
the parson himself is dying ; and it has been held to be
simony to treat with a rector who is ill, though it seems that
if the incumbent has only a toothache there would be no
simony in offering him "terms" for the next presentation to
his benefice.

Forfeiture by breach of condition it would be a forfeiture
of our own trouble and the reader's time to dwell upon, so
we jump at once to forfeiture by waste, which seems to be
founded on the homely saying that "You can't eat your
pudding and have it ;" for if you pull your own house about
your ears, you cannot very well continue to enjoy it.   Tearing down your landlord's wainscot and pulling up his floors
is waste in the eye of the law, but it does not seem that
walking in his cockloft and tumbling through the laths and
plaster is such a waste as would amount to forfeiture.

It is also waste to convert one kind of ground into another,
such as meadow-land into arable.   And it seems that, by
strict right, a paved yard cannot have the stones torn up and
mignonette planted in place of them.   It is otherwise with
the gardens in the centre of squares, which may be meadow
to-day and arable to-morrow, because, as nothing will grow,
there is in fact no difference.

Opening land to search for a mine is waste in general, and
waste of time in particular ; but if there was a mine commenced, the tenant may dig away with impunity.   There is,
however, an old case in the books, of a plug-hole being on
the estate of A, when B, the tenant for years, claimed the
right of opening a mine by *virtue* of the plug-hole.   The
point was reserved for all the judges ; and Holt, Chief Justice, said, " Pooh, pooh ! the plug-hole is not large enough
to let the tenant in."   Another of the judges followed with
the observation, that " he thought at first there was something in the plug-hole, and he had probed it very patiently,

but there was no soundness at the bottom. It seemed at first to savour of something, but if the courts permitted tenants to wedge themselves into the fee through such apertures as these, there must be an end to everything." It went off on this point; and the case has never been opened since for argument.

It is waste on the part of a tenant if he cuts his landlord's timber; but if the tenant cuts his own stick, it is sometimes waste on the part of the landlord to go after him.

Another species of forfeiture is a breach of the customs of a copyhold; as, where the rent is a peppercorn, the tenant must seek out the landlord and give him pepper to the amount specified. The learned and facetious Bracton remarks, that "Where the rent is pepper it is easily muster'd," a joke almost as venerable as the subject by which it is elicited.

The last method of forfeiture is by becoming a bankrupt, when everything goes to the assignee, to enable him to declare dividends, sometimes to the tune of twopence a pound, like black-heart cherries. A bankrupt seised in tail has it instantly cut off, or at least so much of the tail as belongs to him.

CHAPTER XVI.

OF TITLE BY ALIENATION.

ALIENATION is the transfer of property from one to another, a process in which the law delights; "For it is hard," says Coke, "if the lawyers do not get a chance of catching the oyster while it is being passed away from one shell to the other."

Traitors and felons cannot convey their lands; and if it is felony to imitate the signature of A. ROWLAND AND SON, it would seem that the dealers in spurious Macassar cannot aliene their property. A felon may, however, purchase anything he pleases, because *ceo qu'il achctcra la couronne grabbera* (that which he shall purchase the crown will grab, or lay its hands upon).

Infants and idiots may enter into agreements, which are not binding unless confirmed when the infancy or idiocy has ceased ; but it has been said that a *non compos* cannot plead his own non-composity, because if he could, the knave might often play the fool, and write himself down an ass for the sake of getting rid of a bad bargain.

A married woman may purchase without her husband's consent ; but after his death she may decline the bargain ; so that Mrs. Tomkins might buy a house, and having lived in it till the decease of Tomkins, she might then " cry off," and insist on having her money back again.   This is on the principle of the boy, who, having heard an invitation " to taste 'em and try 'em before you buy 'em," ate half a hundred walnuts and expressed himself so dissatisfied with the fruit that he declined purchasing.

A married woman may join her husband in selling her property, but she must undergo a *tête-à-tête* with a judge or a master in chancery, who are empowered to pump her, with a view to ascertaining whether she sells of her own accord, or has been bamboozled or bullied into doing so.   A married woman who has property settled to her separate use, may play at ducks-and-drakes with it if she pleases, and the law, instead of interfering, rather likes the fun of it.

An alien may purchase anything, but can hold nothing, except perhaps his tongue ; for it is useless on his part to say a word against the claim of the sovereign, who may bone on the instant whatever may have been bought by the alien.

Having considered who may get rid of his property, we are next to discuss how it may be done, and a thousand modes instantly suggest themselves.   The law, however, reduces those modes to four—namely, by deed, by record, by special custom, and by devise, which will form the subject of the four remaining chapters.

CHAPTER XVII.

OF ALIENATION BY DEED.

HAVING to plunge into the depths of this subject, we will first take breath on the margin to consider what we are about, and having asked ourselves the question, what is a deed? we shall proceed in our own peculiar way to answer it.

A deed is said by Coke to be a writing sealed and delivered by the parties, but a letter sealed by the postman and delivered by himself is not a deed—and we defy Coke to make it one. It is called in Latin *factum*, meaning something done, but we are of opinion that the word *factum* in law-proceedings should have a wider sense, and imply *somebody* done as well as something. There is no doubt that Shakspere, when he made the witch in *Macbeth* exclaim, " I 'll do, I 'll do, I 'll do," had some legal craftsman in his eye, and the subsequent expression "a deed without a name" proves that he intended an enormous do and a deed to be synonymous. An indenture is a deed cut at the top to resemble the teeth of a saw, which is emblematical of sharp work according to some, but others attribute it to the two parts of a deed having been cut from the same parchment. A deed made by one party is called a deed poll, from its being polled or closely shaven, " and this," says Fleta, " is typical of the client, who is generally pretty closely shaven."

The requisites of a deed are :—1st, persons to contract, and a thing to be contracted for; there must be something to give, somebody to give it, and somebody to take, but if there were any difficulty about the latter, there is the lawyer at hand who is ready to take anything.

2nd. There must be a consideration—but it is to be feared many deeds are executed without any consideration at all—

and there is a case in the American books of a man without
consideration having, on leaving his chambers, hung his hat
on the candle and put the extinguisher on his head ; a deed
which, if he had considered for a moment, he would not have
been a party to.

3rd. A deed must be on paper or parchment, for it has been
decided to be no deed if it be written on stone, board, linen,
or leather. So that an indenture cannot be made with the
sole of a man's foot, though it has been done on the sands at
Ramsgate. Such an indenture is not however binding, and
it is liable to be quashed or squashed, when Neptune enters
upon his usual roll, which he does about breakfast time. A
deed is not good on linen, but we have seen a cotton conveyance, when property, such as a pound of cherries, has been
passed from one boy to another in a pocket-handkerchief.

4th. A deed must consist of the usual parts—the premises,
which have nothing to do with any premises in the bricks-
and-mortar meaning of the word, but simply include the
names of the parties and other preliminary matter,—the
habendum and *tenendum*, or having and holding, which the law
being of a grabbing disposition is extremely jealous of. The
reddendum, which means the rent and is something to be
rendered to the granter, from an immense yearly sum downwards to a peppercorn. The condition, which provides for
forfeiture in case of the rent not being forthcoming. The
covenants or clauses of agreement, some of which run with
the land, which has nothing to do with the case of a tenant
running with the goods ; and the conclusion, which mentions
the execution and date of the document—though a wrong
date does not signify, and a deed dated the 30th of February,
showing it had been executed in no time, has been held valid
provided there is proof of its having been actually delivered.

Reading is requisite to a deed, but as hearing it read
generally has the effect of confusing the parties and preventing them from knowing what they are about, the ceremony of
reading is seldom insisted on. A deed must be signed and

sealed, but a deficiency of penmanship and sealing-wax may be got over by a cross and a wafer, which are sufficient for legal purposes. Delivery is also an essential to a deed, but it is not a delivery in the sense of the London Parcels Company that is here alluded to.

Every deed must be witnessed, which is the greatest safeguard the subject enjoys ; for it is horrible to contemplate what deeds the law might do if not controlled by the presence of witnesses.

We must now explain the several species of deeds, a subject well worthy the poetic muse, which has been successfully wooed by Mr. John Crisp, who, in the *Conveyancer's Guide*, has shed a halo of imaginative light over the sombre darkness of Feoffment and its dreary fellows.

1st. Comes feoffment, which is derived from *infeudare*, to give a feud, and a feud meaning a row, it must be inferred that a feoffment, being the conveyance of a fee, is a thing that it is worth one's while to quarrel and fight about. 2nd. We come to gifts : but gifts very seldom come to us, for they are almost obsolete ; and gift being conveyance number two, we are not surprised that regard to number one has almost superseded it. In the 3rd place are grants, which speak for themselves, and we therefore plunge at once into the 4th mode of conveyance, which is a lease, a style of deed that every one must be familiar with. Exchange and partition, which are the fifth and sixth kinds of conveyance, are also self-evident in their meaning, and we are, therefore, surprised at their forming a part of our fine old inexplicable legal system.

Releases, confirmations, surrenders, and assignments, afford various opportunities for getting rid of property ; but the technicalities attendant on describing them would be too abstruse for the comprehension of the purely elementary student whom these learned pages are designed to edify. Suffice it to say, that a release has nothing to do with a rescue, though it prevents property from being locked up by showing you how to get rid of it. The other modes may easily be learned by those who have any estate of which they are desirous of being legally disencumbered.

A Covenant to stand seised is an agreement to hold property for the use of another, which must be rather a tantalising position. It is sometimes called an innocent conveyance, and perhaps a man may be said to enter into a covenant to stand seised, if he gets into a row and allows the policeman to walk him off quietly to the station-house.

These are the principal modes of conveyance, by which property may be carried off, at a rate surprising to those who have heard only of the law's delays, though the law, when anything valuable is to be disposed of, displays remarkable quickness.

CHAPTER XVIII.

OF ALIENATION BY MATTER OF RECORD.

ANCIENTLY this subject embraced four divisions, two of which, fines and recoveries, having been recently abolished, we are happily saved from the penalty of having to describe a fine, and being made quite ill by explaining the mysteries of a recovery. Two branches of the subject still, however, remain, namely, Private Acts of Parliament, and Royal Grants, which, after stropping the penknife of acuteness on the hone of industry, and nibbing the pen of perseverance, we proceed to plunge into.

Private Acts of Parliament are frequently used to disentangle an estate from the confusion into which the law has contrived to get it by surrounding it with contingent remainders—springing uses—which are generally useless —resulting trusts—it is doubtful if a turnpike-gate is a trust of this description—and other artificial contrivances.

To attempt to put an end to confusion by an Act of Parliament, seems to savour of rendering the said confusion worse confounded. Such acts are very cautiously granted, and are declared to be void if contrary to law and reason : though this is a very nice point, for if it is contrary to law, it may be perfectly conformable to reason ; and if consistent with reason, the chances are that law has been lost sight of.

Royal grants, whether of lands or honours, are conferred by *literæ patentes.*

Grants or letters-patent must always begin with a bill. "Ay," says Spelman, "and end with a bill too ; for, marry come up ! there is no getting letters-patent without paying a pretty long bill for them." The sovereign signs them at the top with his own hand. "Whyche," says Coke, who must claim the merit of having invented the now venerable joke, "*whyche sygne* is a *sine quâ non* in alle letterres patente." Coke, however, with all his waggery was wrong, for the sovereign is not compelled to sign every new patent for life pills, infallible mixtures for the hair, and other articles which are continually being made the subject of royal letters-patent. Royal grants are always to be construed most beneficially for the sovereign and against the party ; while a grant from a subject is construed on exactly the opposite principle. Thus, if a sovereign grants the trees on certain land without the right of coming to take them, the subject can have no other enjoyment of them but such as he can derive from looking at them at a distance. If, however, a subject should grant the sovereign a pint of new milk, it seems that the cow would follow as a matter of course, because there can be no new milk without a cow ; and *à fortiori*, the cow must be fed—so that it is a nice point whether the land in which the cow was turned out would not run with the milk, instead of the milk running with the land, as it certainly would do if the land were granted to the sovereign.

If the sovereign grants anything by mistake, he has the subject of the grant back again ; so that a royal exclamation of " Hallo ! what have I been about ?   I didn't mean to do that," will revoke the strongest grant in existence.   If the property granted is worth more than the king or queen thought it was, he or she may take it back again.   And, in fact, under almost any circumstances, a thing given by a sovereign to a subject is subject to be made the subject of recapture.

Fines have been happily discontinued since the 31st of December, 1833, which, according to a pun in pencil on the 989th page of the fifteenth volume of Petersdorff's Abridgment, is "the *finest* thing that could have happened for the simplicity of the legal system."   The quaint old *jeu* on the *mot* fines is neatly pointed out by a strong italicising of the word *finest*.

Though fines and recoveries were abolished by the 3rd and 4th of William IV., c. 74, the benefit of them was preserved ; but as this benefit chiefly benefited the lawyers, the advantage does not appear particularly obvious.   Thus a tenant in tail may cut off his own tail by means of a pair of scissors, with which the law has provided him, in the shape of the protector of the settlement.   If there is any estate in lands prior to the estate tail, the owner of the prior estate shall be the protector of the settlement.   Where the protector of a settlement is an idiot, the Lord Chancellor, as standing representative of all idiots, comes in to supply his place ; and if a traitor or felon is the protector, the Court of Chancery generally undertakes the arduous character.

CHAPTER XIX.

OF ALIENATION BY SPECIAL CUSTOM.

ASSURANCES by special custom are confined to copyholders and their tenants, whom the law regards as very special customers. A copyholder is strictly speaking, a villain, and those holding under him are *à fortiori*, more villanous ; for copyholds all have their origin in pure villenage. A surrender is an assurance by special custom; and it is managed by A, the copyholder or villain, coming to B, the landlord or his steward, and giving up a rod or a glove to B, who gives it to C, the copyholder elect or villain that is to be, and who swears to perform all the conditions to which A, the ex-villain, was subjected. The last public case of this kind was when that honest fellow, but pure villain, the late square-keeper of Golden-square, resigned the cane to the present worthy villain, who has ever since wielded it. He swore fealty to the trustees, and took an oath of extermination to little boys, at the foot of the statue—which was all according to the custom of the manor.

When an estate is once surrendered, the lord of the fee must admit the surrenderee, and writing up the words " No admittance" will not cut off the right of the surrenderee, who may insist on being let in ; and he may continue knocking and ringing, or kicking up a row till he is let in, for the law will assist him.

The same rule applies to heirs, married women, infants, and lunatics, who must all be admitted on an estate being surrendered to them ; but an infant must be let in through his guardian, as infants often are, and a married woman must be let in through her attorney, as occasionally happens ; a lunatic must have a committee to represent him, but it does

not seem that the committee need have a chairman, or any of
the usual requisites. In lunatics' committees, one is a *quorum*,
but there is always an appeal to the Lord Chancellor, who is,
by virtue of his office, the representative of all monied idiots.

CHAPTER XX.

OF ALIENATION BY DEVISE.

HAVING run through nearly every species of alienation, we
now come to mental alienation, which is often the accom-
paniment of law, or, at least, the characteristic of those who
rush blindly into it.

Alienation by devise is leaving property by will, which
could not formerly be done ; for, in feudal times, it was not
permitted to a man to have a will of his own—at least as
regarded his real property. By statutes of Henry the Eighth
and of Charles the Second—who was commonly called the
Merry Monarch, because, as COKE says, "he was a sadde
dogge,"—real property was made devisable.

The law of wills was, however, altered by the 1st Victoria
cap. 26, which facilitated the transfer of property, personal,
real, and perhaps sham ; for the law loves to encourage the
transmission of property from hand to hand, because, as valuables are never moved without risk of breakage, so, in the
transfer of property, bits may fall to the lawyers.

A will to pass real or any other kind of property need now
be signed only by the testator and two witnesses, who need
not be credible, for the law will recognise a very bad man as
a very good witness.

We shall conclude this Chapter with a few rules for interpreting wills, which have been laid down by the judges, and
picked up by those who heard them.

1st. Wills will be construed to mean what they say, unless

they do not say what they mean, and then the lawyers will go to work to render confusion worse confounded.

2nd. When the intention is clear, the meaning of the words will be disregarded ; and as the intention can only be gained from the words, the lawyers again rush in to complicate the matter. False English and bad Latin will not set aside a will : so that if a man devises his " worsest coat," the legatee will take the oldest coat of the testator ; or if the will specifies a *iocularis bona cœna* to a party of six, it seems that a jolly good supper would pass by these words to the individuals specified.

3rd. Every part of a will must be supposed to mean some-thing, and the law thus tries to put some meaning upon every word,—a process which often ends in making it all amount to nothing.

4th. A will must be construed as unfavourably as possible to the party making it ; so that if he leaves a peg-top to A, a piece of whip-cord to spin it with would pass by such a devise, if such a piece of whip-cord should be in existence.

5th. If the words have two senses,—forming, in fact, a pun, the sense most agreeable to the law will be acted upon ; because it will no doubt be the most disagreeable to every one who has anything to do with the matter.

6th. When two clauses are repugnant to each other, the last clause is to stand ; but the clauses leaving property to one, and being, therefore, repugnant to those who expected the property, are not repugnant clauses in the sense alluded to.

7th. A will is not void for want of the usual legal phrases ; and it is not therefore necessary for a testator to read up all the old learning on the subject of " to wit," " whereas," " hereinafter," and the other terms which constitute the peculiar elegance of legal literature.

PART III.—PRIVATE WRONGS.

CHAPTER I.

OF THE REDRESS OF PRIVATE WRONGS BY THE MERE ACT OF THE PARTIES.

WRONGS are divisible into two sorts, private and public wrongs; but the law takes no cognisance of wrong stockings or the wrong boy, who often gets caught when juvenile mischief has been perpetrated.

Private wrongs are generally called civil injuries, though it is certainly not a very civil injury to give a man a horse-whipping; but we shall learn more of the nature of private wrongs as we proceed with this part, which will be devoted to their discussion.

Private wrongs are generally to be redressed by suit or action in the courts of law; but, as an action may not always suit, it is sometimes allowable for a party to obtain redress by his own act, and thus, in defence of one's self, it is lawful to suit the action to the word, and not only to threaten to knock a man down, but to do it also, if it be necessary for self-protection. A man may also lay about him right and left, in defence of some of those who are near and dear to him, such as his wife, his child, and servant; the last being considered "dear," no doubt on account of the wages and the keep which the master has to provide him with. Care must, however, be observed to prevent the danger of over-doing it; for the law is jealous of a row, and no more force must be used than is required for the purpose of defence ; so that if your child gets a box on the ears, you must not pummel the aggressor too severely. Nor must you turn round and soundly thrash an individual who has trod on your heel, though it may have been done wantonly. Recaption, or taking back what has been taken from you, is sometimes allowable, because it is a remedy at once ; though if you are a poet, and some of your finest ideas are taken from you, it is but a poor remedy to take them back again. You must not, however, recapture your own property, if doing so involves a breach of the peace ; so that the party who has got it need only commence creating a disturbance, in order to defeat your object.

Next to re-capture is re-entry, or taking possession of a place that you are entitled to. This may occur when you have got a place in a railway carriage, which has been unjustly filled by somebody else; but if he happens to get up, you may pop down into it.

A fourth species of remedy by your own act is the abatement of a nuisance ; such as knocking down a gate in a public thoroughfare, and kicking over an apple-stall wantonly placed in the middle of the pavement.

A fifth case of self-redress is the right of impounding donkeys, pigs, and horses, doing damage on your own ground. And if a mad bull trespasses on to your melon-frame, you may take the bull by the horns, if you feel disposed, and distrain him. Or if a cart-horse is floundering about your partridge preserves, you may seize him *damage feasant.*

This power of distraining is also applied to goods, where rent is due, and it is then called a distress, probably, from the result which often follows from it. In treating of what are the articles that may be distrained upon, we may lay it down as a general rule, that the broker and his man may seize almost everything, except a dog, which may, on the contrary, sometimes seize the broker. Animals *feræ naturæ* (of a wild nature) cannot be distrained upon ; so that a

L

broker and his man would come off very poorly in the Surrey
Zoological Gardens, or Wombwell's caravans, where they
might get rent in a way very different from that in which
they had expected it. A bullock walking through a hedge
into a stranger's field, may find himself in custody for the
rent ; and the animal has nothing to do but toss up with the
sheriff's officer, if he is desirous of settling the matter without remaining a prisoner. Tools used in trade cannot be
distrained, and a shoemaker may hold out to the last ; a
carpenter need not consent to be chiselled out of his chisel ;
and a tailor may defy his landlord to take his measures.
Perishable articles, such as milk, may not be seized for rent ;
and it would seem that the plays of a modern dramatist,
being often dreadfully perishable, ought not to be distrained
upon. Things pertaining to the freehold cannot be seized ;
so that your domestic hearth is safe ; for no one can tear up
the hearth-stone and carry off the fire-place or mantel-piece.

Distresses must be made in the day-time, except as to
errant beasts, wandering on to other people's premises. A
landlord may now distrain upon his tenants' goods, wherever
he can find them within thirty days ; and this is, perhaps,
the origin of the term " shooting the moon," or going beyond
the month ; for, a moon being thirty days, the tenant may be
said to have shot it, if he keeps his goods during that time
out of the grasp of his landlord. The law does not allow an
unreasonable distress, such as seizing half-a-dozen handsome
chairs for an arrear of threepence   He must take as a dis-
traint what is nearest in value to the sum due ; and the flat-
iron, in such a case, would be the article he ought to lay his
hands upon. If no rent is due, the tenant may rescue his
goods or animals on the road, provided they are not yet
impounded ; and it seems that if a table is pulled to pieces,
by the landlord and tenant tugging away at it in the middle
of the road, the landlord, if no rent is due, will be liable.

Cattle distrained must be taken to the pound and provided
with food at the expense of the party seizing them ; so that

If they eat very heartily they will cost a great deal, and thus realise the old saying of "penny wise and pound foolish." If a horse eats his own head off, there is a remedy against the debtor, who may be made to pay the expense the creditor has been put to. Replevin is taking the animals or goods back, on giving security for the debt due, or the damage done; but in case of rent, if this is not effected, or the debt paid, within five days, the animals and goods may be put up and knocked down by public auction, the landlord being liable to the owner for the overplus.

While we are on the subject of seizing we may as well add, that heriots, wrecks, waifs, and estrays, described in the first part of this volume, may be seized when and where the party entitled can get hold of them. There are two other methods of remedy for private injuries by the parties themselves; and these are accord and arbitration. Accord is a sort of arrangement, a kind of making it up after falling out; as, if A gives B a black eye, he may apply a salve in the shape of money, if A will allow himself to be salved out in that manner.

Arbitration is a novel method of taking up the time of a barrister without paying him; as frequently happens when a case is submitted to his arbitration, and he makes his award, which is never called for by either party, who get tired of litigation. Beer is sometimes sent for by witnesses in an adjoining room, and the barrister's chambers are converted into a bear-garden, while he is unable to stir from his judicial position with a view to checking the nuisance. When arbitration is had recourse to as a *bonâ fide* method of settling disputes, it is a very wholesome and judicious measure, having all the force of law, with the advantages to be derived from equity.

CHAPTER II.

OF REDRESS BY THE MERE OPERATION OF LAW.

LOOKING for redress by the mere operation of law is almost as idle as waiting for a passage to America in a balloon or an aerial ship, and the analogy is partially carried out by the fact, that there are two ways in which redress by the mere operation of law may possibly be given. These two ways are called retainer and remitter, in the first of which instances a creditor, who is made the executor of a deceased debtor, may pay himself before he pays any one else, by retaining the amount of the debt due to him : and, in fact, giving himself an undue preference over the other creditors. In this case, the mere operation of law is a mere swindle ; but as law is the perfection of reason, the jurists, by a little sophistry about an executor not being able to sue himself, make the arrangement out to be a very reasonable and proper one. The executor, however, cannot retain the amount of his own debt in preference to one of higher degree. As, for example, if another creditor, a publican, had got an execution out against the deceased for beer, while the executor, a milkman, had got no other security for his debt but the wooden tally on which the milk score has been chalked, then the publican comes in, and the executor must —to speak figuratively—"walk his chalks " till another opportunity.

Remitter is where a man who is out of possession of property to which he has a right gets into it again by a wrong title, and, on the principle that " whatever is is right," he is said to have come properly in for it, and to be remitted or sent back by operation of law to his right position. It is, in fact, the case of an individual who, finding he cannot get into his house by the door, pops in through the window, when the law looks at him simply as the head of the establishment, without asking how he got into it.

CHAPTER III.

OF COURTS IN GENERAL.

WE now come to the redress of injuries by suits in courts wherein the law and the parties must co-operate; for the parties are the skittles and the law is the ball, while the lawyer, who sets the ball in motion, may be said to play the game, and have all the fun of it.

A court is defined to be a place in which justice is judicially administered, but it does not appear that justice was ever judicially administered in Pump Court, though a pickpocket was once pumped upon in that court; and, so far, justice was done, though not judicially. The Sovereign is supposed to be always present in every court, but sovereignty would indeed be a burden if it involved an actual attendance at the Court of Requests, the Central Criminal, and a few others we could mention. The presence of the Sovereign is, therefore, only ideal, and we must imagine that royalty is in attendance behind the clock in the Queen's Bench, at the back of the royal arms in the Common Pleas, or under the Chief Baron's easy chair in the Exchequer.

Courts are either of record or not of record—a distinction about as good as that of the philosopher who divided man into those who have been hanged and those who have not been hanged. A court of record is where all the proceedings are recorded on what is called a roll; but this roll is made of parchment, and was, perhaps, originally called a roll because it was bread to those who lived by entering it up and taking care of it.

In every court there must be three parties. The *actor,*

or plaintiff—literally, the doer—for in all lawsuits there is generally the doer and the done—the *reus*, or defendant, though *reus* literally means guilty, and the question, " How will you pay it ?" addressed to every defendant at the Court of Requests before the case has been heard, proves that defendant and guilty are often looked upon as synonymous words ; and the *judex*, or judicial power, comprising those who give judgment ; some of whom by-the-bye give it without possessing it.

There are also attornies and barristers, whom we shall now proceed to give a bird's-eye view of. Every man may appear by his attorney, except an idiot, who must appear in person, for the law regards an idiot as one who is naturally qualified to enter personally into a lawsuit. What an attorney is, everybody who has got an attorney will no doubt be aware, but those who are ignorant on the point may feel assured that ignorance is unquestionably bliss, at least in this instance. We, however, are far from intending to stigmatise all attornies as bad—and the race of roguish lawyers would soon be extinct if roguish clients did not raise a demand for them. No man need have a knave for his attorney unless he chooses ; and, when he goes by preference to a roguish lawyer, it must be presumed that he has his reasons for not trusting his affairs to an honest one.

Advocates or counsel are divided into barristers and sergeants, the former of whom are in the old books called apprentices, from *apprendre*, to learn, because they are not compelled to learn anything. A barrister must eat six-and-thirty dinners in one of the inns of court, and then he must swear in Latin that he will not try and put the Pope on the English throne, or kill a foreign prince in a public thoroughfare, when he will be called to the bar by the benchers. The degree of sergeant is very ancient, and some think that Iago was a sergeant, because he is introduced by the Moor as his " ancient." We know that Cassio was the lieutenant, and, as Iago was his inferior, it is pretty certain that the "ancient" was nothing more than a "sergeant;" for, says Fortescue, "yᵉ sergeantes are yᵉ most anciente of all yᵉ legal officers." The queen's counsel are selected from these degrees, but a sergeant is made by purchasing what is called the coif—a barrister's wig with a bit cut out of the middle, and a patch of black silk sewn over the hole in the centre. This coif costs about a thousand pounds, so that whoever sells them must make a capital thing of it. The barristers in our day have been compared to the Roman orators, whose clients were their dependants; but a counsel would find it very inconvenient to have a parcel of plaintiffs and defendants dangling at his heels wherever he went, and, therefore, the Roman practice has become somewhat obsolete at Westminster. Counsel, however, keep up the old superstition of taking no fees, except a *quiddam honorarium*, but they take pretty good care to have the *quiddam* safe in their pockets before they undertake the cause of a client. Counsel guilty of practising deceit are punishable by a sentence of perpetual silence in the courts; but there are some counsel who are doomed to perpetual silence by their utter brieflessness. These unfortunate individuals, so far from practising deceit, are utterly precluded from practice of any kind.

CHAPTER IV.

OF THE PUBLIC COURTS OF COMMON LAW AND EQUITY.

THE policy of Alfred was to bring the law home to every man's door, but the policy of every man ought to be to keep his door shut, and on no account let the law in if he can help it. For this purpose there was a court in every manor in the kingdom, and justice was of course administered in all kinds of manors. These petty tribunals or legal free-and-easies have mostly fallen into decay: and in accordance with

the motto *de mortuis nil nisi bonum,* we refrain from saying
anything regarding them.

1. The lowest court in England, and at the same time the
quietest, is the court of *pie poudre,* or *curia pedis pulverati,*
so called, according to Sir Edward Coke, "because justice is
there done as speedily as dust can fall from the foot;" but in
our opinion because it was necessary to come down with the
dust in this court as well as in every other. It is a court of
record that may be held in a fair or market, of which the
steward of the owner of the market is the judge, and it has
jurisdiction over commercial injuries done in that very fair,
such as withholding a pie which might have been fairly won
by a toss with the pieman, or unduly abridging a ride in a
roundabout. There is an appeal by writ of error to the
courts at Westminster; so that an individual, having paid
a penny to see the learned pig, is dissatisfied with the amount
of erudition displayed by the porker, and gets a remedy in
the court of *pie poudre,* it is then settled that the pig or
his master may come down and ask for a writ of error.

2. The Court Baron, which is incidental to every manor,
was a court composed of the tenants who were the *pares* or
peers, or equals of each other, and as judges they were no
doubt much of a muchness. These courts have jurisdiction
over claims under forty shillings, but the proceedings may be
removed into the superior courts by what is called a *pone,*
probably because the papers were generally sent up to town
on the backs of *ponies* before waggons were in use, mail
coaches were known, or railroads were thought about.

3. A Hundred Court is only a larger Court Baron, originally instituted to apply to a hundred different villages;
but these hundreds soon came to exceed the number, like a
hundred of walnuts, which are one hundred and eight, or a
hundred weight, which is one hundred and twelve pounds—
so that the term hundred always had a somewhat arbitrary
meaning attached to it. These courts have also fallen into
disuse, on account of the causes being liable to removal, or in

other words, to being walked off by a writ of error to Westminster.

4. The County Court is under the jurisdiction of the sheriff, who used to sit in great dignity and splendour, with the bishop on one side of him and the alderman or earl on the other. The dignity, however, was much diminished when the earl, who got very tired of the business, neglected to attend, and the bishop, who rather liked it, was prohibited from doing so.

5. The Insolvent Debtors' Court consists of a chief and three other commissioners, who hold their offices during good behaviour; so that, it is presumed, if they were to cut jokes while upon the bench, or otherwise misconduct themselves, they would be dismissed immediately. They make circuits to release those debtors who can't get round, and it is their province, at stated times, to go into the provinces.

6. The Court of Bankruptcy consists of a number of town and country commissioners, whose tenure of office is said to depend on their good behaviour, though we have heard of some odd freaks, which have not been followed by a loss of their situations on the part of some of them.

7. We next come to the Court of Common Pleas, which though now fixed, used formerly to follow the person of the Sovereign; so that a barrister wishing to move the court, was compelled to move after it. Common Pleas include all civil actions between subject and subject, and the court has been styled by Sir Edward Coke, the lock and key of the common law; the idea of a lock being suggested, perhaps, by the fact of its affording very pretty pickings.

8. The Court of King's or Queen's Bench, is so called, because the King used to sit there on a bench placed expressly for him; but he was always a mere dummy, and was never allowed to dispose of a cause, or even consent to the taking of a rule to compute, except through the mouth of his judges. This court, though it never moves, is movable, and might follow the Sovereign to York or Exeter; but *semble* that it

cannot be sent to Jericho, unless the King goes there first, when he might insist on its coming after him.   This court takes a very high hand over inferior jurisdictions, and among other things can command magistrates and others to do what Nelson expected every man to do at the battle of Trafalgar.

9. The Court of Exchequer was intended to recover the debts due to the Crown, and it is called Exchequer from the chequed cloth, resembling a chess-board, which covers the table.   This chess-board table-cover was used for counting out the king's money, which was put into the squares; and hence, perhaps, the origin of squaring one's accounts, or putting them into black and white, those being the colours of the squares alluded to.   This court is now thrown open, like the Common Pleas and the Queen's Bench, to any one who will go into them, and in fact the words, "*facilis descensus Averni*," may be applied to the law in general, though for *Averni* some read *Attorney*.   All these three courts had formerly one chief and three puisne judges, but another puisne has been added to each; and as there is said to be a remedy for every wrong, "*nemo me impune lacesset*," may perhaps be translated "no one shall injure me without a puisne—pronounced always *pune*—doing me justice."

10.   The High Court of Chancery derives its name from the Chancellor, who is so called from *cancellaria*, which is so called from *cancellando*, because he can cancel the king's letters patent.   This derivation seems to us rather far-fetched, but it is, perhaps, all the more legal on that account.   By the way, it might almost as plausibly be said that a commissioner is derived from commission, which is derived from the Latin word *comes*, which is in English pronounced comes; because a commissioner must come before he can be present to exercise jurisdiction.   The Chancellor has the custody of the great seal and the Sovereign's conscience, so that by the aid of the former he can always make an impression on the latter. He is visitor of all hospitals, and has the right of popping in at Guy's, and taking the nurses by surprise whenever he feels

disposed, and superintends all charitable uses; so that he in fact might superintend the basket of which the charitable use is, in some cases, granted to those who cannot afford to buy their own baby linen.

The Chancellor is assisted by three Vice-Chancellors, but as there may be an appeal from the latter to the former, it is possible that this assistance may give him more work if he should be called upon to correct the errors of his subordinates. However, by the learning and skill of the present vices, who are well versed in their duties, it has hitherto been *vicé versâ*.

11. The Court of Exchequer Chamber is constituted of all the common law judges put together, and embraces, as they say in the play bills, the whole strength of the company. Appeals from one of the three courts are heard in the Exchequer Chamber before the judges of the two others; which is as it were, cabbaging a fourth court out of the other three, as the tailors manage to crib a garment out of a suit of clothes for which the customer has found his own materials.

12. The House of Peers is the highest court of judicature in the kingdom, but when it sits as a court of appeal it generally comprises the judge whose decision is appealed against, supported by one or two law lords—his personal friends—and a lay peer or two nodding off to sleep over the newspaper. It is a tribunal of the last resort, and certainly the last that any one in his senses would think of resorting to.

13, and lastly, are the Courts of Assize and *Nisi Prius*. Every one knows what is meant by the Assizes, which is in fact going the circuit to deliver the jails, lest the list of prisoners should swell to too great *a size*, and "hence," says Jones, "we get the word Assize." But, by the way, Jones is no authority in these matters. *Nisi Prius* means, as every schoolboy knows, *unless before*, and it applies to cases which are to be tried at Westminster *unless before* the judges come to try them, which everybody knows they intend to do. Such are the several Courts of Common Law and Equity, the "wise economy" of which those who have had to pay a bill of costs will find it difficult to appreciate.

CHAPTER V.

OF COURTS ECCLESIASTICAL, MILITARY, AND MARITIME.

In the time of the Saxons there was no regular Ecclesiastical Court, but the bishop and the alderman used to sit together in the county court in a spirit of mutual confidence, the alderman bowing to the bishop in spiritual matters, while in temporal affairs the bishop returned the compliment by bowing to the alderman.

William the Conqueror, who brought over with him a very miscellaneous set, and introduced shoals of foreign clergy, separated the ecclesiastical court from the civil, and subjected the people to the canon law, which some have thought was so called from its being enforced at the cannon's mouth; but, unfortunately for this theory, Sir Walter Raleigh had not then arrived in England with his sack of potatoes and his cargo of gunpowder. The bishop withdrew from the county court, leaving the alderman, or, in his absence, the sheriff, "alone in his glory;" but King Henry the First restored the union of the civil and ecclesiastical courts,

> " Like a fine old English gentleman,
> All of the olden time !"

On the death of Henry the First, Stephen, who had been brought in upon the shoulders of the clergy, found that they shrugged up their shoulders very much at the idea of this union of the ecclesiastical and civil jurisdiction having been restored. King Stephen therefore repealed the union, his majesty being the first and probably the last that ever could accomplish such an object. The ecclesiastical courts consist of—

1. The Archdeacon's Court, which is the most inferior of all, and is held in the archdeacon's absence by a judge, called the official; so that, being an archdeacon's court without an archdeacon, it is something on the same plan as the tragedy of *Hamlet* with the part of Hamlet omitted.

2. The Consistory Court, which is called Consistory, according to some, because it *consists* of the bishop's chancellor, who acts as judge; but this is a poor pun, which the severer writers do not recognise.

3. The Court of Arches is a Court of Appeal, which is presided over by the Dean of Arches, who probably used to hold his court either over or under an archway.

4. The Court of Peculiars is a branch of the Court of Arches, and has nothing at all peculiar about it.

5. The Prerogative Court takes cognizance of wills, where the deceased has left goods in the different dioceses, which is thought to be too good a thing for the bishop to have a hand in, and the archbishop therefore interferes by way of special prerogative.

6. The judicial committee of the Privy Council is a Court of Appeal, made up of a vast variety of judicial ingredients. It is in fact one of the richest compounds, consisting of all the cream of the Courts of Law and Equity; the principal judges being skimmed off to comprise the judicial committee of the Privy Council.

Courts Military comprised a Court of Chivalry, which has gone nearly out of use; for the days of chivalry being past, a Court of Chivalry would be somewhat of a superfluity.

The Maritime Courts include the Court of Admiralty, which has jurisdiction over all marine matters, except perhaps marine stores, of which the Court of Admiralty takes no cognizance. In time of war there is a Prize Court, to sit upon vessels taken as prizes; but as the judges of these Courts are often quite at sea, there is an appeal to the judicial committee of the Privy Council.

CHAPTER VI.

OF COURTS OF A SPECIAL JURISDICTION.

THE Courts whose jurisdiction was special were never very particular, and much oppression, therefore, arose out of them. They consisted of—

1. The Forests Courts, instituted for the protection of the royal deer or venison, which no one was at liberty to make game of. The Forest laws have, however, happily fallen into disuse; "for the lives and liberties of the subject are more dear," says Petersdorf, quaintly, "and the lives and liberties of the deer more cheap than they used to be."

2. A second species of particular Court is the Court of Sewers; yet, considering the subject of jurisdiction, the court ought not to be over particular. The Commissioners of Sewers are paramount over ditches, and may fine and imprison for contempt; yet when we reflect on the nature of the court, contempt is almost unavoidable.

3. The Court of Policies of Insurance, which was established to do wonders for the merchants; but as it did nothing for them at all, the court fell into disuse somewhat speedily.

4. The Court of the Marshalsea and the Palace Court at Westminster, which are often confounded together, and the suitors in which are frequently more confounded than the courts themselves, by the decisions given.

5. A fifth species of private Courts were those of the Principality of Wales, which were necessary because writs did not run from Westminster into Wales; but as debtors did sometimes run into Wales, the administration of justice in England and Wales was rendered uniform.

6. The Court of the Duchy of Lancaster, which is a sort of minor Court of Chancery, where equity is dispensed in a

small way on the same terms as at the chief establishment There is a Chancellor of the Duchy, who bears about the same relation to the woolsack as the three kings of Brentford did to the throne of England.

7. The seventh species of Private Courts are those appertaining to the Counties Palatine of Lancaster. and Durham, which have dwindled down into insignificance, and were almost entirely hoed out by the Uniformity of Process Act. To this class also belong the Courts of the Cinque Ports, or five principal havens, namely, Dover, Sunderland, Romney, Hastings, and Hythe, to which have been added Winchelsea and Rye, so that the five ports have actually gone to sixes and sevens. Some think that the word cinque has no reference to five, but that it is the old Norman-French for *sink*, and indicates the fact that vessels may sink in the ports alluded to. This, however, is one of those vapid *jeux de mots* which the earlier jurists were very fond of indulging in.

8. The Stannary Courts in Cornwall and Devonshire form the eighth species of courts of a particular jurisdiction, and are established for the use of the tinners who work in mines ; but the miners who have got any tin, are nevertheless looked after by the Court of Chancery.

9. There are several other courts of a private nature within the city of London—not including, however, the Tennis Court—which it is not worth our while at present to go into. If we were to go through all the courts, we should go through the Insolvent Court among the rest ; but as the reader would not derive any benefit from the act, we forbear from doing so. There are Courts of Request, or Courts of Conscience, for the recovery of small debts, held often in a room, where a chairman sits on a mantelpiece, with his legs supported on a fender, while a few commissioners cling to a cupboard in one corner of the apartment, intended to serve for a jury-box.

10. There are also the Chancellors' Courts in the two English Universities, which have jurisdiction where one of the parties

is a scholar, though the other may be what is vulgarly called "no scholard;" so that a fellow commoner might bring an action against a commoner fellow in the courts alluded to.

We have now gone through all the courts of special jurisdiction, which are never allowed to go beyond the express letter of their privileges, which letter, says the humorous Coke, must be consonant to the constitution.

CHAPTER VII.

OF THE COGNIZANCE OF PRIVATE WRONGS.

It is a saying of the lawyers, that "there is no wrong without a remedy;" and wishing that the reader, if wronged, may get the remedy he requires, we proceed to point out the courts professing to give it him.

The wrongs cognizable by the Ecclesiastical Courts may be reduced—like the dog Cerberus—under three general heads: 1st, *pecuniary*, 2nd, *matrimonial*, and 3rd, *testamentary*.

The pecuniary causes comprise all disputes about money matters connected with the church; as, if a curate plying for hire is called off the clerical stand in the Chapter Coffee House to preach a sermon, and then cannot get his money, he may go to the Ecclesiastical Court to recover it.

Matrimonial causes are very often causes of dispute, and of these the Ecclesiastical Court takes cognizance. Thus, husbands and wives who do not agree may become suitors, by suing for a divorce, if there are legal grounds for it.

Testamentary causes are such as relate to wills, over which the Ecclesiastical Courts came to have power by people dying without any will at all, when their property was pounced upon for the good of their souls by certain religious bodies.

The process in the Ecclesiastical Courts is regulated according to the civil and canon laws, and perhaps the phrase not "worth powder and shot," as applied to law proceedings, originated with the great expense which the canon law entailed on those who had recourse to it. The ecclesiastical jurisdiction was however defective, from its want of power to enforce its sentence, and it was wittily said by the great Lord Stowell that the canon law ended in smoke too frequently. Excommunication was the only punishment it could enforce, and as excommunication only disqualifies a man from serving on a jury, being subpœnaed as a witness, or going to law— all of which he is much better out of—the sentence seemed rather to savour of a privilege than otherwise. It is true that after forty days they could lock him up till he was reconciled to the church, but this was, after all, like putting a naughty boy in a corner till he promised to be good ; and excommunication was therefore discontinued by the 53rd of George III. c. 127, except as a mode of spiritual censure.

2. We will now consider the injuries cognizable in the Court Military or Court of Chivalry, which formerly interfered in " contracts touching deeds of arms or of war ;" so that any dispute about a prize fight would probably, in the days of Richard II., have been referred to the court alluded to. The days of chivalry have however departed, and the Court of Chivalry has accompanied the days of *ditto*. It used to be resorted to for redressing usurpations in matters of heraldry ; as, if a man took my crest, I might cut his comb for him ; or if my coat of armour were a tea-urn, stagnant on a rug gules, and some other armiger or esquire disputes my right, we could have contended for the tea-urn and the rug in the Court of Chivalry. So, if my crest be a lion rampant, and my neighbour's lion has no right to be rampant, I might reduce him in the Court of Chivalry to a *couchant* condition. These matters have, however, long ceased to agitate men's minds, though there is a modern case of Sir Hugh de Buggins, a city knight, having run the pole of his carriage, out of pure spite, into the panel of another citizen, who had quartered in his coat of arms a bit of blazonry which the Buggins family claimed the sole title to.

3. Injuries cognizable bv the Courts Maritime or Admiralty Courts come next, and include all causes arising on the high seas, which are called high to distinguish them from the very low seas of Chel and Batter. Wages becoming due on the high seas are cognizable in these courts, but the sea need not be particularly high to give the court jurisdiction; for wages earned in a calm are recoverable equally with those that fall due during a boisterous passage. The Courts of Admiralty have also jurisdiction over beacons, but we defy them to exercise any power over the beacon on the Goodwin Sands, whose conduct has been most refractory, and which has tumbled about with the light in its head, to an extent unparalleled in the annals of light-headedness.

4. We must next consider the injuries cognizable by the Courts of Common Law, and in these we must include all possible injuries whatsoever, for which the courts already alluded to do not provide a remedy. This reminds us of the recommendation of the poet to one who asked a question of the hills, and who was advised, if the hills would, not help him, to " try the groves." To those who have suffered a wrong for which they have asked for a remedy in vain from the courts ecclesiastical, military, or maritime, we say emphatically,

　　" If these won't help you, try the common law."

There are, however, two sorts of injuries which are specially provided for, as when an inferior court delays justice, by declining to go on, or when such inferior court takes upon itself to decide in a case it has no right to meddle with. The first of these injuries is repaired by a writ of *procedendo*, or a writ of *mandamus*, the writ of *procedendo* being an order to proceed, and answering to the popular phrase of " Go it, ye cripples;" for when justice does not move in its proper course it is crippled to all intents and purposes. A *mandamus* is a command from a superior to an inferior court, to go on or do a certain act, and it issues from the King's Bench, when there is a King, or the Queen's Bench, when there is a Queen ; and, "in the latter case," says Spelman, "perhaps a *woman-damus* instead of a *man-damus* would be the proper name for it." The other special injury is that of encroachment—as when a little court attempts to interfere with great matters ; as if the Court of Requests, in Kingsgate-street, should endeavour to do a bit of chancery, upon which a prohibition would issue to put a stop to its impertinence. If the little court should still go on, the little judges may be punished for contempt, and may be made to look even more little than they really are, by the necessity for eating a quantity of pie usually known by the epithet of humble.

CHAPTER VIII.

OF WRONGS AND THEIR REMEDIES RESPECTING THE RIGHTS OF PERSONS.

Wrong being merely the privation of right, the first object of the law is to put a man where he was before ; and, indeed, as far as any remedy is concerned, it very often leaves him just as it found him. Remedies are sought through the medium of actions, and very bad actions they sometimes prove to be. They are divided into personal, real, and mixed, which we shall proceed to give a brief description of.

Personal actions are not exactly such as the term would imply ; for it would be a personal action, in one sense, to pull a man's nose, though such would not be a legal action. Personal actions in law are resorted to for claiming satisfaction for damage done to person or property ; while real actions relate to real property, though really there was so little of the reality of justice about them, that they have been laid aside in practice. Mixed actions partake of the nature of the other two, and are a species of legal grog, in which the real and the personal, like the spirit and the water

are happily blended.   They have, indeed, a double effect, for
they entitle one to the recovery of land, and to damages for
injury done to it; so that this sort of law is like the very
strong gin sold for mixing, and is called a mixed action in
consequence.   These have, however, with the exception of
the action of ejectment, been all abolished; so that the law
is now usually taken neat, instead of being mixed as here-
tofore.

As it is advisable before going to law to know what one
is going to law about, we will now consider the nature of the
injuries for which the courts already named profess to give a
remedy.

Private wrongs or civil injuries are divided into two heads
—namely, such as are with force, and such as are without
force.   An Irish row, where blows are dealt promiscuously on
to the skull of the first comer, is a civil injury belonging to
the first head; but slander is without force, even when the
language is strong, and it therefore belongs to the second
head, of civil injuries—a term which is, by the bye, a misno-
mer, for slander is the most uncivil injury that can be
inflicted on any one.

Wrongs are said to correspond with rights—if things can
be said to correspond which are exactly the reverse of one
another; but the law so jumbles them up together, that it is
sometimes difficult to distinguish them.   Injuries relate to
either persons or property—the former of which affect lives
and limbs, bodies, health, and reputations.   Injuries affecting
life will form the subject of the concluding part; but those
affecting limbs and bodies we will at once proceed to the
discussion of.   These consist of—1st. Threats, by which a
man may be so frightened that his business is interrupted; as,
if one man threatens to give another a hiding and the other
runs away and hides himself through fear, and neglects his
affairs, he may bring an action for damages. 2nd. By assault,
which need not amount to a positive thrashing, or even a blow,
for if A aims at B, and misses him, but hits C by mistake,

both B and C might bring an action against A for damages. 3rd. By battery, or beating ; but even the least touching of another in anger, though the touch may be as soft as batter, amounts in law to battery. But battery is in some cases justifiable, as in self-defence, or in the exercise of an office ; and it has been held that a beadle may batter a boy that is refractory. 4th. By wounding, which is merely aggravated battery ; or, as Finch says, " a wound comes from anger, being wound up to its highest pitch." 5th. Meyhem, which consists in depriving another of a member useful for his defence in fight, as an arm, a finger, an eye, or leg—the defensive property of the last consisting in its enabling him to run away with greater rapidity.

Injuries affecting health are of various kinds, such as selling the sloe-leaf for tea, or its juice for port wine ; pelting people to death with Life Pills, and otherwise victimising the health of the community.

Injuries affecting a man's reputation include slanderous words and written libels. Though it is actionable to print. that which may injure a man's reputation, it does not seem that a printer can have an action brought against him for printing a book whereby the reputation of the author is seriously damaged. To call a man a rogue or a rascal in words, is said to be no ground for an action, though it would be very good ground for the action of knocking him down, without going any further into the merits. Reputation may also be destroyed by malicious indictments or prosecutions ; as, if Brown, out of spite, indicts Smith for forgery, and it turns out that Smith is a blacksmith, and has forged nothing but horse-shoes and other articles, in the way of his trade—then Smith has a very good action against Brown, who has been guilty of a very bad one.

We will now consider injuries affecting personal liberty, of which the chief is false imprisonment—an offence which any man who illegally detains another is guilty of. If a man holds me by the button of my coat in the public streets, and will not let me go, or, if a Jew, in Holywell-street, seizes me, to inquire if I have any old clothes to sell, and refuses to release me, he is guilty of false imprisonment, which I may terminate in four legal ways, though I might probably resort to a fifth, which, if not mentioned in the books, is one which the law of nature indicates.

The four legal ways are—1. *Mainprise;* 2. *The writ de odio et atia;* 3. *The writ de homine replegiando;* and 4. *habeas corpus.* The three first of these writs are now never resorted to, and, leaving the learning respecting them to those gentlemen who, when falsely imprisoned, would rather get free by a roundabout way than by a short cut, we proceed at once to the writ of *habeas corpus.* The attempt to evade this glorious bit of parchment in the celebrated case of Jenks —the Carus Wilson of 1676—led eventually to the passing of the famous *habeas corpus* Act, in the days of Charles the Second. By this statute even a single judge in vacation—or, indeed, any judge, whether single or married, may at any time grant a writ of *habeas corpus* to any one who is illegally imprisoned, if he complains by affidavit of his being so. This has quite done away with the old evil of putting people into prison on suspicion, and forgetting them altogether, as if they had been merely mislaid, like umbrellas left in cabs, which has been the fate of many during temporary suspensions of the *habeas corpus* Act.

Having considered the absolute rights of individuals, we will now look at their relative rights, and contemplate our fellow-creatures in their relative positions of husband and wife, including Mr. and Mrs. Smith ; parent and child, em- bracing Mister Smith and Master John, or Miss Julia Smith ; guardian and ward, as Mister Smith and Young Brown ; or master and servant, in which relationship we naturally con- template Mr. Smith and his flunky. The injuries that may be suffered by a husband, exclusive of those proceeding immediately from his wife, such as sulks and curtain lectures, consist chiefly of abduction or taking her away—not always such an injury as it at first appears—and assaulting or beating her. For these, and other injuries inflicted on a husband in his conjugal character, an action of trespass will give him what the law terms satisfaction—the result of which is often very far from satisfactory.

Injuries done to a parent, by the ill-treatment or ruin of his child, give the former a right to an action on the ground of his having lost the latter's' services. The old law evidently rated the value of one's offspring at servants' wages ; but it is now settled that a parent may bring his wounded feelings into court, as a ground for further compensation ; and it is also settled that his wounded feelings may be made the theme of merriment by the counsel opposite.

The relationship of guardian and ward is considered to be the same as that of parent and child ; and a guardian may go to law for injuries done to his ward—the greatest injury of all consisting very frequently in wasting the ward's estate in litigation. Chancery is, however, the favourite court for matters relating to wards, because Chancery keeps such a tight hand on a ward's estate, that no one—sometimes not even the ward himself—is able to get hold of it.

The injuries incident to the relation of master and servant, are chiefly two—1st, taking a man away before his service has expired. As, if Smith dines with Brown, and is so pleased with the cooking, that he rushes down into the kitchen to inveigle and hire Brown's cook, then it is clear that Smith has done Brown, and Brown has an action against Smith for damages. The second injury consists of battering, confining, or disabling the servant of another ; and it is clear that when Lear asked who put his man in the stocks, the poor old monarch contemplated putting the matter into his attorney's hands, and was inquiring the name of the party against whom to bring his action.

These relative injuries are, however, like Irish reciprocity, all on one side ; for though husband, parent, guardian, and master have an interest in their relations, the said relations have no legal interest in them, and may see them thrashed or carried away without being able to maintain any action for damages.

CHAPTER IX.

OF LEGACIES AND PERSONAL PROPERTY.

THE greatest injury that can be done to personal property is to take it unlawfully away; as, if A illegally distrains and insists on taking the distress away, by which he leaves much distress behind, and refusing to be moved himself, determines on moving the furniture. An action of replevin is the remedy in this case, which gives the goods back, and then tries the right, unless the original distrainer has eloigned or bolted with the goods, when it is useless to try the right, for the wrong has been accomplished. Detaining of goods may be illegal where the original taking was lawful; as, if a bull walks into my preserves, I may distrain him *damage feasant* while he is damaging my pheasants. Now, though it is lawful for me to take the bull by the horns, or even to seise him in tail, yet if his owner tenders me amends, I have no right to detain the brute, but must throw him up or be liable to an action. If I lend a man a horse and gig which he will not restore, but continues to drive himself about, he drives me into an action of *detinue;* when, if it should turn out that the turn-out is legally mine, he will be obliged to give it back with damages for detaining it.

There is also the action of trover, which politely presumes that A has found what does not belong to him, when he has goods belonging to some one else unlawfully in his possession. For injuries done to things personal in the owner's possession, such as spoiling his personal appearance by tearing his coat, the remedy is either an action of trespass or on the case, as the case may happen.

Besides injuries to personal property in possession, there

are injuries to things which belong to a man when he gets them; such as debts, and a few other matters, which the law wishes he may get as early as possible.

A debt is a sum of money due; but, as we are not anxious to go very deeply into debt, we shall not attempt a minute description of what every one must be more or less acquainted with. An action of debt can only be brought for a specified sum; and if I claim 30*l.* I must not prove a debt of 20*l.*, any more than I could recover an ox by an action of detinue if I claimed a horse; though it is certain that I might recover a pair of ducks if I claimed a pair of white trousers.

A covenant is an obligation contained in a deed, to do or omit a certain act; as, if a man covenants to go to Bath, he must either go to Bath, or be liable to a writ of covenant, which will plunge him into hot water. A promise is a sort of verbal covenant; as, if a builder undertakes to build Caius a pigsty by a certain day, and the pigs of Caius catch cold and die because the sty is not completed, then the law not only takes the sty into its eye, but the pigs also, and will give damages to Caius for the injury he has sustained by the neglect of the builder.

Besides express contracts, there are some that are implied by law, including the great original contract—an original, by the bye, of which we should be glad to see a copy—to pay whatever taxes the government may choose to impose; a contract which is very partial and one-sided in some respects. Again, if I employ a person to transact business for me; if, for example, I ask D to hold my horse and then refuse to pay him, he may ask a jury of his countrymen how much he deserves to be paid, which is called an action of *assumpsit* on a *quantum meruit*. There are other cases of implied contract, for the breach of which there is a remedy; as, if a horse is warranted sound and turns out to be a roarer, though it may be true that he is all sound, *vox et praeterea nihil*, there will be a good action on the warranty. The case of a horse that is warranted a good goer, and will not go at all, is exactly the reverse of the case of a print the colours of which are warranted not to run, but which nevertheless do run on the first washing. With this graphic simile we conclude our inquiries into such wrongs as may be offered to personal property.

CHAPTER X.

OF INJURIES TO REAL PROPERTY ; AND FIRST, OF DISPOSSESSION, OR OUSTER OF THE FREEHOLD.

REAL injuries, or injuries to real property, are principally six ; and as every injury is a violation of a right, it follows that if there are six of one there must be half-a-dozen of the other. The six injuries are : 1. Ouster ; 2. Trespass ; 3. Nuisance ; 4. Waste ; 5. Subtraction ; 6. Disturbance. But ouster is the subject which throughout this chapter we intend exclusively to revel in, though ouster does not seem a very lively or promising topic at the first glance ; but when the student hears that abatement, intrusion, disseisin, discontinuance, and deforcement, all come under the head of ouster, it will be seen that there is much variety in the topic ; and as variety is allowed to be charming, a very charming chapter may be counted on.

1. Abatement is where a stranger coolly walks in and takes possession of an inheritance, before the heir has had time to enter ; as, if A, the heir, is in London, and his ancestor dies at Birmingham ; and B, a mere stranger, takes possession of the inheritance before A can get down by the train ; then B is called the abator, because he abates, beats down, or overthrows the heir's rightful possession.

2. Intrusion is where a stranger enters before a remainderman can come in ; as, if I have been standing on the step of an omnibus, with a promise of the reversion of the first vacant seat, and a stranger pushes in before me, and takes the place which I am entitled to, he is an intruder, and defeats my right of possession.

3. Disseisin ; which is a wrongful holding out of him who is seised of the freehold ; and there is no doubt that a fellow who would do this ought himself to be seized by the collar and bundled neck and crop off the premises.

4. Discontinuance ; which arises when he who has a limited estate makes it larger than he is by law entitled ; as, if I take a garret for a week, and then underlet it for a whole year, perhaps getting a quarter's rent in advance, it is called a discontinuance because I suspend or discontinue the estate of the superior landlord. If A opens a theatre, and lets B a box for three months, and the landlord not being able to get any rent, takes possession of the house, which closes in six weeks, and B absolutely insists on sitting in his box, it is termed a discontinuance.

5. Deforcement ; where a man holds lands to which another has a right, and in which it resembles any other species of ouster ; but the law has here loved to make a distintcion without any very great difference. Deforcement seems to have been added to the other four kinds of ouster, on the same principle as adding a fifth wheel to a coach ; or perhaps, says Bracton, " it was designed to throw more intricacy upon the subject ;" which, the shrewd jurist saucily remarks, " is almost as bad as sending coals to Newcastle."

Having treated of ouster, we will look at the remedy ; for the law finds a plaister to every wound, though the law has not yet invented a poor man's plaister for those who cannot afford the more expensive article.

The first remedy is entry, or taking possession one's self ; but as this requires a good deal of self-possession, and is liable to end in a row, it is seldom acted on. A recent Act (1 & 2 Vict. c. 74) has, however, facilitated the entrance of landlords, where there is no rent, or where the rent does not exceed twenty pounds a year—two cases which often come to the same thing in the end ; and the justices may issue their warrant when a tenant unwarrantably keeps possession.

We had prepared a very learned episode on the writ of entry and our Saxon ancestors, with a little bit of antiquarianism about the statute of Marlbridge; but as the writ of entry—of which all this was *apropos*—has been abolished by the 3 & 4 Will. IV. c. 27, s. 36, our learned episode is not destined for the light; and indeed it was hardly suited to the light, for it was necessarily very heavy.

The writ of assize is said to be the invention of Glanvil, just as the patent mangle is said to be the invention of Baker; but as the writ of assize is abolished, it really matters very little to the legal student of the present day who on earth invented it.

The writ of right is another bit of legal lore which has gone quite out since the legal fashions have changed, and the simple has partially superseded the unintelligible. A writ of right was resorted to for the purpose of ascertaining the right of property, which was distinct from the right of possession; for one man may have one and another the other; that is to say, a person may have no right to what belongs to him, or he may have a right to possess what is some one else's property. These abstruse writs and remedies are, however, rendered useless by the 3 & 4 Will. IV. c. 27, which prevents people from popping up every half-century to recover lands, which they can now only claim within twenty years after their right accruing.

CHAPTER XI.

OF DISPOSSESSION, OR OUSTER OF CHATTELS REAL.

Ouster of chattels real arises where a man has got an estate in pledge, and is turned out before the money he has advanced is paid. As, if my tailor takes a seat in my room, saying he will wait till I pay him, and I kick him down stairs, he is ousted from the chair; which, though not strictly a chattel real, is certainly a real chattel. "This illustration is used because it is one of every-day occurrence, and will come home familiarly to all of us," says Jones; but the student must recollect that the tailor has no legal right to continue in possession of the chair till his bill is paid, for this would be often as good as a freehold. The example, therefore, is not strictly a good one; for, in order to constitute an ouster of a chattel real, the party ousted must have a right to possess the chattel real till he is paid the money due to him. There were several remedies for this injury until, one fine morning in the reign of William IV., they were all abolished, and the action of ejectment is left in place of them. This is the only redress also for a tenant for years, who is ousted during the continuance of his term; as, if my landlord comes to my chambers when I am out, and knocks at my door and is let in, and takes a seat, and then turns out my clerk—a mere boy—and, when I come home, refuses to admit me; then this is a complete ejection of me from my chambers during the continuance of my term, and I am regularly ousted from a chattel real. The action of ejectment being now the only remedy for this illegal and ungentlemanly treatment, it may be as well to say a few words about the action alluded to. It is necessary first for the claimant to make a formal entry on to the premises, and remain on them till he is turned off; but as he might sit in a field all night, without any one taking any notice of him, it is provided that he may have a friend in readiness to come up and walk him away; and this friend is called the casual ejector. An action is then commenced against the casual ejector, who writes in a friendly way to the tenant in possession, advising him to come forward and defend his title, for he, the casual ejector, being only in fun, intends letting judgment go by default if the matter should be proceeded with. The tenant in possession, not relishing the joke, comes forward to defend the action, and then the question is decided as between the parties who are really at issue. After possession is recovered, an action may be brought for mesne profits ; but if the profits have been very mean, they are hardly worth incurring the expense of an action for.

An action of ejectment can only be brought where an entry can be made ; and therefore it cannot be brought for rent, because no man can enter a sum of money ; though the lawyers can sometimes walk into the pockets of their clients.

CHAPTER XII.

OF TRESPASS.

Any unlawful act of one man, by which another is damnified, is a trespass ; and, indeed, the word has so large a sense that every one is more or less addicted to trespassing. If A comes and tells me a long story, he trespasses on my time ; but if he will not go away when my dinner is announced, he trespasses on my patience, and I am compelled to get rid of him by ouster, or by ringing the bell, which is equivalent to an action of ejectment.

But trespass, in the sense we are about to use it, is merely an unlawful entry on another man's ground ; as if A gets over my wall into my yard, where my clothes may be hanging to dry, he breaks my close, and perhaps also breaks my clothes-line.

A man is answerable for the trespass of his cattle ; and I am liable if my horse treads on my neighbour's corn, or my donkey dances among his chickens ; or if my bull rushes into my neighbour's china shop, he need not take the bull by the horns, but may proceed against me personally for the damage.

Entry on another's land, without the owner's leave, is not always trespass ; for any one may go uninvited into a public house ; but if he begins alleging that he

"Wont go home till morning,
Till daylight does appear,"

and seems inclined to act upon this anti-domestic sentiment, the landlord may at once treat him as a trespasser. By the common law, any one may go on another's grounds to hunt the fox and other ravenous beasts of prey; but a bill-discounting bailiff is not a ravenous beast of prey, within the meaning of the common law privilege which allows the hunting of such animals.

As in an action for trespass, not wilful and malicious, the plaintiff gets no costs unless he recovers more than forty shillings damages, we do not recommend the article for general use to legal customers.

CHAPTER XIII.

OF NUISANCE.

NUISANCES are of various kinds; for instance, it is a dreadful nuisance to meet a mad bull in a *cul de sac;*—and, indeed, this is a nuisance which might affect one's corporeal hereditaments. The three kinds of actionable nuisances are, however, overhanging a man's dwelling by building a roof that projects over his roof, so that water runs from the gutter of one to the top of the other; for, as Finch says, "pouring the liquids and gutturals from one roof to another is not consonant with the law, and is at variance with the strict letter." 2nd. Stopping up ancient lights, or building so near my window that I cannot see; though, if a wall is run up which merely interrupts my views and ruins my prospects, I have no remedy, for it is entirely my own look-out, and I must make the best of it. 3rd. Corrupting the air with noisome smells is also a nuisance; and Bracton, with that inveterate love of small punning which disfigures all his works, insists that "a noisome *smell* must proceed from a *smel*-ting house, which is, therefore, held to be a nuisance." There are other nuisances which we need not enumerate; but it should be remembered that enjoyment of a right must be proved before its infringement by nuisance can be the subject of an action. Thus, if I complain of my neighbour blocking up my windows on one side, I must prove that I have enjoyed those panes in my side for twenty years uninterruptedly.

To erect a new ferry on a river near another ferry, is a nuisance to the old one; and the erection of Hungerford Suspension Bridge must be rather a nuisance for Waterloo. A school set up close to another is, however, not considered a nuisance in law, though, if the boys at both are noisy and mischievous, it is a sad nuisance to the neighbourhood.

Any one may abate a nuisance by his own act, but he cannot have an action for damages also; therefore, if A carries on some trade which corrupts the air with a noisome smell, and B waters the roads with Eau de Cologne, or purifies the air of the neighbourhood by burning pastilles, he cannot afterwards bring an action, for he has made choice of his remedy.

CHAPTER XIV.

OF WASTE.

WASTE cannot be committed by one who has the property entirely to himself; for every man may do as he likes with his own. And thus, if I have a joint of meat at my own table, I may cut it as extravagantly as I please, for there is no remainder-man, or reversioner. But if I am dining at an ordinary, and others have to come after me, it is waste if I hack the joint so that I leave nothing for those who are to follow.

Waste may be either prevented or corrected: but when we say *may* be, we are far from meaning that it *will* be; though the law affects to give two remedies, between which,—as in the celebrated leading case of the stools—the client may fall to the ground, after having been advised that he had excellent ground to go upon.

Waste may be prevented by injunction; as, if a tenant is about to cut down trees without leave, or fell timber, he may be directed not to stir his stumps by the Court of Chancery.

The remedy used to be by a writ of waste; but as this is abolished, we should be guilty of waste—of our own and the reader's time—were we to go into it. An action must now be brought on the case, which is generally the case with reference to all matters that used to be the subject of real actions.

CHAPTER XV.

OF SUBTRACTION.

SUBTRACTION, as an injury to real property, is neglecting to swear fealty or to pay rent to the lord of the soil; who, in the present day, is content to dispense with the feudal services if he can secure the filthy lucre. Formerly, I might have attended my landlord in the wars, as an equivalent for my premises; but my landlord never shows fight except when I get into arrear with my rent, and then he calls loudly for quarter. The only remnant of military tenures now left, is the ancient chivalric custom of shooting the moon; which is a sort of knightly, or rather nightly, ceremony; when the landlord is kept in the dark as effectually as possible.

The only remedy for subtraction is distress; but the greatest distress of all is that of the landlord himself, when he finds not only the rent subtracted, but the goods subtracted also.

There are some services due by custom, which may also be the subject of subtraction; as, if I am bound to grind my corn at a certain mill, or have my corns cut by a certain chiropodist. If there is a custom to this effect, and I refuse to become a customer, I may have an action on the case brought against me, as the case may happen.

M

CHAPTER XVI.

OF DISTURBANCE.

DISTURBANCES, as applied to real property, are said to be of five kinds; but there are other disturbances beyond these five, where everything is at sixes and sevens.

1. Disturbance of franchise is where a man has the franchise of taking toll and is disturbed; as, if I were to seize the money-taker on Waterloo Bridge and pitch him over the parapet. The remedy given him by the law is to sue for damages, if, after being dashed to pieces, he could sufficiently collect himself to go to law with me.

2. Disturbance of Common comes next; but it is not what is ordinarily termed a common disturbance, though it may sometimes lead to one. For example, I may send an uncommon quantity of animals to enjoy the right of common, and thus interfere with the rights of my fellow-commoners; as, if I walk my calves on to the ground to such an extent that my neighbour cannot find room for a pair of ducks, I am guilty of disturbing his right of common, and he may bring his action for damages. Inclosure is also a disturbance of common; but this may be done to a certain extent, for the lord may erect a windmill on the common, even though the cattle should be scared at such an uncommon sight and run away from it. He may also, with the consent of two-thirds of the commoners, inclose his waste for the growth of timber, so that he may, says Mr. Selden, "plant pines while the cattle are pining away for want of sustenance, or sow horse chesnuts, though many a chesnut horse may thus be deprived of pasturage."

3. A third species of disturbance is that of Ways; as, if a

man has a right of way over my ground, and I place a rope across it to trip him up, or plough a furrow into which he falls ; in which case having got damaged he may seek further damages.

4. Next comes Disturbance of Tenure, where a stranger drives a tenant off the premises ; but the stranger must be strange indeed who would think of doing so.

5. The fifth and last species of disturbance is Disturbance of Patronage, which is hindering a patron from presenting his clerk to a benefice. But if I felt inclined to patronise my clerk I could not present him to a benefice, and it is doubtful whether I can even give him a living, though he certainly is a pluralist in one sense, for he cleans my boots and carries my wig to Westminster. For this disturbance the patron may have a writ of *quare impedit*, which means, wherefore am I impeded ? or, as Selden translates it, " why this impedence ?" the word impedence being a manifest corruption of impudence. The clerk himself is never allowed to be plaintiff ; for it is presumed that he undertakes with diffidence the cure of souls, and he is not allowed to be indecently struggling for the loaves when, having other fish to fry, he should be looking to the fishes.

CHAPTER XVII.

OF INJURIES PROCEEDING FROM OR AFFECTING THE CROWN.

AFTER having said that the king can do no wrong, we shall be, perhaps, charged with impudent inconsistency in beginning to talk about injuries proceeding from the crown ; but he that writes a law-book must be prepared to commit himself now and then, or he will not be equal to his subject.

The way in which the jurists get over the anomaly alluded to is, by saying that if the king does wrong it is entirely through mistake ; a plea that, in the case of one who has merely "mistaken" another's pocket for his own, has never been considered effectual. Personal injuries from the sovereign to the subject are held by the law to be quite out of the question; for even an assault from a royal hand would show a familiarity highly complimentary to the subject, on the principle, perhaps, of the celebrated case of King Arthur, who had a custom of kicking his courtiers down stairs; "a custom," says Mr. Locke, " by which they, the courtiers, were more honoured in the breach than his Majesty could have been in the observance."

It is, however, thought just possible that injuries to property may emanate from the sovereign; but in such cases he is presumed to have been deceived by his agents—to have been in fact the dupe of some rascally pettifogging attorney, in whose hands the monarch is, by a complimentary fiction, supposed to have placed himself. The vulgar cry of "It's all my attorney's doing," which is often set up by a sneaking client, who has been goading his lawyer on, and then throws all the odium on the latter, is thus thrust into the mouth of the sovereign as an excuse for the injustice he has been guilty of.

The method of getting a restitution of either real or personal property from the crown is by a petition of right, when if the king chooses to say, in bad French, *soit droit fait al partée* (let right be done to that party or fellow), then if on inquiry he establishes his claim, the party gets his property back again. These proceedings are taken in the Petty Bag Office, "because," says Finch, "it is very petty of the sovereign to bag the subject's property."

For an injury from a subject the crown may bring any action consistent with the royal prerogative; but the king could hardly commence proceedings for work and labour, or goods sold and delivered. We cannot imagine the sovereign sending in a regular bill for governing the nation, and going to law to recover the amount, while the task of framing a fair scale of charges would be exceedingly difficult. We cannot suggest a reasonable sum for such an item as "going down to the house to open Parliament in person—engaged half a day;" and we should be equally puzzled to estimate the value of "attending to prorogue," or taking "instructions for royal speech from prime minister." Majesty is consequently paid in the lump, irrespective of the work done; and as no dispute can arise on this subject, there is generally no occasion for the sovereign to resort to an action at law, which is thought to be too plebeian and common-place a remedy for royal grievances.

Inquisition, or Inquest of Office, is an inquiry by the king's officer as to whether the sovereign is entitled to certain property, and is as though the king were to say, "I shrewdly suspect so and so belongs to me. That fellow who has got hold of it has, I think, no right to it. Go you and look into the matter, and if the property is mine, take it by all means, and hand it over." A party who impeaches the title of the crown must also prove his own; so that it is not enough to succeed in the usual legal way, but he must beat the sovereign with both hands,—in other words, give it him right and left, in order to obtain the fruits of victory.

If the crown has given anything unadvisedly, such as granting a patent improperly, it may be remedied by *scire facias*, two verbs meaning "to know and to do," implying that the sovereign did not know what he was doing,—the old excuse for royalty when it has been engaged in a "do" of any kind. An information on behalf of the crown, filed in the Exchequer is, when the attorney-general gives the court to understand that so and so is the case; and, as a wink is as good as a nod to a blind horse, so is this wink of Mister Attorney as good as a nod to Justice, which is said to be blind; and it sets to work to inquire into the matter immediately.

A writ of *quo warranto* issues when any one exercises a franchise,—a liberty which the crown thinks to be an unwarrantable liberty,—and asks what right the party has to take it.

This writ was greatly abused in the latter part of the reign of the Merry Monarch, so called from its being a good joke to make a king of one whose regal qualities were, but for their mischievous tendency, truly ludicrous. A bridle was put upon this branch of the prerogative in the reign of William and Mary, and a further curb in the reign of Anne; but "as this," says Plowden, "was only bit by bit reform, the saddle was ultimately put on the right horse, when, by the statute 32 Geo. III. c. 58, it was enacted, that no one, after six years' enjoyment of a franchise or office, should be disturbed even by *quo warranto*, applied for by virtue of royal prerogative."

The writ of *mandamus* is a command to admit a person to any office or place; but I cannot have a *mandamus* commanding my admission to such a place as the pit of the opera, if I have not paid for it. A *mandamus* may issue compelling the election of a mayor, lest a city be left wholly mayorless, and thus fall a prey to all the horrors of civic anarchy.

"We have now gone through the circle of civil injuries," says our original commentator; and, if we do not echo him, it is because, comparing our labours to going round a circle, is very like an admission that we have written so far to no end whatever. We, however, gladly adopt his comparison of our system of remedial law to an old Gothic castle with moated ramparts, embattled towers, and trophied halls; for all these things are emblems of the difficulty we have in getting at a remedy when we want one.

Much has, however, been done by law reform since Blackstone wrote, and much in the way of amendment may yet be looked for.

CHAPTER XVIII.

OF THE PURSUIT OF REMEDIES BY ACTION; AND FIRST, OF THE
ORIGINAL WRIT.

In treating of an action at law, we naturally begin with
the beginning, which is much easier than to say what will
be the end of it. The first step is the easiest, and it is truly
a step, for when it is once taken, a party may be said to
have regularly put his foot in it. By way of security that
the writ would be followed up—for the law does not like
being tantalised by a mere taste of a client's money—it was
usual to have pledges to prosecute, and the patriotic individuals, called John Doe and Richard Roe, have immortalised
themselves by lending their names, without reserve, to all
persons for the purpose alluded to. We need hardly say
that the national debt is a mere flea-bite in comparison to
the amount of the liabilities under which the misguided
Doe and the reckless Roe have placed themselves. We do
not wish to go very minutely into the description of a writ,
for it is a document which few are desirous of cultivating an
acquaintance with. Writs are made returnable, which does
not mean that they may be returned by being thrown in the
face of the party serving them, of that an endorsement may
be made on the *postea* by kicking him out of the house,
though the books show that this has been done in numerous
instances. The return of the writ is the day on which the
defendant is to appear, and which is often the day by which
he has managed to disappear altogether.

CHAPTER XIX.

OF THE SUMMARY OR EQUITABLE JURISDICTION OF THE COURTS OF COMMON LAW.

To make a distinction between the equitable and the ordinary jurisdiction of the Courts of Common Law, is as much as to say that their jurisdiction is ordinarily not equitably exercised.

The court will interfere summarily if its regulations are infringed or abused, and if its officers misconduct themselves; though, if one of its ushers should become intoxicated, it is difficult to see how equity would step in and deal with him. The summary jurisdiction of the court is set in motion on the motion of counsel, and must be founded on an affidavit; so that it is necessary to make a parson swear, if the party is a clergyman. The court either refuses the motion, when counsel takes nothing by his motion, except the fee, which is a motion of course; or will grant him a rule calling on the opposite party to show cause why the thing asked should not be granted: and if this cannot be done, the rule, like that of the Emperor of Russia, is made absolute.

If this rule is not attended to, the remedy is to get another, called an attachment; but as the second rule may not succeed any better than the first, it may be possibly jumping into the fire out of the frying-pan when one rule has failed to incur the expense of another. An attachment takes the person, and half-pay officers, who are said to be unattached, may frequently be taken by the sort of attachment alluded to. As the courts are not always sitting, many small matters may be decided by a judge at chambers, forming a little *multum in parvo*, or full court of justice, in an apartment a few feet square, and appearing quite an *naturel*, without the gown, the wig, and the rest of the judicial properties. A judge's order, if disobeyed, may be made a rule of court ; but if the party against whom it is directed considers that four heads with wigs on are better than one without, he may appeal to the judicial quartette, or full court, to rescind the solo order made by the solitary judge sitting " alone in his glory " at chambers.

CHAPTER XX.

OF PROCESS.

THE first step in a suit is the process, or writ of summons, calling on the defendant to appear ; so that it may be compared to a species of incantation scene. If the plaintiff keeps on calling, and the defendant keeps on not coming, a *distringas* may be obtained to enable the former to enter an appearance for the latter, which is, as it were, going to law against a lay figure ; for the defendant may never be found at last, even after all the expense of an entire action has been gone to. A *distringas* is sometimes asked for with a view to outlawry which is a very melo-dramatic position for a man to be placed in, on account of a mere debt ; and he has only to appear in order to put an end to it. If Rob Roy, the bold outlaw, had marched into Westminster Hall and entered an appearance, his outlawry would have been, *ipso facto*, reversed, on his paying the costs of the day and all other expenses.

Thus much for process, which is only intended to get the defendant into court, and signifies much the same as, " Dilly, dilly, dilly, dilly, come and be killed,"—the process by which, in former times, ducks were invited to be victimised.

CHAPTER XXI.

OF PLEADING.

The Pleadings, though now in writing, were formerly carried on by word of mouth, and the parties used to meet to talk each other down with declarations and pleas, until the court, by giving its opinion, put a stop to the quarrel. He who could jaw the longest, had of course the best chance under the old system.

The pleadings begin with the declaration, anciently called the tale, though it was by no means like the tale of Othello, a "round, unvarnished one." By the way, as a round tale could come to no definite end, the law is perhaps right in disregarding such a tale, as savouring of rigmarole. The declaration sets forth the plaintiff's grievances in a most exaggerated style ; and in making his complaint, he lays it on alarmingly thick, in conformity with the old maxim, that some is sure to stick when such a plan is resorted to. He, in fact, twists the matter into every possible shape, like the ingenious individual who attends fairs and races, professing to fold "a single sheet of paper into six-and-twenty different forms."

After the declaration comes the plea, in which the defendant sometimes simply gives the lie to the plaintiff, and at other times the latter shuffles and prevaricates to such an extent, that the former is completely flabbergasted. The facts of the case then become so thoroughly mystified, that they are lost sight of altogether, and the whole matter becomes a question of law, when the parties themselves, no longer understanding their own dispute, give the thing up to the lawyers, who fritter away the real cause of contention in demurrers and nice points, that are only nice to those who get nice pickings out of them.

Pleas are of two kinds : dilatory pleas, and pleas to the action. Dilatory pleas, like the order on board a steam-packet, to " Ease her," are only to make the action slower. Such pleas are soon answered, and the other party can " go on a-head " with the action immediately afterwards. Dilatory pleas are—1st. To the jurisdiction. As, if the Court of Requests should propose to try a right of way, then its jurisdiction might be denied by a plea, unless it was a right of way through the mob, which usually chokes up the path to its own fountain of justice, the commissioner's seat on the mantelpiece. 2nd. To the disability of the plaintiff. As, if he should be an infant, or a monk, or an outlaw, or all three at once, he is said to be disabled from coming into court ; but a disabled soldier, who has lost his limbs, is not thought unfit to go into legal action, though when he comes into court he may not have a leg to stand upon. 3rd. In abatement. As, if the plaintiff should die, though he may have had a good action, his good actions do not live after him, but must, as Shakespeare says, be " interred with his bones."

A plea to the action either gives the plaintiff the lie direct, by denying his declaration, or prevaricates, by confessing that there was some truth in it at one time, but that the grievance has been somehow or other atoned for. This is called con-fession and avoidance ; but the avoidance of a just claim too frequently predominates. A flat denial is called the general issue, though to say what the issue will be is generally quite impossible.

Special pleas in bar are very numerous ; and one of these is the plea of justification, or " Sarve him right," as one of the old jurists humorously terms it. *Son assault demesne*, is also a plea in bar, meaning that the plaintiff began the assault ; so that the defendant may put his black eye into the pleadings against the plaintiff's swelled nose, and if the blackness of the defendant's eye is older than the swelling of plaintiff's nose, and if the nose can be shown to have been the consequence of the eye, then, says Stephen, " the eye will get the aye, and the nose the noes, from the jurymen who will have to give the verdict."

Another plea in bar is the statute of limitations, to prevent actions being brought except within certain periods; " for if there were no limit to the time," says Spelman, " we should have the name of the Wandering Jew continually in the paper, as plaintiff in the Courts at Westminster."

There is one more plea in bar, called an *estoppel*, or, as " the boys " would call it, a regular stopper to the action. It arises when the plaintiff has done something or other by which he has estopped himself; as, if at backgammon one party does not take a man that he might have taken, he may be huffed, and is clearly estopped from taking it afterwards.

After the plea comes the replication, or reply, which is the plaintiff's " Yes, you did," to the defendant's " No, 1 didn't." The defendant may then rejoin, by saying, " I tell you I didn't," when the plaintiff may put in a sur-rejoinder, saying, " You may deny it as you please, but you did though for all that ;" when the defendant may rebut, by refusing to have it at any price, and the plaintiff then winding up by way of sur-rebutter, with " You're another;" the parties are at last supposed to be tired out, and to have come to an issue. This occurs when there is something distinctly affirmed on one side, and denied on the other, divested of any of the rigmarole and prevarication by which the parties are for a long time kept from arriving at anything definite.

CHAPTER XXII.

OF ISSUE AND DEMURRER.

An issue is either on a matter of law, or on a matter of fact ; for the law is not always so matter-of-fact as it ought to be.

An issue on a matter of law is called a demurrer, which

confesses the facts, but picks a hole in the law, or, in other words, demurs to it.

An issue in fact, is when the parties have been giving each other the lie about the facts, throughout a series of pleadings, until they have at last come to a dead stand-still by a flat contradiction ; which renders it necessary for some one to decide which is wrong and which is right, when they both agree to "put themselves upon the country," or throw themselves on the usual kind indulgence of a British jury box.

A demurrer is, however, argued solemnly before the judges, who are supplied with a demurrer-book four days in advance, that they may read it up, or cram themselves, so that when the matter comes on, they appear to be quite *au fait* at it. If the issue be one of fact, it is made up into what is called a paper book, and a little historical sketch of the action, nicely written out on parchment, is called the record ; which is preserved among the national archives for the benefit of some future Hume, who may be desirous of writing the history of his country.

These were formerly in Norman-French, and were a badge of conquest ; and, as our plays are all originally in French, it must be presumed that they are a badge of conquest also. Edward the Third established a sort of legitimate legal drama, by insisting that the law proceedings should not be mere adaptations from the French ; and he patronised forensic native talent, by making the barristers speak their own language, or leave the law alone altogether. The proceedings however continued to be enrolled in Latin ; but it has been declared by " the ingenious Sir John Davis," whose ingenuity we have not been able to detect, that the law is all the better for being locked up in a strange and unknown tongue ; an opinion which, if the law were so completely locked up that no one could get at it at all, we should perhaps be disposed to concur in.

Cromwell was the first who threw the Latin to the dogs, and indeed it had been nothing but dog Latin from the first ;

though on the restoration of Charles, the Latin was also restored, till about the year 1730, when, by way of giving a job perhaps to the native dramatists, it was again ordered to be "done into English," by the statute 4, c. 26, of George the Second. Technical terms are still used in Latin, for the very good reason, that being perfect nonsense, it would be utterly impossible to turn them into English. The proceedings used to be written in what was called a court hand, but as no one could read it, and every one about the court made a wretched hand of it, this remnant of legal mystery has been at length abolished.

CHAPTER XXIII.

OF THE SEVERAL SPECIES OF TRIAL.

THOUGH there is only one right method of doing anything, the law of England suggested no less than seven modes of trial. Two of these are abolished, and three more are hardly ever used, so that the seven modes have dwindled down to two for all practical purposes.

1. Trial by record, is when a matter of record is in issue and the record must speak for itself, "for that," says Coke, "is in black and white, and one cannot say that black is white as I have heard some of our witnesses."

2. Trial by inspection, as if the defendant pleads that the plaintiff is dead, and some one comes and says he is the plaintiff, the judges shall determine by inspection, whether he be the plaintiff or not, and *semble* that a near-sighted judge may use a quizzing-glass.

3. Trial by certificate, and 4, trial by witnesses without the intervention of a jury, are now obsolete, and we therefore plunge into 5, trial by battle, which, though it is abolished, demands for the mere fun of the thing a word or two in the way of explanation. The custom of fighting it out was intro-

duced by William the Conqueror, who having pitched into the people, naturally encouraged them in pitching into each other. In a case of trial by battle the parties were compelled to fight till the stars appeared, when a suit was decided in a twinkling, for if the tenant could stand his ground so long he obtained the mastery : but if one cried Craven he was beaten, for he solicited quarter, and "hence it is," says Mr. Brand in his Antiquities, "that the Craven soliciting quarter made Craven-street the quarter of the solicitors."

6. Wager of law, which is abolished, but though law can no longer be wagered it is still a mere toss up, and has so far retained its gambling character. As it is however put an end to by an Act of William the Fourth, we shall lay the wager on one side and prepare ourselves for the seventh species of trial, which will be the subject of the ensuing chapter.

CHAPTER XXIV.

OF THE TRIAL BY JURY.

It is diﬁcult to get the British bosom into a sufficiently tranquil state to discuss this great subject ; for every Englishman's heart will begin bounding like a tremendous bonse, at the bare mention of trial by jury. This splendid palladium of our rights and umbrella of our liberties has sheltered us according to some since the time of Woden, but as it is very doubtful whether twelve honest men could be got together in those primæval, or, as Mr. Selden calls them, primeevil days, we must date the invention of trial by jury at a later period. The trial by jury is of course a subject that every true-born Briton with a quarter of a pint of Saxon blood in his veins is prepared to revel in ; but as the imagination starts wildly off, reason whispers "ease her—stop her," and feeling our ardour checked we proceed to give a common-sense account of what trial by jury really is or really ought to be. When A puts himself on the country and B does the like, then A and B have thrown themselves on the indulgence of a British jury box. When the jurors are called, and sworn, they may be challenged; that is to say, they may be called out of the box, by either party to whom they do not give satisfaction. The challenging being disposed of, (if any,) and the jury sworn, which is accomplished in three quartetts, all swearing together in unison, the trial commences by the counsel's speech, which is sometimes a very great trial for those who are obliged to listen to it. If he can support his case by his evidence it is well and good, until the other counsel makes another speech and brings other testimony of an exactly opposite character. This gives the first counsel a right to reply, which causes much bewilderment to the jurymen, who are further puzzled by the summing up of the judge, the usher's cries for silence, and the perpetual talking of the briefless barristers. In this condition the British jurymen are expected to agree in their verdict, and if they can't they are hurried out of court and locked up in a kitchen, or perhaps a coal cellar, till they are agreed, when the twelve honest Britons are released from their imprisonment.

It would be right down blasphemy to doubt the integrity of a British jury, and, indeed, "trial by jury" is a popular motto for a banner with several societies of Odd Fellows; but we have nevertheless heard of that great bulwark of our liberties tossing up occasionally, when a verdict could not be otherwise agreed upon. It has been held that if jurors do not make up their minds before the assize terminates in a particular town, the judge is to drive them on to the next place in a cart, but as the verdict would not be worth the expense of carriage, it is usual to discharge the jury rather than carry it about the country, till it has made its mind up. Such is trial by jury! the bulwark in which John Bull can walk triumphantly, the buttress of our rights, the clothes-prop of our liberties, the cloak-pin of law, and the hat-peg of equity.

CHAPTER XXV.

OF JUDGMENT AND ITS INCIDENTS.

THE judgment of the Court speaks for itself, or rather the judge speaks for the Court, when the Court delivers its judgment. A man may be arrested on a judgment, unless the judgment gets arrested first, which is sometimes possible.

Judgments are of four sorts :—First, Where the facts are admitted but the law disputed ; as if a man says, " I know I am wrong, but I will trust to a quibble of the law to decide that I am right," which is called judgment on demurrer. Secondly, Where the law is admitted but the facts are disputed ; when it may become a question of hard swearing, which is judgment by verdict. Thirdly, Where both law and fact are admitted by defendant, who says, " Fire away and do your worst," which is judgment by default. And lastly, Where the plaintiff has commenced an action against law and fact ; when, finding that he has put his foot, or rather both his feet, in it, he consents to judgment, as in case of a nonsuit. After judgment comes execution, unless the party, wishing to have plenty of fun for his money, or rather having plenty of money to pay for his fun, indulges in a series of expensive appeals, which we shall consider in the next chapter.

CHAPTER XXVI.

OF PROCEEDINGS IN THE NATURE OF APPEALS.

APPEALS were formerly of four kinds, and consisted of—First, A writ of *attaint*, by which the verdict of a jury was declared to be tainted and corrupt ; or, in other words, it was suggested that the " twelve honest men" were " a dozen consummate scoundrels." This, however, has been abolished, as well as the writ of deceit; and the *audita querela* having become obsolete, there is nothing left in the nature of an appeal but a writ of error.

Formerly, if there was a word misspelt in the proceedings, a writ of error would lie; so that Mavor's spelling-book was in fact a higher authority than the statute-book. A cockney clerk, who confounded his *v's* and *w's*, might have ruined a good cause, and the parties to an action were literally spell-bound, that is to say, bound by their spelling, until the legislative released them from the trammels of orthography.

A writ of error is a happy device of the lawyers to induce suitors who have been unfortunate in one court to try their luck in another. Thus, when the Queen's Bench has got all it could out of a cause, it may be taken by writ of error to the Exchequer Chamber, where the lawyers may squeeze something more out of it, and it may afterwards serve as a bone of contention in the House of Lords, where it will admit of further pickings. A writ of error may be so called from the fact that it is a great mistake on the part of any one who resorts to it.

CHAPTER XXVII.

OF EXECUTION.

EXECUTION is the putting the sentence of the law in force; and, considering the terrible execution which is done by the law, there cannot be a more appropriate word for the final step in an action.

A writ of execution to take possession of land may be acted upon by the delivery of a twig, a knocker of the door, or a bell-handle; for it has been held that the wire will draw the house after it.

Execution against the person is now, happily, almost abolished, except on railways, where any one who has lost his

ticket, and refuses to pay a second time, may be made a prisoner. Execution against goods and chattels may be had for
debt; but the sheriff cannot carry away the produce of a
farm, except, perhaps, the chaff which, if the debtor happens
to be of a facetious turn, will certainly be offered him.

Another species of execution is by *levari facias*, where
the sheriff holds a levy, which he sometimes accomplishes
by walking off with the contents of a drawing-room. The
power over the person is now much restricted; but goods
may be seized to a very pretty tune, the execution being exceedingly rapid, though the debtor sometimes anticipates the
creditor by a quicker movement. When judgment has been
obtained, and still the plaintiff cannot get his right, he may
throw some good money after bad by bringing a fresh action
on his judgment; but he must have very poor judgment
indeed who would easily be persuaded into doing so.

CHAPTER XXVIII.

OF THE GENERAL NATURE OF EQUITY.

EQUITY is said to be the very spirit of our law; but, like
all spirit, it seems very liable to evaporate. Disregarding
the figurative mode of considering equity and law to be
allied, we look at the fact that in England they are separate;
and we are inclined to believe that equity has just enough
law to deprive it of its justice, while law is so much itself as
to prevent equity from entering much into its composition.

It hath been said that equity applies peculiarly to cases of
fraud, accident, and trust; but law has quite as much to do
with these matters, for the law revels in a fraud, delights in
an accident, because an accident may be the subject of an
action, and luxuriates in trust, because, when trust is given,
legal proceedings may arise from it. It seems, indeed, to be
admitted by all our best jurists, that law and equity are the

same in spirit, if not in form ; and we, after carefully comparing the two, have come to the conclusion that they are
" much of a muchness." Every one who applies to a court
of equity must allege that he has no relief in law, and indeed
there is seldom much fiction in this, for the law brings
seldom relief to any man, except by relieving him of his
superfluous cash or his property.

The mode of trial in equity differs from a trial at law in
many ways, but chiefly in the mode of examining witnesses,
who are supplied with written interrogatories, which are
generally couched in such mysterious language that the person
to whom they are addressed cannot, if he would, give a
straightforward answer.

In equity all proceedings must be taken by bill ; but here
again, we find a strong resemblance between equity and law,
for the bill is inseparable from both ; and it has been quaintly
said, that it would have been well if equity began only with
a bill, but unfortunately it always ends with one.

CHAPTER XXIX.

OF THE MATTERS COGNISABLE BY COURTS OF EQUITY.

THE Court of Chancery has the guardianship of infants,
idiots, and lunatics, who are all persons that cannot help
themselves ; and the courts of equity consequently come in
and help themselves out of the property of these unfortunates.
There is at first sight something parental in the care which
the Court of Chancery professes to take of those who cannot
take care of themselves ; but if an infant, an idiot, or lunatic,
is without money, and consequently really requires some
friendly hand to aid him, the Court of Chancery will have
nothing to do with him. Equity has also the superinten-
dence of charities, and indeed will interfere in almost any
matter where there is property to administer ; but it will

have nothing to do with empty pockets, for Chancery, like nature, abhors a vacuum. It differs from law chiefly in this respect, that whereas the latter will entertain itself with any bone of contention, however dry, the former will see plenty of meat on the bone before having anything to do with it. There are some cases in which law and equity have a concurrent jurisdiction ; but he must be in a bad way indeed, who is the victim of such concurrence, for the word means literally a running together, and when law and equity run together, they generally finish by running away with the property which has got into their joint clutches. It has been pithily observed that an estate which is the subject of litigation both at law and equity is like money thrown into a sack which is open at the top as well as at the bottom. Equity has, however, in many cases, an exclusive jurisdiction, particularly with reference to trusts and the rights of a married woman, whom Chancery professes to benefit by setting her and her husband at loggerheads, if she has any separate property.

Such are some of the principal matters cognisable in courts of equity, into which we have not ventured too far, lest we should have some difficulty in finding our way out again.

CHAPTER XXX.

OF PROCEEDINGS IN THE COURTS OF EQUITY.

THE first proceeding in equity, as we have already said, is a bill, which must be in the style of a petition, humbly praying for relief, and the prayer is answered much as Jupiter granted the petition of the frogs in the fable.

A bill must contain nothing scandalous or impertinent ; but we have seen some lawyers' bills that have been really scandalous, to say nothing of the impertinence of sending them in ; but these are bills of another kind, and it is perhaps not necessary to allude to them. If the defendant does not appear to answer a bill, he is said to be in contempt, when he may be attached, and until recently he would have been declared a rebel; but, if it were rebellious not to answer a bill, the whole country would be in a constant state of rebellion, for bills of every description are being treated with the utmost contempt in all parts of the kingdom. No writ of rebellion can, however, now be issued; but a defendant may be committed to prison if he does not answer; when he is only let out on purging himself of his contempt, the purge consisting of a pill in the shape of costs, and a draft to liquidate it afterwards.

If the defendant appears, he may demur, plead, answer, or disclaim; and, as Chancery loves complication, it allows a defendant to do all four at once, which of course throws a beautiful intricacy over the whole business. Demurrers, pleas, and answers, speak for themselves; but disclaimers require some explanation. They renounce all pretence to the matter in dispute, as, if a bill were filed calling on a modern composer to transfer the copyright of his music, he might disclaim with good reason, alleging that the music was not his, because he had stolen it.

There are also supplemental bills and bills of revivor; so that a defendant never knows what he has to answer, and he may be so harassed with bills of revivor that, instead of acting as revivors, they may be the death of him.

The mode of proving facts is by interrogatories in writing; but the questions must not be leading ones, though they may mislead as much as possible. If the witnesses reside in the country or beyond sea, a commission may be appointed to examine them; but such evidence is always suspicious, for when it is very far-fetched, there is no knowing how much credit can be given to it. When all this has been done, the cause is said to be ripe for hearing, and sometimes it is not only ripe, but has actually run to seed; and indeed, during the process of ripening, the suitors are often in the position of the horse who is left to starve while the corn is growing. On the cause coming on, counsel are allowed to talk the subject thoroughly out, but sometimes only two or three talk, and the others stand with briefs in their hands, bowing their concurrence in the sentiments of their leaders. By this time the mind of the judge has become so mystified that he usually takes the papers home to get his ideas free from the labyrinth in which counsel may have succeeded in involving them. When the decree is delivered, minutes are taken down, and hours are taken up in the delivery. Still, the decree is seldom final, but is generally interlocutory; that is to say, it leaves the door open for further litigation and more costs, before the matter is brought to a settlement. Occasionally, Chancery plays into the hands of law, by sending an issue to be tried, which is always a little grist for the legal mill; and the cause generally comes back again to the Court of Equity with a great deal of additional difficulty attached to it; and thus the suit gets as it were a new lease tacked on to it. Another mode of keeping the game alive is to refer certain matters to the Master, who sends the cause back again for another decree; and in fact a chancery suit becomes a shuttlecock to be kept up as long as possible by the numerous battledores that have an opportunity of getting a shy at it. Lest the suitor may not have had quite enough of it,—for law is a good deal like " the green-eyed monster which makes the food it lives upon," —he is allowed to ask for a re-hearing, and subsequently a bill of review, with finally an appeal to the House of Lords. It might be thought that these would be more than enough for the keenest legal appetite, but there are some determined litigants who have " stomach for them all."

PART IV.—OF PUBLIC WRONGS AND THEIR REMEDIES.

CHAPTER I.

OF THE NATURE OF CRIMES AND THEIR PUNISHMENT.

THE law relating to crimes and punishments forms what is termed in every country the criminal code ; though, if the code does only that which is right, it seems unjust to call it criminal. With us, in England, it is denominated *the pleas of the Crown*, because the sovereign is supposed to be hurt by every injury done to the public. So that if A hits B on the head, the blow is supposed to fall on the Crown, in a double sense, and the sovereign comes forward, nominally, to pro-secute.

The criminal law, say the commentators, was, down to the end of the eighteenth century, remarkably rude ; but we think there was something more than mere rudeness in doom-ing a man to be hanged for cutting down a cherry-tree ; and Plowden allows that " he must have had a black heart indeed, (observe the pun on the black-heart cherry) who suggested placing such a law on the Statute-book."

Crimes and misdemeanors are nearly the same thing, except that the former are rather of a deeper dye ; and many are of opinion that we get the word crimson from the sangui-nary hue which some crimes are invested with. One of the deepest offences is imagining the death of the sovereign, because it is possible that a person who imagines the death of the sovereign may take a fancy to murder him.

Punishments are not intended as an atonement of an offence, but to amend the offender and serve as a precaution for the future. Thus, the law imprisons—or, in some cases, hangs—a man to-day, that he may know better to-morrow.

It is, however, difficult to say what should be the measure of punishment, and many wise men have failed when they tried their hands at it. Josephus alludes to a law of the Egyptians, that every one having poison in his possession should be bound to take it; which would be very hard on Mr. Butler, the respectable chemist of St. Paul's Churchyard, and would entail on Messrs. Savory and Moore the necessity of consuming several pounds of arsenic. The Locrians had a law demanding an eye for an eye, which rendered gouging a recognised part of their judicial system; but as some evil-disposed persons selected people with one eye as victims, the law was altered, with an eye to equality, and it was decreed that he who struck the only eye out of a one-eyed man, should lose both his optics;—an enactment, by the bye, which led to some very horrid spectacles. This law of retaliation, however, often caused much injustice; for if a Locrian had a decayed tooth, which he wanted extracted, he had only to knock out the tooth of some respectable dentist, who would be bound by the law to take out tooth for tooth; and thus he might lose at once a valuable molar and the price of his professional services. The law of retaliation was once tried in England, during the reign of Edward the Third, when it was founded on the principle of inflicting on one the same injury that he designed unjustly to inflict on another. This was, however, found inconvenient, and only lasted a year; for one man might threaten to knock another into the middle of next week, but it would be impossible for the law to carry out this threat against the individual who had uttered it.

In England it has always been difficult to apportion the quantity of punishment due to different crimes; but some

general rules have been usually acted on.   Thus, stealing a
loaf on account of hunger is a grave and serious offence ; for
it is a melancholy business, and the punishment is no joke ;
but wrenching a knocker from a door and running away with
it, is neither grave nor serious, because there is some fun
about it, and the penalty, to be in character, is proportionably
ludicrous.   The criminal law of this country formerly made
hanging a matter of such fatal facility, that " Hang me," and
" I'll see you hanged first," are to this day familiar phrases
amid all classes of English society.   Excess, however, always
brings an end to an evil ; and the sanguinary system of capital punishments having been allowed a frightful abundance of
rope, has at last nearly worked out its own destruction.

CHAPTER II.

OF THE PERSONS CAPABLE OF COMMITTING CRIMES.

WHEN we talk of persons capable of committing crimes,
we do not mean to imply that any particular capability or
talent is necessary to make a criminal.   It is, however, customary to say that So-and-So is more rogue than fool,—a distinction that seems to recognise a certain affinity between
crime and cleverness.   Incapability to do wrong is simply a
want of will ; and no crime is complete unless there is a will
followed by a deed.   Though the student must not suppose
that all wills and deeds are of themselves absolutely criminal.

The first incapacity for crime arises from infancy—or baby-
hood ; for directly a child is *doli capax*—up to snuff—or, as
some translate it, capable of nursing a doll—the infant is liable, in
many cases, to punishment.   No one who is under seven can be
found guilty of felony, " for it is thought," says Foster, " that
the moral qualities are all at sixes and sevens until after that
period."   Much, however, depends on there being proof of a
guilty knowledge of doing wrong, in which case we find from
Chitty, that the merest chit may be subjected to punishment.

The second excuse for crime, is lunacy, or idiocy ; in which case a man is said to be not of sound memory, and is of course liable to forget himself. There is, however, some difficulty in distinguishing real from sham lunatics ; for it is not in real life as it is upon the stage, where mad folks walk about with wisps of straw sticking in their hats, or carried in their hands, to show their insanity. If this practice were generally adopted, the public would be much safer ; for if every lunatic were compelled to carry a wisp, it would be seen that he was a man of straw, and consequently not responsible.

Thirdly ; there is artificial madness, or drunkenness, which our law regards as an aggravation of the offence, perhaps on the plea that there is *in vino veritas*, and that a man who commits a crime, when drunk, is a true criminal, or, as Coke would say, " a criminal in spirit."

There is, fourthly, a deficiency of will where an injury is done by misfortune or chance ; as, if I go into a theatre by chance, and have the misfortune to find a bad actor playing *Macbeth*, an injury is done to me, and the offence may amount to murder ; but, as the perpetrator is the victim of misfortune, the act is not, legally speaking, criminal.

Fifthly ; ignorance or mistake will constitute a defect of will ; as, where a beadle runs after and thrashes the wrong boy, or if I turn round, on missing my pocket-handkerchief, and collar an innocent party, who, in self-defence, levels me to the ground. Here the various injuries, being inflicted in ignorance and mistake, will not subject the parties to punishment.

A sixth species of defect of will arises from compulsion, or necessity ; but this seems to be a very questionable excuse, and resolves itself into the juvenile plea of " I couldn't help it." The ordinary case of compulsion is supposed to be that of a wife commanded by her husband ; but as it is often quite the other way, our law holds a wife responsible for many offences, particularly those that are *mala in se*, for as Bracton quaintly hath it, " These *mala* are not merely *mala* in the case of a male, but of a female also."

Compulsion may also arise from fear; as, if I kill a man from fear of his killing me; but my fear must be reasonable, for I have no right to get myself into such a nervous state that I am to mistake my valet for an assassin, and shoot him dead when he enters my room with my shaving-water. If I am told that if I read a facetious book it will make me die of laughing, I am not justified in assassinating the author or the publisher, for my fear must be such, "*qui cadere possit in verum constantem non timidum et meticulosum.*"

"Fear that might touch a man with nerves of leather;
Not one whom you might knock down with a feather."

There is one more case of necessity which our law does not recognise as an excuse for crime, but rather as an aggravation of it, and a reason for severer punishment. The necessity in question is a want of food to support life, which is the only necessity that our jurists do not consider strong enough to justify an unlawful action. This doctrine is said to be sanctioned by the Jewish law, which provided that "a thief who stole from hunger, should restore sevenfold, and give all the substance of his house"—a penalty that presumes the possession of substance as well as house, which they who really steal from hunger are never in possession of. It is, however, said that, in this country, no man who is in want need commit crime; and when the provisions of the Poor Law are considered, it must be allowed that it is unnecessary to commit crime, when destitution gives you nearly—if not quite—the same advantages. The workhouse, it is true, is not quite so comfortable as the prison, but there is in the latter the *mens conscia recti* for those who prefer gruel and self-approval to remorse and more liberal rations.

To these cases of incapacity to commit crime, we have only to add that of the sovereign who can do no wrong,—a maxim for the truth of which we refer the student to the chapters headed " Richard the Third," " Henry the Eighth," and a few others we could name, in the History of England.

CHAPTER III.

OF PRINCIPALS AND ACCESSORIES.

CRIMINALS are either principals or accessories ; as, in a dramatic murder, the principal is he who enacts *Macbeth*, while the accessories are they who give him his cues, and otherwise aid or abet him. It is even doubtful whether the barber who dresses his wig is not an accessory before the fact, while the critic who praises his performance is clearly an accessory after it.

In some offences there are no accessories, but all are principals ; and in the sort of murder we have just alluded to, all would no doubt wish to be. In high treason all are principals, because the offence is so great ; and in trespass all are principals, because *de minimis non curat lex*, or in other words, because the offence is so little. Very small criminals are pounced upon all in a lump, and the law crushes them beneath its foot as an elephant would an ant-hill. *De minimis non curat legs* would be in each case appropriate. An accessory before the fact is one who causes the commission of a crime, and though he has suggested one crime, he may be accessory to another ; as, if A orders B to shoot Titius, and B, instead of shooting Titius, gives him some British brandy, of which Titius dies, then A is an accessory to the poisoning, and may be punished—like all accessories before the fact— in the same manner as the principal. Accessories after the fact, are such as relieve or harbour a felon, knowing him to have committed a felony ; or buy stolen goods, knowing them to be stolen. The purchaser of modern music is an accessory after the fact to a theft on the part of the composer, who has stolen the ideas of others. By the French law, receivers of stolen goods were punished with death, a law which, if put in force in this country, would have decimated Field Lane, and utterly depopulated the greater part of the Minories. Accessories before the fact are in most cases punished in the same way as principals, and it is very clear that in the case of *the Crown on the prosecution of Banquo against Macbeth and wife*, the latter, though only an accessory before the fact, deserved as severe a punishment as her husband. In the case of *Friar Lawrence re Romeo on the demise of Paris*, the friar was only an accessory after the fact, and therefore in harbouring and assisting Romeo he would, by the present law, have only rendered himself liable to two years' imprisonment.

CHAPTER IV.

OF OFFENCES AGAINST RELIGION.

This chapter will, for obvious reasons, be brief; and indeed the crimes and punishments to which its title refers are now happily seldom heard of.

Fire used to be a favourite penalty in former days, but this has completely gone out, and has been superseded by what the wag Coke would have called a more sensible edition of Burn's Justice. Protestant dissenters and Roman Catholics were formerly subject to much legal oppression; but as the Toleration and Emancipation Acts have relieved both from their disabilities, we shall not rake up old grievances. Blackstone excused the severity of these laws on the plea of their being seldom used; but it would be as just to turn a tiger loose upon a multitude, and tell the people not to mind, as the brute could not devour every one of them.

Among other similar offences may be ranked that of swearing, which is regulated by a sliding scale that lets in, or rather allows a man to let out, an oath, on terms proportionate to his position. Thus a soldier or a sailor may swear as low as a shilling, and a person under the degree of a gentleman must pay two shillings for each oath; but a gentleman who is a blackguard, and chooses to swear, must pay five shillings for the privilege.

Conjuration, witchcraft, and sorcery, were formerly capital offences, but they have latterly been considered capital fun, and been practised with much profit by Wizards of the North, and other professors of the art of magic.

Simony, or the purchase of an ecclesiastical benefice, is also an offence in the eye of the law, but it generally contrives to keep itself out of the eye of the law, and thus no notice gets taken of it.

Sabbath-breaking is likewise prohibited by the law, though it is difficult to say what the offence really consists of. You may not bait a bull, but you may bait a horse on Sunday ; and an attempt has been made to constitute baking a crime, but the roasting they have got who have supported this view of the case, has put an end to their efforts.

Drunkenness is punishable by a fine of five shillings, or sitting six hours in the stocks ; but these stocks have now gone quite out of fashion, and are not to be met with in any stock-market. A splitting headache is, however, an obvious penalty for drunkenness, in addition to the fine,—a penalty which, though not inflicted by the letter of the law, emanates entirely from the spirit.

There are one or two other offences that fall under this division of the subject, but as they carry with them their own punishment in addition to that awarded by the law, it is not necessary to notice them.

CHAPTER V

OF OFFENCES AGAINST THE LAW OF NATIONS.

THE law of nations is a large subject and rather heavy, but we have no doubt we shall succeed in making light of it. The law of nations may be infringed : 1st, by violation of safe conduct, which conduct it is by no means safe to pursue, or committing hostilities against a foreigner in the time of peace, such as worrying an Italian organ boy, an offence against international law, which the police ought to prevent as much as possible.

Secondly; infringement of the rights of ambassadors, the chief of which appears to be the right of the ambassador to run into debt without having his goods seized or his person arrested.

Thirdly; piracy—consisting of robbery on the high seas, such as following at the stern of a vessel and sheering off with the bowsprit; but it is a nice point, whether picking the pocket of the captain when his back is turned would be piracy, for though it is robbery on the high seas it could hardly be considered as a proof of that reduction to a savage state of nature, which, according to Coke, is the condition of one who is guilty of piracy. " There be land pirates " according to Shakspeare; and the Corsair who reprints a spurious edition of a book is one of this class of delinquents, who go under the name of *hostes humani generis*. They would indeed be enemies to the human race did they multiply copies of all the trash that is written.

Any commander running away with any ship or boat is a pirate, and therefore if the captain of the Bachelor should run away with the Bride he would be guilty of piracy. Any one endeavouring to cause a revolt on board is adjudged a pirate, felon, and robber, and shall suffer death; so that if I were, for mere fun, to take advantage of the absence of the captain of the twopenny boat, to mount the paddle-box, order the boy to go on easy, and inform the stoker that he was free, I should have incurred, according to the strict letter of the law, the liabilities of piracy. A statute of Victoria has, however, abolished hanging for piracy, except in cases where there has been an attempt to murder, so that I might have some capital fun with the crew and captain of a boat without the fear of capital punishment.

The attempt to prohibit the slave trade has also given rise to treaties between some nations, and the right of visit has created some dispute ; but the visit is indispensable to ascertain if negroes are on board, for the dealers in slaves would swear black was white unless there happened to be ocular demonstration to the contrary.

CHAPTER VI.

OF HIGH TREASON.

THE word treason, which means treachery and breach of faith, is borrowed from the French, and as the French use the article a great deal more than we do, they are welcome to have their word back, for happily we seldom require it in England. When disloyalty reaches so far as to attack majesty itself, it is called high treason ; but all this sort of thing has long since been voted excessively low, and low it is in every sense, for it has been summarily put down as it deserves to be.

It has been held that treason can only be committed against the sovereign in possession, and that allegiance is due to the individual who occupies the throne; so that if a French prince were to invade England (which we should like to catch him at), and to declare himself king of this country, it would seem that we should be obliged to acknowledge him. We think that without any sacrifice of our loyalty to her present majesty, we may say that when a French prince invades England, when he is allowed to get to Windsor, when he declares himself king without being summarily walked off to the first station-house as a rogue and vagabond, —then we may acknowledge his sovereignty.

It is high treason to compass or imagine the death of the king; but compassing does not mean stabbing him with a pair of compasses ; nor does imagining mean a mere act of imagination, though it implies perhaps taking a fancy to killing the sovereign. An attempt on the sovereign's life is a compassing or imagining his death; but when Sir Walter Tyrrel, being a fearfully bad shot, aimed at a hart and sent his arrow into the heart of Rufus, it was not treason; and as it was shooting out of all compass, it could not be called compassing.

There must always be what is called an *overt* or open act to constitute a case of treason. It is said the tyrant Dionysius had a man executed for dreaming that he had killed him; but by our law, the person who has such a dream must walk in his sleep, and thus be guilty of an overt act before he can be accused of a treasonable intention. By a recent statute, it has been made penal to throw any matter whatever at the sovereign, with intent to injure or alarm her; and, therefore, though it is settled that a cat may look at a king, whether a horse may shy at a queen, has become since the act of the 5 an l 6 of Victoria, a very nice question.

Words alone cannot be treason, but they may be rendered so by writing, for *scribere est agere*—to write is to do, "which," says the facetious Spelman, "is often the case; for if I write a book that does not sell, and I get a large sum for it, *I do* the publisher; but if the book sells, it is ten to one but *I do* the public." Here Spelman is wrong, for his book may sell, and he may himself be done by the publisher. There is, however, an objection to make mere writings the subject of treason; and though Sidney was executed for some papers found in his closet, his attainder was afterwards reversed;—a privilege for which he would doubtless have given his ears; but as his head had been already cut off, they were not at his own disposal.

Levying war against the king in his realms is also treason, and resisting the king's forces by defending a castle against him is levying of war; as if Jack Straw, or the Elephant, having some military billeted upon them, were to defend the respective castles against the soldiery. Adhering to the king's or queen's enemies in the realm is high treason; but if I saw a boy throw a stone at her gracious majesty, I may run after him and stick to him till I catch him, which is in some sort adhering to an enemy of the sovereign. It is also treason to comfort a pirate ; " but," says Spelman, " if I may not harbour a pirate by affording him a bed in my house, I may at any rate give him his gruel, which is one comfort any how." It is also high treason to counterfeit the sovereign's great or privy seal in wax, for the law waxes very severe in this instance. Coining money, which was formerly treason, is now only felony, though it seems there is no punishment for a manager of a theatre who is said to be literally coining money when he gets a succession of overflowing houses. It is useless to furnish a catalogue of all the acts that were formerly called treasonable ; but we shall name one as a sample of the whole lot of them. By the statute 3 Jac. 1, c. 4, any natural-born subject who became reconciled to the pope, was guilty of treason. Thus, if I had been on visiting terms with old Pius, and there had been a coolness between us for some trivial cause—perhaps a game at whist, or the non-return of a morning call—and if I was afterwards reconciled to the old gentleman, I became liable to have my head cut off as a traitor.

By the statute of Philip and Mary it was made treason to clip or deface the coin, because it was thought an insult to majesty to rub out its eye, melt down its nose, or play any other tricks with the royal portrait on the public money. Among the Romans it was treason to deface the statues of the emperor ; but the statue of one of the Georges, in Golden Square, has long been a mark for the boys, who have had a cut at it from father to son, proving themselves chips of the old block, by chipping the old block whenever they could get an opportunity of doing so. The punishment of high treason is now to be drawn to the place of execution and hanged In ordinary executions the culprit is hanged, and not drawn, except by the artists of some of the illustrated newspapers, who keep up the barbarous practice of drawing condemned criminals.

CHAPTER VII.

OF FELONIES INJURIOUS TO THE KING'S PREROGATIVE.

THE periodical lexicographers have puzzled themselves and each other as well as us, about the derivation of the word felony. As they all make different suggestions, we decline adopting any, and throw out on our own account the notion that felon is a corruption of fee-long, because a long fee is necessary to get up a defence for felony. This definition is, doubtless, far fetched, but not so far fetched as that of some of the legal antiquarians, who have travelled into Greece to get the word φηλος, an impostor, as the origin of the word alluded to. Our own suggestion we consider the best, because felony is on all hands allowed to be a crime involving a loss of property : and the fee-long or long fee certainly implies an enormous sacrifice of assets. The felonies against the king's prerogative are six, which we shall briefly specify.

1st. Offences relating to the coin, which were formerly so severely dealt with, that it was almost death to be found with a bad halfpenny in one's pocket, and to utter a suspicious sixpence was regarded as a piece of unutterable villany. All previous statutes have however been repealed by the Act of William the 4th ; and thanks to this measure, followed by that of the 1st of Victoria, the law now lies in a nutshell. We however always observe, that though the law does lie in a nutshell, it requires a good deal of jaw, and a long crack over it, before it is come-atable.

By the new Act it is an offence to manufacture coin, but there is no harm in making money ; and it is also criminal to utter a white-washed halfpenny for a halfcrown, which would be a very desperate trick, for the uttering would probably turn ont an utter failure. Having false money in your possession with intent to utter it is likewise a misdemeanour; but it is a minor offence for a singer to have a false note in his chest, and to utter it before an audience.

2nd. Felonies against the king's council, which formerly included assaulting a privy councillor by a blow or even a kick; but these kicks are now on the footing of common assaults, and attempts to kill are felonies without any distinction as to the rank, except in the case of royalty, of the intended victim.

3rd. Serving foreign states was formerly a felony, except, says Coke, "serving them out, which was always allowable." The statutes on this subject are now repealed, and any one may enlist in the Kamtschatkan Greys, the Sandwich Island Buffs, or any other outlandish regiment, if he first provides himself with a royal license.

. 4th. Felony by embezzling the sovereign's stores, or rather his warlike stores; for if I go to his store closet, and steal a lump of his sugar, it is not felony under the statute. To set on fire any of the royal dock-yards or ships is a crime still punishable with death; and it is also arson to burn an arsenal.

5th. Desertion in time of war, by sea or land, is a felony, and in peace it is a grave offence; so that the sentinels in the park must not desert their posts to run after refractory boys who may irritate the military to any extent, by keeping just beyond the verge of the promenade to which the soldiery are limited. Endeavouring to seduce him from his allegiance is punishable with transportation or imprisonment, and holding a pot of beer up as a temptation to draw him off his beat, is probably within the statute.

6th. Administering oaths for a seditious purpose is felony punishable with transportation; but administering oaths indiscriminately when in a state of intoxication, to any one who happens to pass by, is only punishable with a fine of five shillings.

CHAPTER VIII.

OF PRÆMUNIRE.

THE offence we call *præmunire* means introducing a foreign
power into this land, as if I asked the pope to pay me a visit
at my chambers, or invited him to tea; in which case I must
also have introduced papal provisions, which was in the eye
of the law an offence of the gravest character. The statute
16 Richard the 2nd was called the statute of præmunire, and
it enacted that no one should procure translations, &c. at
Rome or elsewhere; so that the present dreadful custom in
which our dramatists indulge, of getting translations from
the French, would have subjected them, in the good old days,
to the penalties of a præmunire. Accepting provisions from
the pope also incurred a præmunire; so that if the pope sent
me a Bologna sausage, it was a papal provision which I must
not have accepted. Contributing to the maintenance of a
popish ceremony beyond sea was a similar offence; and if the
statute of præmunire were now in force, as in the days of
Henry the 8th, it would play old Harry with the Boulogne
Boarding Schools. There were a few other offences that
came under the head of præmunire, but as the law relating
to it has become obsolete, we refer the curious to 1 Bulst.
199 , Bro. Abr. t. Corone, 196; 1 Hawk. P. C. 55, and other
lively authorities on this very tantalising topic.

CHAPTER IX.

OF MISPRISIONS AND CONTEMPTS AFFECTING THE KING AND GOVERNMENT.

MISPRISION, like a great deal of our treason and treachery, is derived from the French, and comes from the word *mespris*, a contempt or neglect for the proper authorities. Misprision, like electricity, is either negative or positive ; and like electricity also, it is a very shocking business.

Negative misprision is a misprision of treason; that is to say, a knowledge of treason without revealing it, which makes the party knowing it an aider and abetter, "though," says Coke, "such a culprit can scarcely be called a better, for he is just as bad as the principal." The concealing of treasure trove is also a misprision; as, if I were to find a whale, which is a royal perquisite, and say nothing about it, but put the whale, or rather the proceeds thereof, into my own pocket, I should be guilty of misprision, and liable to fine and imprisonment.

Positive misprisions are called contempts or high misdemeanours ; such as the mal-administration of public affairs, which is an offence very common with Cabinet ministers. This is punishable by banishment; but banishment from Downing-street is generally the highest penalty inflicted on such offenders.

Refusal to join the *posse comitatus*, or make one of a mob of boys and vagabonds running about at the heels of a constable, when required, is also misprision ; and refusing to come home from beyond the seas, in obedience to a writ, is a misprision that many of our fellow subjects at Boulogne, and other parts of the continent, are continually guilty of.

Contempts and misprisions against the royal person or the

government are also punishable; but "What is to be done," beseechingly inquires Puffendorf, "when the government makes itself contemptible?"

Contempts against the king's title are the denial of his right to the crown,—an offence occasionally committed by some deluded maniac who fancies he ought to be on the throne of England, instead of in the garret which such a person usually occupies. Contempts against the royal palaces are also misprision; but this is sometimes the fault of the architects who build them, and Buckingham Palace is a standing incentive to misprisions of this description, for no one can look at it without thinking it utterly contemptible. Fighting in the king's palace or courts of justice was formerly punished by death; so that a quarrel between two of the royal housemaids, or a set-to between an usher and a refractory bystander in Westminster Hall, would have subjected all the parties concerned to the penalty of hanging. This severe statute is now repealed, and a row in court, instead of being a capital felony, is generally regarded as a capital joke by all but those who are immediately concerned in it. It is also a misprision to use threatening words to a judge; but the judge of a court of request often hears all sorts of threats addressed to him, amid which he can only scream out "I'll commit you if you're not quiet," though, as he has only one impotent usher to protect him from a mob of desperate suitors, he never can get his menace executed. Assaulting a plaintiff or defendant, and endeavouring to intimidate a witness, also amounted to misprision; but the latter offence has become so common among counsel themselves, under the very eye of the court, that the judges are obliged to wink at it.

CHAPTER X.

IN treating of offences against public justice we shall begin with the most penal, and then fall down upon those which, growing "small by degrees and beautifully less," may be considered as next to nothing in the scale of criminality. . Embezzling or falsifying a record is a felony. And it is a grievous offence to steal a writ ; but as people often get more writs given to them than they care to have, it is not very likely such an offence would be committed.

It is felony in a gaoler to use too much duress towards a prisoner in order to make him accuse another; as if Mucius the Arcade beadle had got the boy Paulus in custody by the scurf of the neck, and were urging him to confess that the infant Spurius had thrown a stone, it would be evident that Mucius the beadle would be guilty of felony.

A third offence against public justice is obstructing process ; such as pumping on an officer about to serve a writ, or jogging the hand of the signer or sealer, so that he could neither sign nor seal the awful document.

An escape out of custody is also an offence against public justice ; but when a prisoner has once made his escape, it is a game the authorities are very anxious to catch him at.

Rescuing a prisoner is another offence against public justice ; and it is a felony even to lend him a disguise to elude justice ; so that it is dangerous for the keeper of a masquerade warehouse to lend out his dresses promiscuously to all sorts of characters, some of whom may be escaped convicts, who are very likely to form part of the company at a Cockney carnival.

Returning from transportation used to be a capital offence ;

so that quick returns brought very small profits; but the law is now relaxed, and the offence is punishable with transportation for life, or until the convict makes his escape a second time.

Receiving stolen goods, knowing them to be stolen, is also an offence against public justice; as if the audience at a new play receives with laughter a joke that has been cribbed from Joe Miller or somebody else, the public well knowing the same to be stolen.

Compounding a felony is punishable with fine and imprisonment; as if some one steals my handkerchief, at the same time "filching from me my good name," marked in red cotton in the corner, it is not allowable for me to take my property back, and promise not to prosecute; for if I did such a thing, even with reference to a mere pocket handkerchief, I should get a wipe from the hands of justice.

Common barretry is the offence of exciting and stirring up lawsuits and quarrels, or setting parties at loggerheads with one another; but as this only brings grist to the mill, the law does not very often take notice of an offence which it finds tolerably lucrative.

Maintenance is the maintaining a person with money to go to law; but indeed it seems only fair that a person inducing another to go to law, which may probably strip him of all he has got, should at least undertake the responsibility of his maintenance.

Champerty is an agreement with either plaintiff or defendant to divide the profits of the suit; but this is a dangerous game, for however just the cause, there may be at the end of it nothing to divide but a heavy lawyer's bill.

Conspiracy to indict an innocent man is also punishable, and so is the offence of sending threatening letters; but it does not seem that a letter from a tailor, threatening proceedings unless he receives the amount of his little bill, can be considered a threatening letter under the statute.

Perjury, and subornation of perjury, are both very serious

offences, for which a man's ears were formerly nailed to the pillory; and the old saying that "walls have ears," arose probably from the number of ears that were nailed against the wall, when this part of the law was acted upon. The celebrated speech of Marc Antony, in which he asks the Romans to lend him their ears, shows that these articles were moveable in the days of Julius Cæsar.

Bribery used to be a common offence among the judges, until Edward the Third stuck up a notice that no fees should be paid to puisnés; until which time the legal dignitaries were in the habit of almost asking to be remembered, and virtually saying, "Judge, your honour?" to the parties whose causes they tried, much in the same spirit as the demand made at the cab-stand of "a copper for the waterman."

Embracery is an attempt to influence a jury by promises or persuasions; as if the plaintiff were to rush into the box and throw his arms round the necks of the twelve honest men about to try his action. Embracery is a kind of huggery of the jury which there is nothing to justify; for a party to a suit should embrace nothing but the opportunity of getting it tried as soon as possible.

There are one or two other offences which suppose misconduct in the judges; but this is an event that with the benches of the courts filled as they now are, cannot by my possibility happen.

CHAPTER XI.

OF OFFENCES AGAINST THE PUBLIC PEACE.

THE first offence against the public peace is the riotous assembling of twelve persons; but our peace has often been more disturbed by the riotous assembling of two or three cats under our window, than by the largest and noisiest mob of human beings. In case of an assembly of twelve or more refusing to disperse, the riot act may be read to them ; but as it is impossible to hear a word of that lively and interesting statute in the midst of an uproar, it would be just as well to read a chapter of the last new novel, or a scene from the last new play—either of which, by the way, might be more efficacious in driving people away than even the riot act. If they do not disperse, they are guilty of a transportable offence ; and *semble*, that any one beginning to sing, " We won't go home till morning," may be specially punished as a ringleader. Unlawfully hunting in a legal forest or park is felony punishable as simple larceny ; and if I were to go hunting among the woods and forests up and down Regent Street, or in either of the Parks, I should, indeed, be guilty of very simple larceny. Sending threatening letters, demanding money, is transportable ; but I cannot transport an attorney if he sends me a letter threatening to sue me if I do not pay my tailor.

Pulling down floodgates, picking the locks of canals, and taking away the dreary or venerable piles of any sea-bank or wall, are all felonies punishable with transportation. Destroying and walking off with a turnpike-gate is a similar offence ; but any one may regularly clear the toll if he has a proper ticket.

Affrays (from *affraier*, to terrify), are fights between two or more persons, to the alarm of the bystanders, any of whom may interfere to part the combatants, and probably get for his pains some pains of another description. The constable is actually bound to interfere at all risks ; and poor Pummell, the Kensington beadle, has in this way come in for an immense quantity of pummelling.

Riots, routs, and unlawful assemblies, require at least three persons ; " for," asks Hawkins, " who would go to the expense of rout cakes and rout seats, for a rout at which less than three individuals are to be present ?" Rioting and routing are meeting to do any unlawful acts whatever. Unlawful assemblies include drilling without authority ; but a sergeant may attend a preparatory school, and drill young gentlemen from three to eight, without any special license.

Tumultuous petitioning was made an offence by a statute of Charles the Second; so that more than twenty persons must not sign a petition to the King or Parliament, on any matter of church or state, and they are thus prevented from begging the question.

Forcible entry is likewise punishable by imprisonment; but perhaps the old custom of kicking down stairs is the best mode of treating any one who forces himself upon you, when you wish to get rid of him.

The offence of riding or going armed is a crime, because it is likely to terrify the people: though in the present day the people are not so easily terrified; and when they see the ancient knights armed *cap-a-piè* in the Lord Mayor's Show, the people, instead of being terrified, only laugh at the knights alluded to.

Spreading false news was punishable by fine and imprisonment; and a penny-a-liner who furnishes a flaming report of a fire that never took place, or the dry particulars of a storm that did not happen, ought not to be sheltered from the consequences of his deception.

False prophecies were formerly very general, and are even now punishable with fine and imprisonment; thus, if in an almanack I predict rainy weather, and it is fine, the fine may be imposed upon me, for having imposed upon others.

To send a challenge is also penal; but a puffing tradesman may challenge competition to any extent; for it is not in the nature of a duel, because it seldom ends in his giving satisfaction.

The last offence against public justice to which we now refer is that of libel, the truth of which was formerly no justification; and as "the truth is not at all times to be spoken," it is still only a justification in cases where it is proper that it should be published. We had prepared a very splendid panegyric on the liberty of the press; but, availing ourselves of the liberty of the press, we take the liberty of omitting it.

CHAPTER XII.

OF OFFENCES AGAINST PUBLIC TRADE.

SMUGGLING is an offence against public trade ; but it is so frequently practised by the fair sex, that it has been held to be a fair proceeding, if it can be managed without detection.

Another offence of this class is fraudulent bankruptcy, like that of Antonio, the Venetian bankrupt, who having made an alarming failure and a terrific sacrifice of his friend, was compelled to take the benefit of the (fifth) act of the *Merchant of Venice.* Usury was formerly highly penal ; but it may now be practised almost without restriction ; for the· law says, to protect yourself against usury, you must use— your—eye—and keep a good look-out after your own interest. Cheating is an offence against trade, which is very commonly practised ; "for it is wonderful," says Roger Bacon, "how much lighter a pound of sugar becomes in your own scales ;" and, indeed, the ingenuity of the tradesman is chiefly shown in attaching an undue weight to trifles.

Forestalling the market is an offence at common law ; as if I were to waylay a cart full of turnips going towards Covent Garden, and purchase them all, I should probably send turnips up to a frightful premium, by forestalling the market.

These are all the offences against trade which the law at present punishes ; though perhaps the most serious offence against trade is the very ordinary one of getting into a tradesman's books without the smallest intention of paying him.

CHAPTER XIII.

THE chief offence against the public health was, in former times, that of spreading the plague, which is happily now extinct; though we have a tolerably severe substitute for the plague, in the Income Tax.

A second offence against public health is the adulteration of food or wine; but the bakers frequently grind their bones to make our bread; for cheating is bred in the bone of most of them. Wine also is frequently mixed, and more particularly port wine, though cape is sometimes known to be waterproof.

We now come to offences against the public police; in which we do not mean to include such petty offences as calling a policeman offensive names, which is a juvenile error frequently committed by boys in a state of buoyancy.

First in the catalogue of those offences stands the enormity of forging any document relating to marriage, such as a license or a certificate; though the fetters of matrimony may be forged at any time by any ordinary Smith, or Jones, or Thomson.

Polygamy is also a very serious offence; but it is a crime that generally brings its own punishment. Two or more wives must be a somewhat fearful infliction; for it has generally been held that one is a dose, under ordinary circumstances.

Outlandish persons, calling themselves Egyptians, or gypsies, were formerly subjected to the severest penalties; but now they are only treated as rogues and vagabonds. They are in the habit of robbing farmyards and telling fortunes, pretending to the gift of prophecy, which is no gift at all, for they make people pay pretty dearly for it. It has been ingeniously said, by an acute punster, that these fortune-telling gypsies are more plagues than prophets.

Personation of some one entitled to money is also an offence; but it is often committed on the stage by gentlemen with thirty shillings a week, who personate heirs to the vast estates of testy old men in farces and comedies.

We now come to common nuisances, which include annoyances in highways, bridges, and public rivers, all of which may be put down in a summary manner. Some nuisances, however, cannot be remedied,—such as being splashed with mud on the highway, having your hat blown off on a bridge, or running aground in a river. Since the introduction of railways, a new class of nuisances has sprung up, the worst of all being, however, the nuisance of holding shares that do not bear a premium or return a dividend.

Offensive trades come under the head of nuisances, and melting tallow is said to be indictable; though every man who burns dips or rushlights is *pro tanto* a melter of tallow.

It is a nuisance also to keep a disorderly inn, but an inn where there are no orders, must be chiefly a nuisance to the landlord. Making fireworks or squibs is punishable by fine, but a good squib is never objected to. Eaves-droppers, or such as listen under the eaves of houses, are a common nuisance, and are indictable at the sessions; but they are also punishable with the water-jug, which is now the better practice. Last but not least in the catalogue of nuisances comes the common scold, or *communis rixatrix*, who used formerly to be placed on a stool and ducked; from which practice it is thought the word duck came to be applied to a wife by her husband.

Idleness is a high offence against public economy; but our law makes a distinction between idleness from choice and idleness from actual necessity, for it only punishes the latter, though the former would seem to be the most blameable. Idlers from necessity are treated first as disorderly persons if they have nothing to do, but a second offence brings them under the head of rogues and vagabonds; and as nothing can come of nothing, they are—unless they take to picking pockets—tolerably sure to fall eventually under that denomination.

Persons exposing wounds to excite compassion, such as going about without legs for the purpose of collecting alms, may be imprisoned on conviction before a magistrate.

Luxury has been the subject of restraining statutes; and formerly extravagance in dress, diet, and the like, could be severely punished. In the reigns of Edwards the 3rd and 4th it was made penal to wear piked shoes, but the nobles kicked at it, and it was repealed accordingly. There is still a statute existing which ordains that no man shall be served at dinner or supper with more than two courses ; "but how," asks Sir John Fortescue, "is the law to know whether at supper I follow up my plate of sprats with a welsh rabbit, and wind up with a piece of cold pudding saved from my dinner, making three coursés in defiance to the strict letter of the Act of Parliament."

Next to luxury comes the offence of gaming, which was once so rigidly prohibited that none but nobles and gentlemen were permitted to play at bowls and skittles, so that the aristocracy of Henry the 8th's time no doubt patronised all the public houses that could boast of good dry skittle grounds. In George the 2nd's time an Act was passed to put down "rolly polly and other games," but "gammon and spinach" does not seem to have been mentioned in that wholesome statute. Gambling debts are called debts of honour, because they are in violation of the law, which, however, does not go at high game in its punishment of gaming, but makes thimble-rig the object of its greatest rigour.

There is another kind of game which by means of the game laws has been made the peculiar care of the legislature. Persons preserving game are qualified to kill it ; but potting a hare does not give a right to become a sportsman. The severity of the game laws has been greatly relaxed within the last few years, and as further amendment is likely to take place, we forbear from letting fly at them, but return the shafts of indignation to our agitated and quivering quiver.

CHAPTER XIV.

OF HOMICIDE.

HOMICIDE is of three kinds, justifiable, excusable, or felonious. When the law tells a man he may go and be hanged, it is justifiable, and, indeed, necessary to hang him ; but the necessity must be bitter, indeed, which causes any one to adopt such a line as the halter. It is said to be justifiable to commit homicide to prevent a robbery ; but if a boy were in the act of picking my pocket, I do not think I should be justified in stabbing him to the heart with the ferule of my umbrella, or braining him with the knob at the handle of it.

Homicide by accident is excusable, as if Servius makes a joke which sets Publius laughing till he splits his sides and dies of laughing ; then Servius has been guilty of accidental homicide, for which the heirs of Publius could not have him punished. If, however, Publius is on horseback, and Servius whips his horse, causing it to run away and kill a child, then Publius is innocent, but Servius is guilty of manslaughter.

Homicide in self-defence is excusable ; but I am bound to run away as far as I can, before I turn round upon my assailant ; and it is only when I get into a *cul-de-sac*, such as Panton Square, where there is no thoroughfare, that I am justified in making a stand against my pursuer, and killing him, if he will not be satisfied with any milder treatment.

Felonious homicide is either self-murder or the murder of another ; and as they are neither of them pleasant themes, we forbear to make them the subject of comment. The law itself was formerly guilty of this crime to an enormous extent, and the legislative murdered more persons than ever fell by the hand of private assassins. Within the last few years, these legalised atrocities have been very properly abolished.

CHAPTER XV.

THE first offence against the person is meyhem, which we have already touched upon. It consists of depriving a man of any limb that may be of use to him in fight; but does not extend to his nose, which gives him no advantage over his adversary; but, perhaps its very absence would tend to terrify a foe, and thus prove as good as an extra weapon. By the old law, any one guilty of meyhem was sentenced to lose the limb of which he had deprived another; but this was found inconvenient; for if a man cut off the arms of six people at once, he could not receive his punishment, because it would be impossible to amputate his arm twelve times over. This offence, when accompanied by an attempt to murder, is now punishable by death, along with many other delinquencies of a similar character.

The second offence against personal security is stealing an heiress, by running away with her against her will; but this rarely happens in these days, for heiresses either have no will of their own, or are quite willing to be run away with.

Assaults, batteries, and woundings, are minor offences, and may be punished by fine or imprisonment. One species of battery is more atrocious than the rest, namely, that of beating a clerk in orders; but there are some clerks who act quite contrary to orders, and who would be all the better for a little wholesome battery without the benefit of clergy being allowed to them.

False imprisonment is an offence we have already alluded to;—though if the imprisonment is false, it cannot be real, and it seems to be only fighting with a shadow to make it the subject of punishment.

The last offence against the person is that of kidnapping men, women, or children, called in the civil law spiriting them away; because probably they were plied with spirits till they were utterly intoxicated and incapable of taking care of themselves. The only relic of kidnapping in the present day is the custom of smugging a boy for a Guy on the fifth of November. This, however, savours somewhat of child-stealing, which is punishable by transportation for seven years, or two years' imprisonment.

CHAPTER XVI.

OF OFFENCES AGAINST THE HABITATIONS OF INDIVIDUALS.

THE offences immediately affecting the habitations of individuals are only arson and burglary, to say nothing of the minor offences of runaway rings at the bell and wrenching off of door-knockers.

Arson is the malicious burning of a house, or outhouse; but an attempt to burn is not actually arson. And the surrounding a building with Talacre coal, which notoriously refuses to burn, would not be considered felonious.

Burglary is breaking into a man's house, which the law of England figuratively styles his castle, looking upon the steps across the area as the drawbridge, and the gutter that runs along the top as the battlement, while the donjon-keep is probably either the iron safe, or the copper. Oxford-street is in the eye of the constitution a series of castles, and the wife of each honest tradesman is of course a *châtelaine*.

"A burglar," says Coke, "is one who entereth a mansion-house at night to commit a felony," as if any one goes to dine with the Lord Mayor, intending to pocket any of the city spoons—not the aldermen, but the plate—he is guilty of burglary.

Four things are necessary to constitute a burglary in law ; namely, the time, the place, the manner, and the intent, to which may be added occasionally the dark lantern, the crow-bar, and the opportunity.

The time must be night, for there is no burglary in the day; and it was formerly difficult to determine what was really night, and what was day, till the statute 1st of Victoria, c. 86, was passed, which declares the night to be from nine in the evening till six in the morning ; so that the burglars are apt to say, "that's your time of day!" when they are planning a burglary.

As to the place, it must be a mansion-house ; but a coal-cellar, or a larder connected with a house by a covered way, is considered a mansion-house for housebreaking purposes.

If I hire a shop and never lie there, it is no dwelling-house, and burglary cannot be committed therein ; but I shall very likely lie in my shop, even if I do not sleep there, for I should be sure to puff my goods enormously.

The next essential to a burglary is the manner ; for manners do not only make the man, but they also make the burglar: there must be a breaking and an entry, either by breaking a pane, or picking a lock; but a burglar must be at great pains, for he could not make an entry through a very little one. Getting down a chimney is a breaking and an entry, and, indeed, it may sometimes be both ; for the burglar may break his leg, besides finding himself regularly in for it. A partial entry is sufficient after a breaking, as if a burglar gets stuck in the middle of a window-frame, and can neither get one way or the other, he has made a burglarious as well as what Coke would call a bunglarious entry. Walking into a house in the day-time, committing a felony, and breaking out at night, is a burglary ; but it would seem that the thief must have broken out in a fresh place to constitute the offence alluded to. The intent is also requisite to complete a burglary ; for if a man walks from the top of his own house on to that of his neighbour, and tumbles through on to his neighbour's bed in the middle of the night, there will be a breaking and an entry, but no burglary.

The punishment of this crime varies according to circumstances; for when accompanied with an attempt to murder, the penalty is death; but in other cases it is transportation or imprisonment.

CHAPTER XVII.

OF OFFENCES AGAINST PRIVATE PROPERTY.

LARCENY, malicious mischief, and forgery, constitute a leash of offences against private property, which we will now proceed to touch upon.

1. Larceny, or theft, is either simple, or compound; the first being plain theft, and the second accompanied by aggravating circumstances, though being robbed is generally considered to be of itself an aggravating circumstance. Simple larceny was further divided into grand and *petit*, or petty, the grandeur consisting in the goods stolen being worth more than twelve pence; while a robbery for eleven pence three farthings was always thought to be a very petty proceeding. Simple larceny is the felonious taking and carrying away of the goods of another, which it is said could not have happened when things were held to be common: but a gingham umbrella is held to be very common, and yet it is larceny to walk away with it.

To constitute larceny, there must be a taking; though if I steal a hundred blue pills, it is doubtful whether I must take them all, in order to have the charge of theft brought home to me. There must at all events be a carrying away. Though in a larceny of a horse, it is not necessary that the thief should carry away the horse; for if it were *vice versâ*, and the horse carries away the thief, it is still clearly a robbery. The taking and carrying away must be felonious; for if I take a pinch of snuff and carry it away, I cannot have done so *animo furandi;* but more likely *animo sneezandi;* and it is therefore no felony. There can be no larceny committed with reference to real property, or of things adhering to the realty; as if a bill-sticker sticks a bill against my wall, it adheres to the realty, and there would be no larceny in pulling it down; but I should be much obliged to any one who did so. Things savouring of the freehold, such as corn, or grass, could not formerly be the subject of larceny; but *semble*, that herbs for stuffing might have been; for though they savour of the land, they savour still more of sage and onions. Taking a shrub by day or night is, however, now larceny; but taking rum-shrub without any felonious intent, is not punishable. Stealing animals, *feræ naturæ*, is not larceny; and there is no property in either a rat or a rhinoceros, unless they are enclosed; as a rat caught in a trap, or the rhinoceros "at home" in the gardens of the Surrey Zoological.

We now come to the punishment of larceny, which was made death by Draco, who is said to have written his laws in blood; but it is possible that he wrote them in red ink, which may account for the mistake the historian has fallen into.

Our ancient Saxon law hanged people for simple larceny of anything above the value of a shilling; and, indeed, the rope was so common in olden times, that the word Eu-rope is supposed to be derived from the European practice of wholesale execution. Even until the 7 & 8 of George the 4th, c. 29, the laws were very severe, and it was a hanging matter to plunder a vessel in distress; so that stealing a bottle of ginger-beer from the cabin of an above-bridge steamboat during a collision, would have been in those days death without clergy. Simple larceny is, however, made punishable with transportation, imprisonment, or whipping, by the statute alluded to. Whipping is generally applied to juveniles, who are often called whipper-snappers, because they often snap in two the whips they are beaten with.

Mixed, or compound larceny, is an offence much stronger—
like everything used for mixing—than simple larceny, or larceny "neat as imported." The distinction consists in the fact
of the former being committed in a house, or on a person ; and
when accompanied by force, it is called robbery.   Putting in
fear is sufficient without actual violence ; as if a man shakes
his fist in my face, and asks alms, as though he would say,
" Your money or your nose," it is a robbery, if I give it
him—meaning the money—to prevent his giving it to me
after another fashion. .

Malicious mischief is the second offence against private
property, and is punished by various terms of transportation or
imprisonment.   Destroying corn, or hay, or even hops, comes
under the head of malicious mischief; and it would seem
that going to a dancing-room with the intention of turning
it into ridicule, might be such destruction to a hop as to
amount to malicious mischief.   Taking possession of marine
stores from a stranded vessel, and selling it, is also a malicious mischief; but if I find in the Strand a vessel—say a
saucepan—containing marine stores—say kitchen-stuff—I
am liable to no very severe penalty for selling it.

The third offence against private property is forgery, or
the *Crimen Falsi*, which was formerly capital, without the
benefit of clergy, though, by the way, as forgery implied an
ability to read and write, clergy, which was the same thing,
could have been no benefit whatever ; for he who could not
plead clergy, that is to say, who could neither read nor write,
could not have been found guilty of forgery. Uttering a note as
true, when it was really false, was formerly death, so that
the principal tenor at a theatre would have deserved hanging
twenty times in a night, if the utterance of false notes had
in those days been considered capital. By the 11th of George
the 4th, and the 1st of William the 4th, all the sanguinary
laws against forgery were repealed : and transportation for
life, or for lesser periods, is now the penalty of the crime
alluded to.   The lowest kind of forgery is, however, punish-

able with fine or imprisonment, or both, and includes the forgery of the plates on hackney-coaches, or the conductor's or driver's badge, which becomes a badge of fraud under such disgraceful circumstances. Some kinds of forgeries are allowable, and the forging of a horse-shoe is most certainly winked at by the law, if the law has it in its eye, by standing too near the anvil. " But," says Spelman, "a smith's fiery furnace, is not a thing for authority to set its face against." Such are the principal infringements of the rights of property; and our Synopsis having comprehended them all, we can only hope that the reader will have comprehended them also.

CHAPTER XVIII.

OF THE MEANS OF PREVENTING OFFENCES.

HAVING frightened our readers out of their wits by talking about crimes, it is high time we should begin to say how they are to be prevented.

One mode of preventing an offence is by binding over a suspected party to keep the peace, as if Valerius threatens to knock Marcius into the middle of the ensuing week, Marcius may get Valerius bound over in a heavy penalty, and perhaps find others to be security for his good behaviour also. Thus Marcius is protected; for if he is found to have been precipitated by Valerius suddenly in advance of his age, the recognizances of Valerius will be forfeited.

A man may be bound over to good behaviour, if he is found to keep bad company; though it does not seem that the manager of a theatre can be bound over to good behaviour for keeping the very worst company that can be found; for if he could, there would always be many against whom it would be advisable to enforce the penalty.

CHAPTER XIX.

OF COURTS OF CRIMINAL JURISDICTION.

THE method of inflicting punishments will be the last subject of our inquiries; though our readers may possibly think that they know sufficiently what an infliction is, from having perused the previous portion of our learned treatise.

We shall now describe the Courts of Criminal Jurisdiction, which are all independent of each other, and can pursue their executive vagaries in their own peculiar way without appeal or interference of any kind.

1. The highest criminal court is the High Court of Parliament, before which the nation, in the character of a policeman, may bring up a corrupt minister, and after giving him in charge, may insist on his undergoing a trial. This is the grand privilege of the whole people acting through their representatives; but what is everybody's business is nobody's business; and though corrupt ministers are seldom scarce, no one takes the trouble of impeaching them.

2. The Court of the Lord High Steward, is a court instituted for the trial of peers indicted for treason or felony, as if Duke Humphrey, the hospitable nobleman with whom some of us have so frequently dined, were to commit a highway robbery upon me, he, supposing him to be a peer, might be tried by the Court of the Lord High Steward for the delinquency.

3. The Court of Queen's Bench has a plea side and a crown side; the latter taking cognisance of all criminal cases—"but the crown side does not mean," says Puffendorf, "that side of the Court which has the royal arms with the crown fixed up against the wall of the building."

4. The Court of Admiralty, which has jurisdiction over

crimes committed on the sea, or on the coast, as if I am bathing at Margate, and any one runs away with my clothes, the Court of Admiralty is open to me, for I may stand on my naked right, and the law will throw its cloak completely over me.

5 & 6. The Courts of *Oyer* and *Terminer*, and general gaol delivery, which are held by the Judges, who go round twice a year, to hear and determine, and deliver the gaols, by hanging, transporting, imprisoning, or acquitting, and in some way making a clearance of all the prisoners.

7. We now come to the Central Criminal Court, established by the 4 & 5 of William 4th, c. 36—a Court which is an odd compound of judges, for it may comprise the Lord Chancellor and the Lord Mayor, with a sprinkling of Aldermen, and even a spice of judicial seasoning from the Sheriffs' Court. This tribunal is a sort of common sewer for carrying off all the iniquity of London and Middlesex, as well as certain parts of Kent, Essex, and Surrey. It is a kind of criminal cesspool, and some of the scavengers of the profession were formerly in the habit of frequenting it.

8. The Court of Quarter Sessions of the Peace, for the trial of minor offences, when the chairman and the bar divide their time between small talk and small delinquencies.

9. The Sheriff's Tourn, or turn, when the sheriff takes a turn at judicial work ; and

10. The Court leet, which, as the Scotch would say, has very *leetle* occupation ; or, to make use of the more healthy English pun, the Court *leet* is now nearly obso-*leet*.

11. The Court of the Coroner, to which we have made an allusion in another portion of our work ; and finally,

12. The Court of the Clerk of the Market, to punish false weights and bad measures ; though the prime minister cannot be punished for his bad measures in the Court alluded to.

There are a few criminal courts having a partial jurisdiction, but they are nearly all obsolete ; and Bacon says,

"partiality is such a bad thing, that courts of partial jurisdiction ought to grow obsolete as quickly as possible."

The Courts of the two Universities have been already referred to ; but they are virtually dead, or at least in a state
of hibernisation, from which they are not likely to be
awakened.   The Vice Chancellor of each University may
claim cognisance of any indictment preferred against any
scholar ; but the Vice Chancellor has something better to do
than keep his eye on the criminal procedure throughout the
country for the purpose of availing himself of the privilege of
trying any matter of knocker-wrenching, or nocturnal bell-
ringing, in which a member of the University may have been
concerned.

Lastly, we have to notice the police courts of the metropolis, the acts relating to which have been amended by the
2 & 3 of Victoria, c. 71 ; but further amendment is very
desirable.   These courts are chiefly distinguished for their
efficacy in putting down, or, at all events, thrusting out
of the way, the frightful cases of fruit-selling, destitution, and
other flagrant crimes with which the metropolis would be
overrun but for the summary treatment they experience at
the hands of the police magistrates.

CHAPTER XX.

OF SUMMARY CONVICTIONS.

A SUMMARY conviction is a conviction summarily arrived
at by a judge without the intervention of a jury.   In former
times this sort of conviction was so very summary that the
justices condemned a man before they summoned him, which
certainly saved the trouble of hearing a tedious defence, and
perhaps examining witnesses.   There is an appeal to the
Quarter Sessions, but this is often going out of the frying-pan

into the fire, for the justices in Quarter Sessions are usually more summary than they are when exercising separately their ordinary jurisdiction. In most cases a conviction, like a gooseberry, may be quashed in the Court of Queen's Bench, when that great constitutional crane, a *certiorari*, has been put into requisition to lift the conviction up to the higher court from the lower one. Every offence punishable by summary conviction must be prosecuted within three months; "for if it were not," says Sir John Suckling, "we should have a summary conviction happening for some offence committed in the winter, which would be quite out of season." Contempts are punished in a summary way by attachment, though attachment seems really an odd way of meeting contempt under ordinary circumstances. Contempts are either direct or consequential; and when the judges wish to be very consequential, direct contempt must be sadly derogatory to their dignity. There are various kinds of contempts, but the greatest contempt of all is that which is generally felt for the Courts of Request; a contempt that sometimes breaks out into a volley of abuse showered down on to the heads of the commissioners by the disgusted suitors.

If contempt be manifested in the face of the court, as by throwing his ignorance in the face of a commissioner, or telling him he is a fool to his teeth, the party may be instantly apprehended; though in the Courts of Request the usher is usually old and imbecile, while the whole court is scarcely equal to the meanest apprehension.

In Chancery any one may purge himself of contempt by a draft affidavit.

CHAPTER XXI.

OF ARRESTS.

An arrest may be made four ways :—1. By warrant; 2. By an officer without warrant; 3. By a private person also without warrant (as if that disagreeable private individual, Publius, unwarrantably holds me by the button-hole, which is really an arrest); and 4. By a hue and cry, or a hullabullo, in which the law luxuriates.

1. Of arrest by warrant, which Sir Edward Coke once said could not be issued till an indictment had been actually found, but while this was being done the suspected party might he actually lost, and the indictment would then be found to be useless. Warrants formerly did not run into any county but that for which they were originally intended ; but as the delinquents used to run into another county, the custom of backing warrants was resorted to. This process is effected by the Justice of the second county putting his name on the back of the warrant issued in the first ; and a criminal who has escaped to a colony may be arrested on a warrant endorsed by a colonial Judge. "So that," according to the wag Tomlins, "he may be brought to a full stop in a distant *colon-*y." By the 6 & 7 Victoria, cc. 75 and 76, French and American criminals may be captured here in return for a privilege allowed us of taking into custody in France and America certain delinquents who may have gone there for congenial society.

2. Arrests without a warrant may be effected by a justice of the peace, the sheriff, the coroner, and the constable, all of whom may apprehend any one for an offence they have seen committed, as if there should be an assault, and a blow is given under the sheriff's eye, he is justified in taking the assailant into custody.

3. Any private persons present at a felony may arrest the felon, and if they kill him it is not murder, but if he kills them they have the satisfaction of knowing that it is murder to all intents and purposes.

4. The last species of arrest is the hue and cry, or running after a felon with horn and voice; such as the *cornet à piston* and the lul-li-e-te, which may be kept up from town to town like a tin kettle at a dog's tail, after a suspected felon. The statutes relative to hue and cry have, however, been all repealed by the 7 & 8 Geo. IV., and the hue and cry may be practised as a solo by a single peace officer, or any private man that knows of a felony. Any one maliciously raising the hue and cry may be punished as a disturber of the public peace, for then he becomes little better than the dustman, the itinerant vendor of fish, or any other noisy individual.

It was customary in former times to offer rewards for apprehending felons, and 40*l.* were given by the 4 & 5 W. & M. c. 8, to any one who would capture and prosecute to conviction a real highwayman. Such a character is now obsolete, and is likely to continue so, unless the highwayman, finding his occupation gone upon the road, should take to the rail, and, riding on a high-spirited locomotive, stop the goods train, exclaiming "Your luggage or your life" to the affrighted stoker.

CHAPTER XXII.

OF COMMITMENT AND BAIL.

HAVING now got our delinquent regularly into custody, let us see how we are to deal with him; for we must either commit him or take bail, and this brings us to the subject of the present chapter. When a person is charged before a justice with any offence, the circumstances may be inquired into, and if there is no ground for suspicion, the prisoner must be discharged; as if a man is accused of stealing a horse, and it turns out to be a mare's nest, the suspected party must be set at liberty. In doubtful cases the prisoner must either be locked up or bailed. There are some offences for which an immediate committal must take place, and " as to bail," says Coke, " the law will not have it at any price." Murder and treason are bailable only in the Court of Queen's Bench. Other courts must send the suspected assassin or traitor to prison, where he may have every comfort consistent with his safe custody. He may have his dinner from the nearest hotel, if he is rich enough to pay for it ; but the law gives him none of these luxuries, except perhaps his gruel, in the end. The law has no right to hurt a hair of his head, and he therefore does not undergo the operation of having his hair cut, which convicted delinquents are compelled to endure.

CHAPTER XXIII.

OF THE SEVERAL MODES OF PROSECUTION.

THERE are several modes of prosecution ; but if we were asked to recommend any one mode, we should be disposed to tell the querist to toss up a halfpenny and decide for himself.

Presentment and indictment are two of the forms which we shall now proceed to describe ; but as a presentment is generally the preliminary to an indictment, the latter will be the subject of our remarks.

An indictment is always brought in the name of the sovereign, who is the supposed recipient of all the black-eyes, blows, and bruises, which are made the subject of an indictment for an assault. An indictment must always be presented on oath by a grand jury, whose grandeur is generally explained to them in a charge from the judge, who says— " Gentlemen, you are a very ancient body ; you are as old as King Ethelred :" but if they were told they were as old as Methuselah, they would be just as wise.

The grand jury then hear the evidence, which they generally get at by asking twenty questions at once, mistaking the beadle for the witness, and examining the door-keeper every now and then, by way of change. If they think the accusation groundless, they write on the bill "not found;" but they used formerly to indorse it with the word *ignoramus*, which has been discontinued on account of its seeming to refer less to the bill than to themselves. If they think it a true bill, the indictment is said to be found, though the prisoner often considers that all is lost when a bill is found against him. Indictments formerly required a great deal of bad Latin, and worse English, to render them valid, while a departure from a technicality was fatal to the whole. Thus, in the case of a murderer whose name was Richard, but who was called, in the record, Dick, it was declared upon the Dicktum of all the judges, that Dick was not his proper name, and he was therefore discharged. By recent statutes, however, amendments are allowed to be made.

Besides indictments there are informations, which are sometimes at the joint suit of the Crown and the informer. The King or Queen leads, and the informer, who is often a Knave, merely follows suit. Other informations are at the suit of the Crown alone, and are filed *ex officio* by the Attorney-General, who does so by virtue of his office, though, when we look at the large fees, we cannot say that virtue is in this case its own and its only reward.

There is also a species of information in the nature of a *quo warranto*, to which we have already alluded. It issues in cases of the usurpation of an office, as, if Spurius is beadle of an Arcade, and Lucius insists on walking up and down with a staff performing the functions of beadle, Spurius may have a *quo warranto* to ask Lucius what warrants his interference, after which Lucius may be ousted at once.

These are the only modes of prosecution known to the English law, and on the subject of indictment and information we have indited all the information we possess.

CHAPTER XXIV.

OF PROCESS UPON AN INDICTMENT.

WHEN an indictment is found, the culprit is not always to be found, and it is usual in cases of small misdemeanors to issue a *venire facias*, calling on the delinquent to come; but he is sometimes as bad as a waiter at a tavern, for, call as long as you may, he will not come at all. In this case you must issue a *capias*, which is equivalent to clutching him by the *cape*, or laying hold of him by the collar; but it often happens, says Hawkins, "that even with the aid of a *capias* you may keep capering for months after a delinquent, whom you may be utterly incapable to catch." If an offender absconds, you may pursue him to outlawry; but you might as well pursue him to Jericho, for any benefit you will derive from the chase. Formerly an outlaw might be slain by every one he met, which was probably the origin of the complaint of the Irishman, that he had been " murthered fifty times."

After an indictment is found, it may be removed by *certiorari* into another court, a *certiorari* being a sort of legal spring-van, by which actions and prosecutions may be carefully removed. The old lawyers used to let out a *certiorari* as they would a truck, but it became a vehicle of so much mischief that in criminal cases it is now seldom used.

CHAPTER XXV.

OF ARRAIGNMENT AND ITS INCIDENTS.

ARRAIGNMENT is calling the prisoner to the bar; but it does not mean that he is made an utter barrister, for he is called upon to utter nothing but the words guilty or not guilty, in reply to the charge. He is told to hold up his hand, and it was once thought necessary to a trial that this should be done, until there happened a case of a prisoner without arms, who was implicated in stealing a venison pasty, and, on being asked to hold up his hand, he declared that he could have had no hand in the offence, nor even a finger in the pie, which led to his acquittal.

A criminal either stands mute, confesses the fact, or pleads, which are called incidents to the arraignment ; but the most startling incident of all is standing mute, because it is a piece of pantomime which the Court is seldom prepared for. A prisoner stands mute when he makes no answer at all, but proceeds to take a sight at the jury who are about to try him. If he answers foreign to the purpose, he also stands mute, as if he is asked, "Are you guilty or not guilty?" and "Don't you wish you may get it?" is the only reply that can be got out of him. If, having pleaded not guilty, he then refuses to put himself upon the country, he also stands mute ; but the law will nevertheless try him, for the law will have the country put upon. In former times a prisoner might be put upon the rack, but this is now abolished, though the mind may be upon the rack just as much as ever. The penance for standing mute was in ancient times very similar to a trick we have seen performed at Greenwich Fair by strong men, and was accomplished by putting heavy weights on the culprit's chest, beginning with a ten pound weight, and gradually increasing the pressure till the delinquent either died or pleaded. There is the case in the books of one poor fellow, who having had a three-volume novel thrust upon him, was completely flattened, though he had supported half a ton without the smallest inconvenience. By an Act passed in the reign of George the Fourth, standing mute amounts to a plea of not guilty ; but if silence gives consent, the opposite conclusion would seem to be the proper one.

Another incident to arraignment is simple confession, which is much too simple for the law, and the law, hating simplicity of any kind, discourages confession. The prisoner is generally advised to retract and take his chance, "for the law," says Hawkins, "is a toss-up, to which Hamlet is supposed to refer when he says, 'Man pleases not me, nor woman neither;' which proves that the Prince of Denmark had learned the game of heads-and-tails during his visit to England."

Accomplices may sometimes be admitted as witnesses, and are called king's evidence, if they will add to the villany of their offence the treachery of betraying their fellow-culprits.

CHAPTER XXVI.

OF PLEA AND ISSUE.

Pleas are of five sorts, whereof the first is a plea to the jurisdiction; as if a man is indicted for murder before the Secondary, he may take a primary objection to being tried by such a very secondary court.

Second, a demurrer to the indictment, by which the prisoner asserts that the crime laid to his charge is not the crime it is alleged to be; as, if I am arraigned as a poacher, and I have only poached an egg, I may demur to the indictment.

Third, a plea in abatement, which was formerly available for the mis-spelling of a name; but as the law has, as we have before hinted, burst the spell that bound it, we proceed to

Fourth, special pleas in bar, of which there are four kinds, namely, a former acquittal, a former conviction, a former attainder, or a pardon. A former acquittal is a good plea, for if the law finds a criminal not guilty, the law must then take him as it finds him, or rather it must not take him at all. A former conviction is also a good plea, if there has been no judgment, for if the law will not act up to its own conviction, and has betrayed a want of judgment, it is not the culprit's fault. A former attainder is likewise an allowable plea, for a person attainted is dead in law, and the law has no right to set him up again like a skittle already down, to have another shy at him.

Lastly, a pardon may be pleaded in bar, for though " Forget and forgive " is a good motto, it is not right that the law should forgive first and forget afterwards.

The fifth plea is the general issue, or not guilty, to which the Clerk of the Crown somewhat illiberally replies, that the prisoner is guilty, and he (the Clerk of the Crown) is ready to prove him so. This announcement is flippantly made by the two monosyllables *cul* and *prit*, *cul* being the short for culpability, and *prit* being neither the long nor the short, but rather the substitute for *paratus verificare* (I am ready to verify). From these two very vague abbreviations we get the word culprit, but when we get it we see no very great significance attached to it.

When the Crown and the culprit are at issue, the latter is said to have put himself upon the country, which means that he has thrown himself on the kind indulgence of a British jury-box. He is then brought to trial, with a description of which we intend to try the patience of our readers in the ensuing chapter.

CHAPTER XXVII.

OF TRIAL AND CONVICTION.

OUR Saxon ancestors had various methods of trial by purgation, such as poking people into the fire, or plunging them into the water, an arrangement which was said to be preserving innocence from false witnesses. For our own parts, we had rather run the risk of hard swearing, than incur the certainty of a severe roasting, and it is clear that if this mode of trial were in operation, no one would be found innocent but he who, like the celebrated Chabert, could keep a red-hot poker in his mouth as coolly as if he were sucking a lollipop. In the water ordeal alleged witches were thrown into pools, when, if they sunk, they got on swimmingly, for they were considered innocent ; but if they happened to swim, it was said they were indebted to witchcraft for their preservation, and they were hanged accordingly.

Another species of purgation was trial by corsned, or morsel of execration, which was a large lump of cheese or bread, that was to be swallowed entire by the suspected party, and if it went down without choking him, he was considered innocent. It is said that Godwin Earl of Kent was suffocated by the morsel of execration ; but the story does not go down with us, for we are utterly unable to swallow that which is, in every sense of the word, a crammer.

The trial by battel, or single combat, was a little more reasonable, though equally barbarous. Hawkins, who is constantly being betrayed by excessive vanity into an idle pun, says that the trial by battle was a striking scene ; but as we have referred to it in a former chapter, we shall resist the temptation of taking another view of it. By the way, if in these trials a prisoner might have appeared by attorney, they would still be popular, for the practice of subjecting the lawyers to ordeals, and particularly that of being ducked in a horse-pond, would be quite in conformity with the vulgar and absurd prejudice existing against the whole legal profession.

The fourth method of trial in criminal cases is that by the peers, which is often a farce, and if "one trial will," as the grocers say, "prove the fact," it is the trial of the Earl of Cardigan.

The trial by jury is, however, the grand boast of every Englishman, who enjoys the privilege from his birth, so that even the baby may consider trial by jury the bulwark of his little liberties. It is difficult to get up the steam of patriotism on this subject after having let it off in a previous chapter ; but, with enthusiasm for our stoker, we will make the attempt to take a few more turns ahead on this inspiring topic. The effort is, however, vain ; for our pen seems to stick in our throat, emotion chokes our inkstand, and our pen quivers with sensibility. We therefore give up the sentiment as hopeless, and by plunging into the cold facts, we give a damp to our patriotic ardour.

When the trial is called on, twelve jurymen are put into a box without a lid, and their names being read over, the prisoner may challenge or call out those who are not likely to give him satisfaction. To prevent all this challenging ending, like many other challenges, in smoke, and hindering the trial from proceeding, the number of challenges is limited to thirty-five in treason, and twenty in cases of felony.

When the jury is sworn, the trial proceeds as in ordinary cases, and prisoners are now allowed counsel; but this is merely taking them into the frying-pan out of the fire.

After the examination of witnesses on both sides, and the speeches of counsel, the jury must give their verdict, but if they cannot agree, they are locked up, and thus become prisoners themselves, like the alleged culprit they have been trying. If the British jury—the great palladium, &c. &c.—should give a verdict against the law, or against the direction of the judges, a motion to set it aside will smash the palladium in a few minutes, and batter the bulwark to pieces.

If the prisoner is acquitted, he is set at liberty without any fee, but though he has not stood mute, he will usually stand liquid, in the shape of beer, to his friends, who have come to congratulate him on his innocence.

If found guilty, either on his own confession or by verdict, he is brought up for judgment, which will be the subject of another chapter.

CHAPTER XXVIII.

OF THE BENEFIT OF CLERGY.

THE benefit of clergy is now abolished in every case; but in accordance with that desire to show our learning, which is

so common among law writers like ourselves, we proceed to
offer a few useless observations on that which is obsolete.

Formerly no man could be admitted to the privilege of
clergy unless he had the *tonsuram clericalem*, that is to say,
unless his head had been shaved ; but as this let in lunatics
and bald-headed persons to the benefit of clergy, the distinction was soon abolished, and all men who could read were
considered as clerks.   Laymen who took the benefit of clergy,
were marked with a hot iron on the thumb, and this burning
probably gave rise to Burn's Justice, of which we have all of
us heard.

Thus much for the benefit of clergy, which exists no
longer, except in the practice of paying half crowns with briefs
for the benefit of the clerks.

CHAPTER XXIX.

OF JUDGMENT AND ITS CONSEQUENCES.

In criminal proceedings judgment comes last ; but if judgment in some cases came first, much mischief—which of
course includes law—might be avoided.   After conviction a
defendant is asked what he has to say in arrest of judgment,
which is in most cases merely tantalising him, for let him
say what he will, he is seldom allowed to get off.   He may
plead a pardon if he has got one to plead, but if not, judgment must be pronounced against him according to the offence
he has been guilty of.   If felony is the crime, it involves
forfeiture of property and corruption of blood, being a sort of
moral vaccination which corrupts the blood, but is supposed to
make the patient healthier by purgation, which is the case
with a criminal who is supposed to be a new man when he
has undergone his punishment.   The goods of a convicted
felon are forfeited to the crown, and a housebreaker when
found guilty must lay his crowbar, his skeleton keys, and his

bull's eye, at the foot of the throne. He may, however, sell his property at any time previous to his actual conviction, and this is frequently done by culprits before their trial, which causes the market to be overstocked with implements for burglary on the eve of the commencement of the Sessions at the Old Bailey, and other criminal courts.

Corruption of blood was abolished in all cases except high treason and murder, by the 54th Geo. III. c. 145, which acted as a refiner, running throughout almost all the criminal veins and arteries of this happy land.

CHAPTER XXX.

OF REVERSAL OF JUDGMENT.

A JUDGMENT may be reversed either with or without a writ of error; a nice distinction reminding us of the subtlety with which one of the elder jurists divided the whole human race into two classes, namely those who had and those who had not been hanged.

A judgment may be reversed without a writ of error, when it is given by persons who have no right to form any judgment at all, as if I say to my servant that he may go and be hanged, I in fact pass sentence of death upon him, but my judgment, being a piece of gratuitous severity on my part, is *ipso facto* reversed. So if the Commissioners of a Court of Requests insist on trying a peer of the realm for high treason, and proceed to deliver judgment—which by the way is generally impossible, for they have usually no judgment among the whole lot—there is no occasion for a writ of error to quash their impertinence, which perishes from sheer want of strength.

A judgment may be reversed by writ of error from inferior courts to the Queen's Bench, and from the Queen's Bench to the House of Peers. Error, as its name implies, supposes there has been some mistake; so that if a man has been hanged by mistake, his heirs may have a writ of error as a matter of course.

An attainder may be reversed by Act of Parliament, but this reversal of attainder is too expensive to be easily attained. Outlawry is reversed by simple appearance, and really the very simple appearance of some who have been outlawed is sufficient to dispel the illusion as to their being anything like the bold outlaws of whom we read, including the celebrated Roy, whose occupation of robber was well denoted in his abbreviated name of Rob.

CHAPTER XXXI.

OF REPRIEVE AND PARDON.

A REPRIEVE is a temporary withdrawing of a sentence, which is in certain cases allowed. As if a criminal between his trial and his punishment becomes *non compos*, he must be reprieved, for it is presumed by the law, that if he had his reason, he would have some reason to offer why his sentence should not be carried into effect. So if my tailor having brought an action against me, gets a verdict, and the annoyance of the law proceedings drives me out of my wits, it seems that he could not recover his money until I recover myself. A denial of identity is also a plea in bar of execution ; but this plea seems to savour of that of insanity : for if a prisoner denies his own identity, he, in fact, alleges that he is somebody beside himself.

When reprieve will not avail, there is only the hope of pardon, which is the most amiable prerogative of the crown. It is really the brightest jewel of all, throwing the Nassuck diamond into the shade, and making it appear as paste in comparison with the brilliant gem called mercy, which is so becoming to the sovereigns by whom it is worn. There are a few cases to which a royal pardon does not apply, but these are of rare occurrence. In cases of private justice, the sovereign cannot pardon ; for if Titius gives me, gratuitously, a black-eye, it is taking an unpardonable liberty with my eye, for which Titius deserves the lash ; and though I may settle the matter with Titius in a twinkling, the sovereign cannot pardon him, for it is *injuria mihi*, or all my eye.

In cases of parliamentary impeachment, the royal pardon cannot be pleaded ; but when the impeachment has finished, the royal pardon may be extended, and parliament will have had the trouble of impeaching for nothing.

The manner of pardoning, is by warrant under the great seal, and not as it is usually represented on the stage, where a culprit kneels, and says " Sire," while the sovereign raises him by the hand, and expresses a hope that " all his kind friends around him will be as lenient to any little errors they may have observed in him, and that he may have the pleasure of exercising his royal clemency, with their kind permission, every evening till further notice." Having described the manner of a royal pardon, we have only to speak of its effect, which is to make the offender a new man, even when he happens to be an old one. A pardon is like brimstone and treacle, for it purifies the blood, and with this luscious illustration, we draw this chapter to a close.

CHAPTER XXXII.

OF EXECUTION.

There now remains nothing but execution, which is a painful subject, and happily requiring a very few words, for hanging is now rarely resorted to, though once the law of England seemed not to know where to stop, but we cannot add, that it did not know where to draw the line.

The sheriff is bound to execute a criminal, but he may get a substitute ; and in former times a substitute was such a

catch, or as some called it ketch, that the executioner got
the title of Jack Ketch, by which he is still vulgarly known.
Having carried these commentaries to the close ; having
brought them as it were to the scaffold, we will from that
very scaffold ; review in a concluding chapter, the whole legal
building, a structure which, if we were to wander from pole
to pole, we should never see surpassed.

CHAPTER XXXIII.

OF THE RISE, PROGRESS, AND GRADUAL IMPROVEMENT OF THE LAWS OF ENGLAND.

WE now propose to take a survey of the whole juridical
history of England ; and boldly grasping the constitutional
theodolite, we proceed to take the levels, mark out the gradients, and observe the cuttings along the whole line of British
Law.   The periods and intermediate stations through which
we intend to pass are six :—1. From the earliest times to the
Norman Conquest, a short and not a very easy stage. 2. From
the Norman Conquest to the reign of King Edward I., which
will be very up-hill work. 3. From thence to the Reformation, in which we shall observe that the gradients were somewhat rapid. 4. From the Reformation to the Restoration of
Charles II., where the cuttings were very severe. 5. From
thence to the Revolution in 1688, where the tunnelling must
be heavy considering what was gone through. And 6. From
the Revolution to the present time, where we arrive at the
terminus of our work.

1. And first let us look at the Ancient Britons, who, we are
told, " never committed their laws to writing, possibly for
want of letters "—a reason that reminds us of the excuse of
the angler who did not go out fishing because in the first place
there were no fish. Though in our day we hear of French
without a Master, the Druids were not such clever fellows as

to be able to achieve writing without letters, or penmanship without an alphabet. Antiquarians tell us no trace of a letter is to be found among the British relics, and if they have been looking for some correspondence with the Druidical postmark, we are not surprised at the search for letters having proved vain.

When we consider the number of different nations that broke in upon Britain, we must not wonder at the hodgepodge they made of our early laws; for what with the Romans thrashing the Britons, the Picts pitching into the Saxons, and the Normans drubbing the Danes, it is impossible to say who gave its early judicial system to England, though it is clear that they gave it to one another in magnificent style.

The first attempt to model the constitution was by Alfred, who, having whacked his enemies, might be called a modeller in whacks, and who divided the whole country into hundreds, as we have since learned to divide our walnuts and our coals. He made himself the head reservoir of justice, and laid it on—sometimes rather too thick—to every part of the nation. He was the first literary monarch who ever sat upon the Saxon mile-stone, which was the substitute in those days for the British throne, and we hail him as a brother author: for he wrote the first law book that England ever saw. Among the Saxon laws we find the constitution of Parliaments, the election of magistrates, the descent of the crown, and other institutions preserved to the present day; and not only preserved but potted and garnered up in the bosom of the British Constitution, where we hope they will long remain.

2. The Norman Conquest made considerable alteration, and introduced the forest laws, which threw the game into the king's hands, vesting every beast of the field or fowl of the air in the sovereign, as in one vast hamper, which hampered the people to the very last degree. William also introduced the trial by combat, for he wished the people to learn to lick each other, having taught them to lick the dust.

During this period of our legal history, feudal tenures came into full growth, and they at last had the effect of irritating the barons in the reign of John to demand that splendid piece of parchment which every one puffs but nobody reads—as is sometimes the case with a well advertised book—that enormous palladium of our liberties, called Magna Charta. We shall not describe the contents of this glorious specimen of penmanship, for every Briton of course has it at his fingers' ends, and having learnt it at school, hangs it in his study at home, that he may remember that it regulates the time and place of holding a court leet among other privileges even still more precious than the one to which we allude.

3. The third period commences with Edward the First, our English Justinian—a title that savours of quackery, like the Irish Paganini, the American Braham, and other foreign editions of distinguished men. Among other achievements, he first established a repository for the public records, which perhaps stood on the very ground now occupied by the horse repository in St. Martin's Lane.

The laws went on improving until the time of Henry the Seventh, when that monarch and his ministers being hard up, resorted to every method of making money, and only considered what was "likely to pay."

4. Our fourth period brings us to Henry the Eighth, who introduced the bankrupt laws, and several other legal measures ; having imbibed a taste for law studies while lodging at Honey and Skelton's, the hair dressers at the top of Inner Temple Lane—and it is said that the rival family came to be called the house of Tu—dor, because there are two doors to the house alluded to—a piece of antiquarian affectation and learned foppishness, in which we do not believe.

The children of Henry the Eighth did little for the law ; but Elizabeth extended the royal prerogative, which she seemed to consider as elastic as a piece of Indian rubber, and she used it to rub out many of the dearest privileges of the people.

On the accession of James the First, he found the sceptre too heavy for his hand, a discovery that was subsequently made by James the Second, who very prudently dropped it, when he could no longer manage it, instead of holding on like Charles the First, who was little better than half a sovereign and ultimately paid the forfeit of a crown.

5. The fifth period brings us to the Restoration, and this reminds us that the British constitution is a good deal like Smith and Baber's floor-cloth manufactory at Knightsbridge, which has been destroyed, restored, rebuilt, repaired, burnt down, and raised up at least half-a-dozen different times. The British constitution seems, like a cat, to have nine lives, for it has received within our recollection several death-blows; but, no matter from what height it is thrown down, it always comes upon its feet again. It was in the period after the Restoration, that the *Habeas Corpus* Act was passed, which is said to be a second *Magna Charta*, and must therefore be a good deal like butter upon bacon, for if *Magna Charta* was a bulwark and a palladium, we did not require another bulwark and another palladium before the first had been regularly worn out.

6. From the revolution to the present time is the sixth and last division of our subject, and we are happy to say that this period has been fertile of really useful reforms. These amendments have been noticed in other portions of this work, and it is needless to recapitulate them here.

Thus have we traced our rude plans and maps of our laws and liberties. We have endeavoured to evince a proper admiration for the great monument of law, which, in the capacity of showman, we have sought to exhibit in such a way as to render it attractive to the public at large. We have attempted to do for the law what Van Amburgh has done for the tiger, and it has been our effort to show that the law is not such a formidable monster, tearing to pieces every one that comes within its grasp, as is too generally supposed. We have been anxious to show that it

may be approached playfully, and without horror, until a
familiarity is established between the student and the law,
as pleasant as the understanding between the brute-tamer
and the brute.   Let us hope we have shown that Blackstone,
like another black individual, is not· so dingy as he is
painted.

FINIS.

BRADBURY, AGNEW, & CO., PRINTERS, WHITEFRIARS.

www.ingramcontent.com/pod-product-compliance
Lightning Source LLC
Chambersburg PA
CBHW030643030726
47497CB00006B/1934